MURDER
ON
U.S. RTE. 116

MURDER

ON

U.S. RTE. 116

AN IT'S NEVER
TOO LATE MYSTERY

DONNARAE MENARD

Glenn R. Sennett

Chapter One

Took Farm, Orchard, Vermont (1978)

Hiding in the crux of the ancient apple tree was perfect. He was small enough of stature to be invisible among the twisting branches and thick leaf cover. So much better than standing out in the open on top of the stone wall where any roving eye would pick him out in a heartbeat.

Two rows further on, across the open space, stood the vacant barn with its eastern end collapsing to the ground. That was his destination. He'd been there before and knew it was safe. Except today, two men—one with a camera, the other a yellow legal notepad—had circled the hundred-twenty-foot structure a couple of times. Too far away to hear, he watched as they gestured and pointed, pacing from the downed edge to where the structure looked solid. He was still seventy feet away.

His entry, the pig door, was approachable through the brambles and the burdock. Not a place he wanted to crawl through on the ground. It was a relief when the men disappeared around the corner.

That small comfort lasted until their return ten minutes later with a woman and three other men. The minor irritation had grown into a crowd. Lowering one foot to the bottommost branch, he prepared to retreat back toward LaPlatte Brook.

The watcher chewed the nail on his forefinger. He had already destroyed both thumbnails and one pinky.

What are they doing? Duffers are screwing up everything.

It was hot. He'd come from across the further fields, through the brook, and into the orchard. Not only was he hungry, but at that moment felt on the verge of a faint. Tremors passed through his fingers, and he wasn't sure how much longer he could hold on. If something didn't happen fast, he'd fall out of the old apple tree.

Swiping at an inquisitive honeybee, he looked again toward the haymow and the cool, dim security the barn offered. It wasn't much, but so far, it had worked for him. He cast a look over his shoulder, beyond where he had dug up the few wild plants he knew he could eat, scanning across the wide brook for any movement indicating he was being tracked.

Beyond the brook, where the new houses had been put in, he'd seen a woman watching from a window. She had spied him walking around, casing the house. Looking for an open window, an unlocked door. Hell, a big dog door, any way to get in and get some food.

He'd noticed her when she moved the curtain. Then he'd walked out of sight, between the house and the garage. But when he emerged on the far end, she had changed windows, still watching.

There was a lawnmower by the deck. After a big show of checking the gas, he pulled the cord and mowed the backyard. Nice even, straight rows, like it was his job, and he had every right to be there.

Eventually, the woman disappeared from the window. Putting the mower back where he'd found it, the man sprinted for the woods and was soon out of sight.

He had to watch out for people like that. Nosy busy-bodies who would drop a dime and bring the authorities. He wasn't going back. No matter what. He could be safe in the barn filled with old junk, stinking of pig and wet dog.

Turning his gaze back to the sagging red building, he sighed in relief. They were gone, all of them. Gone. Slowly, he lowered himself from the branches. The deer had trodden down the hay beneath and provided a nice path directly to where he wanted to go.

Chapter Two

Katie sat at the side of the table, and not in the middle seat, either. She specifically didn't want to be in THE ONE chair. As in, the one who was the sponsor, or the requestor, or the final voice in the decision. THE HEAD of the family chair. It didn't matter that she was the owner of the family farm. And the last of the family.

"More or less," she muttered.

"What's that, Katie?" Raymond Dean asked.

The Deans owned the only other property on Fire Lane 61. Katie had known Raymond and his brothers her entire life. He, like her friends; Rick, Ruth, and Stan Baldwin, was there at her invitation. She was over her head on this project, and she knew it.

Kitty-corner across the old farmer's table was Amos Surette. On his right was Percy Burke, and on the end, Steve Libby. Percy and Steve were partners, with Steve being the mouthpiece and the CEO. Amos had brought Steve and Percy because they had the expertise she needed. It would come with a bill she didn't need, but if she didn't at least listen, she'd kick herself later.

"So, we've taken a good look over the project," said Steve. "Amos was right. From our standpoint, the repair work for your barn has a lot of potential as an excellent learning tool for our students. How about you give us a thumbnail sketch of how it got so dilapidated?"

Even though Rick was sitting at the end of the table in THE ONE chair, all eyes found Katie on the side. She sat back, considering what the builders would want to know.

Rick encouraged her to go ahead. "Short and sweet."

Katie stared at the plate of cookies for a few more moments. Her thoughts refused to make a nice straight line. Finally, she exhaled and started talking.

"This piece of property has been in my family for four generations. Before it was a working farm, it was a stagecoach stop."

Percy cut in. "It has historical significance, then?"

"The house does, but the historical society says so many changes have been made inside that it could be in question," Katie said. "The barn was added later and used as part of the dairy business until my grandfather passed away fifteen years ago."

"I think you should get a second opinion on the house," Percy said. "But that's a subject for a different time."

"Anyway, the barn hasn't been used since for anything more than a storage space for my grandmother's junk collection. There may have been some damage happening for years, but I wouldn't know. The only two people who would have had any real knowledge have both passed. Ruth says the barn showed a significant tilt about eight years ago. Then, over one winter, the foundation gave, and the rear corner collapsed. Lumber was pulled off to shut in what was left. That's it, I guess."

She didn't add that she hadn't been here in years, or that the lumber had been cut up for firewood by the two old women. It was none of these strangers' business.

"But you want to save the barn?" Percy asked.

Raymond, Rick, and Stan were nodding.

"Yes," Katie said, tentatively.

In actuality, she wanted it terribly, but she was afraid to give her hopes to these men she didn't know. Amos, who had been trained by Steve, and now worked independently or in the employ of another trained specialist, had sworn Percy and Steve would treat her fairly. Her New England upbringing prevented her from putting all her cards on the table until they had shown theirs.

Steve had a pen in his hand. He wasn't doing as much writing as he was rocking it back and forth against the opposite forefinger.

"This is how Harwood Architectural Renovation works," he said. "We are a teaching organization, specializing in vintage heavy beam construction. Our students work with old tools, old ideas, and—whenever possible—with what was part of the original structure. We aren't so much about building new as bringing the old back to life. We have moved structures from one place to another, but that's not our forte.

"If you hire a contractor to come in and do the repairs," Steve went on, "he's going to go for all-new. If that's what you want, we stop here. In that situation, you'll foot the bill for everything that comes in or happens. This is a school where students, like Amos, learn the nuances of the techniques for heavy wood beam construction. Like I said, using historical methods and how work was done before there was a special tool for everything and workmen didn't need as much actual knowledge. In other words, we are educating the men and women who will work to save our heritage."

"Just barns?" Stan asked.

"No," said Steve. "Any wooden I-beam or center beam structure. That could be houses, churches, schools, covered bridges, anything with wood bones."

"We've built outhouses as well," Amos said.

Katie ignored her wide-grinning friend. "That all sounds pretty pricey."

"It can be. But here's the rub for you. This isn't a tear-down-and-rebuild or roof replacement. This is more a soup-to-nuts on a part of the standing structure. Whole different can of worms. We bring in two different sets of students. They get three days to evaluate, measure, and consult. Each student, or group if they team up, presents their plan. We select the best one, tighten the screws and, with a contract, begin the refurbishing."

Katie understood what Steve was saying about the school, but didn't get what happened between the students' soup and their ending up with nuts. She sat through the next forty-five minutes, listening to the discussion of fees and charges. But after Percy and Steve left, she was hard pressed to break down everything they had said, even to herself. Somewhere in the conversation, fifty thousand dollars had been spoken, and that was where she had remained focused. The only other thing she had really understood was that, because she owned a gravel pit, she wouldn't have to buy the hundreds of yards of it needed to put in a solid foundation.

I don't have that kind of money. Or access to it, either.

She tried to think of a polite way of escaping from the discussion with Rick and Raymond, but was stymied.

Monique, Amos's wife, came in from the living room carrying six-month-old Lydia. It was time to take the baby home and tend to the goats. Raymond and Stan also headed off.

"You'll need time to stew this around," Raymond told Katie at the door. "Then we'll work on figuring out the finer points."

While Ruth collected dirty cups and silver, Katie put a skillet on the stove. She worked at chopping onions, shallots, and green peppers. While they sizzled, she threw in ground beef, Swiss chard, cut-up yellow beans, and an assortment of leftovers. They would be dining on another one-pot wonder that evening.

"Biscuits or cornbread?" she asked Rick.

"Finish up that cornbread." Ruth cut the old man off, leaving him with his mouth open and no words coming out.

Katie ducked her head. She knew both Rick and Charlie would choose biscuits if offered a choice. There was no more discussion about the barn until they all, plus Charlie, who boarded, sat down to eat.

* * *

"Ain't that gonna be kinda expensive?" asked Charlie.

He'd listened during the dining table discussion until there was a lull. But it was the same thought everyone else shared.

"There's no way this would be cheap," Rick pointed out. "The deal with Harwood Restoration is that you don't pay for the labor or planning crap."

"Clean up your mouth," Ruth snapped.

"Yes, honey." Rick quickly changed the subject. "There's a fee for the company to work on the project. We'd be responsible for the concrete and all the other building supplies that can't be salvaged. We just won't be paying for the labor. And the two hundred thou is the top price."

The telephone rang. Katie got up, hoping it was an animal call which she, as the town animal control officer, would have to respond to. That would get her out of the house and away from this discussion. But on the other end of the phone, Marlie was bubbling along. Just hearing her girlfriend's voice brought a flush of heat to Katie.

"Hey, listen to this," said Marlie with a laugh. "I'm actually getting out of work on time. I'll be leaving soon. Is there anything you need me to pick up?"

Marlie had been reinstated as a Vermont deputy sheriff, but assigned a slot in the Northeast Territory surrounding Irasberg and Troy, Vermont. She had accepted that, if having to be stationed far away from where Katie was, had to be her path back after hightailing it off the job when Gregory Ames threatened to expose her sexuality to the public, so be it. But that didn't mean she had to stay up north on her days off. Her new boss had offered her the option of split days off with a weekend day, or two days together during the week. She had opted for Tuesday and Wednesday. Now, at the end of her Monday night shift, she was packed and ready to go.

"No, we're good." Katie grinned over her shoulder towards the table. Ruth held up a plate.

"Marlie, do you want me to save you some supper?"

"Are you kidding? I'm starving. I won't be able to wait that long. There's a hot dog diner on the way. I'll stop there. Nine-thirty or ten, okay?"

"Drive safe," Katie said, but Marlie was already gone.

"Well, there will be snacks waiting when she gets here," Ruth said, covering the rest of the sheet cake with Saran Wrap.

Ruth went back to clearing the table, while Rick took chicken scraps out to the biddies. Charlie and the dogs followed behind. Outside, Bonnie, the rescued pig, lay with her chin resting on the stoop, waiting in anticipation. Now and then, tidbits fell off onto the ground, and she was quick to help clean it up.

* * *

It was closer to ten-thirty when Marlie arrived, and Katie, worn out by the stress of her meeting with the guys from Morrisville Junction, had dozed off on the couch.

Waking her with a kiss, Marlie whispered, "Go to bed. You have tomorrow off, and I don't have to go back until Wednesday evening."

Chapter Three

Marlie came down for breakfast long after Rick had left for the feed store, and Ruth was gone to help Grace Dean in the goat dairy. Katie walked out of the cat room to find her friend pouring coffee and dropping bread into the toaster.

"Good morning, sleepyhead." Katie had gotten up much earlier.

There was no one around. Standing at the sink, washing her hands, and watching the cardinals and songbirds emptying the feeder, Katie didn't realize Marlie was taking tiny sideways steps toward her. Then, with her head full of crinkly hair lying on Katie's shoulder, she whispered, "Did you miss me?"

* * *

It was almost lunchtime when Ruth came into the yard, grunting with the weight of the wagon towed behind her. Marlie, who had been lying in the grass playing with two of the leftover kittens, jumped up to help.

"Holy cow flop, Ruth! How come you didn't take some of these vegetables down to the farm stand?" she asked.

"Are you kidding? This is what's left after we filled the farm stand. Dang garden is going hog wild." Ruth hefted the first basket just as Katie came out the front door. "Let's get it inside. Peppers are coming in, too. With all this zucchini, we can make up some chutney." She stopped to look at Katie and frowned. "How come you two are all wet?"

Katie hesitated for a second. Over Ruth's shoulder, she could see Marlie with two kittens in one arm, a bag of green beans in the other, and a startled look on her face.

"I spilled a cat box all over me, and Marlie tried to help. It was a real mess. We just felt the need for a bath. Are we canning all this?" Katie grabbed the second basket and hustled the old woman in through the kitchen door.

"Going to have to." Ruth dropped her basket on the floor in front of the sink. "Grace's garden is going nuts over there. The farm stand is filled up, and market day is three days away. These won't be fresh then."

Grace had doubled her truck garden space this year. To her amazement, both sites were flourishing to the edge of vegetable hysteria. She had started canning and selling jars at the farm stand, as well as putting by for her family. Down in the cellar, the shelves Rick had knocked up during the winter were filling up, and there were still weeks to go.

Irma had left boxes of canning jars in the barn, and Katie bought pints as needed. But as she lugged a cardboard box of summer squash and zucchini behind Ruth, she was still concerned they weren't going to have enough for over the winter, or that they were going to have all of one and not a mix of others. Grace's green thumb extended up her whole arm. Katie, on the other hand, had two brown thumbs. Once inside, she spoke of her concern.

Ruth rubbed her face. "I've been thinking that, too. There are a lot of beans still growing." She walked over and looked at the phone. "Maybe we should change up what we're doing."

The hair rose on Katie's arms. When Ruth took on that attitude, it could be dangerous to anyone standing close enough to get roped into her scheme. Ruth lifted the telephone receiver and dialed her good friend Blanche. Over her shoulder, she said, "Marlie, take the cart down and tell Grace we'll take that case of spotty tomatoes, and whatever she's got left for long tail onions. Katie, put on the big pot to boil so we can peel them tomatoes." She turned back to the receiver. "Hello, Blanche? Ruth. What have you got for extra canning jars? Yeah, quarts are fine."

Marlie stepped outside, ready to grab the last paper sack of beans, then head down to the farm. But the wagon was empty. Without so much as a shrug, she picked up the handle and headed across the road and down the small slope.

***

Ruth and Marlie peeled and chopped, while Katie ran around town, picking up no longer needed cases of mason jars. Some were coated with a thick layer of dust, chipped, or stained, but she knew the answer would be hot water and soap for most of them—and the dump for the rest.

On the way into the village, a long blue Pontiac convertible roared past, doing well over the speed limit. The top was down, and a woman in oversized sunglasses, head and neck wrapped in a bright scarf of tangerine, red, and yellow, waved back over her head. Katie couldn't tell if it was a salute as she passed or if the woman was flipping her off. "There's never a cop around when you need one," she muttered.

It wasn't the afternoon Katie had planned. This was her day off, too, and she had wanted to do something fun with her friend. But Marlie seemed to be having a great time. Rick was due home. The kitchen was covered with sparkling clean canning jars waiting to be filled and sealed jars lying on their sides atop towels on every flat surface. The cats, who had been shut in the cat room all day, perked up their ears when the rumble of Rick's truck pulled in.

"What's that terrific smell?" he asked, coming across the living room. But once inside the kitchen door, he stopped dead. Katie was lifting the wire rack out of the hot water bath, Marlie was spooning a tomato mixture from the big soup kettle, and Ruth was writing out labels by hand. The look on his face said Uh-oh as he took a step backward. He wasn't fast enough.

"Good, you're here," Ruth said. "We're going to have grilled hot dogs and beans for supper, but before you start lighting off the charcoal, can you check one more time in the barn and make sure we don't have any canning jars hidden away? I specifically would like some pints."

Katie grinned at the pained look on Rick's face. Picking up the heavy bucket of leftover vegetable ends, he headed back the way he'd come in. "I'll feed the chickens and Bonnie while I'm outside," he said.

Solomon and Walker, as well as Bonnie, who had been left on their own all afternoon, happily followed in his footsteps.

"I don't think we're going to need any more jars right now," Marlie said. "The pot is almost empty."

Ruth gave a tired sigh. "I know. I just need a few minutes to rest before I start working on supper."

Katie lowered the new, and last, rack of jars into the hot water bath. "Stay put, Ruth. There's enough tomato and zucchini left over for supper with the hot dogs, and all this has to cool before we do anything else."

She filled a glass with iced tea and shushed her elderly friend out to the living room.

"Marlie, let the cats out. I'll fix their dinner. That will shut them up," she said over her shoulder as she went.

"I'll start washing up," Marlie said, pushing open the door to the cattery and heading toward the sink.

"Absolutely not," said Katie. "We'll eat, relax, then clean up."

The hot dogs were charred just right. The tomato, zucchini, summer squash, and onion base was perfect with the handful of macaroni Katie had thrown in. They ate on the front porch where there was a soft breeze, and the dogs and pig could have rolled in the grass if they hadn't been begging at Rick's knee.

"Just enough garlic," Rick said. "I'm stuffed. What's with all the soup?"

"It's not soup, idjet," said Ruth. "More like stewed tomato and vegetables. That's what I'm putting on the labels. Tomorrow morning, we'll take a mess of it down to the farm stand."

The doors of the Schoolhouse Thrift Shop and Farm Stand opened at seven, self-service. At ten, Monique and Ruth, or her friend, Donna, went down to man the till until three. Then, just like tonight, they'd shut the doors at seven.

"Monique told me this afternoon that we're getting quite a number of people stopping for produce," Ruth said happily. "I'm hoping they'll take more of the canned goods. The yellow beans are pretty much gone by. Too bad some wolf is helping himself to some of the pints."

***

All afternoon while the women were working, the odor of stewing vegetables had filled the air. When they had gotten underfoot, the cats and dogs were put outside where they vied with the pig for a place in the sun and a view through the screen door into the kitchen. The wide-open windows let the heat out, and once Katie started adding herbs and spices to the vegetables, a mouthwatering smell wafted on the breeze. The wind carried the proof of their work down over the lawn, across the narrow dirt strip of barn road, and up into the barn loft.

Wayne, the man hiding in there, stayed near the collapsed end. That set of loft windows remained closed. It was dark, and the floor had a slight tilt. Since Steve and Percy from Harwood Architectural had left, there was no reason for anyone to climb the ladder.

The wind was not concerned with the fragile fears anyone held of the creaking timbers. Twisting, turning, finding each crevice and chink, it carried the good smell with it, even into the dark corners of the barn. Wayne sniffed noisily. His stomach growled. Even as he shoved another handful of dry cereal into his mouth, he damned to hell whoever was cooking.

Rick fired up the grill. When the charcoal was burning hot, he laid down a row of Smithfield garlic red-skinned hot dogs. The natural casings swelled, then split, sending the juices splattering onto the coals, and the Fourth of July smell grew stronger on the wind.

Wayne crawled further along inside the building to an open loft window and peeked around the edge. He could see the side lawn where the road swung past the house and curved back and down around to cross between the backside and the barn. On the right side, the hens were lined up along the inside of their fencing, watching just as he was. But where they might have a view, he saw nothing. He knew there were several people on the lawn enjoying the hot dogs, but even if Ruth had been the only one inside, he wouldn't have chanced walking up to the door and sneaking up into the kitchen.

* * *

Katie picked up plates and, after telling Marlie to stay outside, went directly to the sink. Ruth followed on her heels with the drink glasses. "Do you want some help, or should I start chopping for the chutney?" Ruth asked.

"You're going to do that tonight? I can help." Katie pulled her hands out of the hot dishwater.

"Nope. Going to use the salad-master to grind it up. It's gotta meld before it's canned." Ruth went into the pantry, returning with the black and white box containing the salad-master and all its attachments.

* * *

When he was no longer able to resist the smell of hot, home-cooked food, Wayne lifted the trap door, exposing the wall-mounted ladder down to the first floor of the barn. On the west end, the area was littered with Rick's tools from when he and Philip had worked through the winter on the old tractor. The way was clear.

Sun streamed through the wide-open barn doors. Once outside, Wayne moved at a crouch to the two-tiered wooden fence, staying below the lowest set of rails as he scanned the farmhouse yard.

The dark-skinned young woman was sitting in the grass, while the old guy leaned on the porch support. But where were the others? Wayne moved to the right. The half-grown dog, who wasn't a problem, was out there with the old guy.

Just then, Katie stepped outside next to Rick. Moments later, Ruth appeared with a bucket of new vegetable ends, headed toward the chicken coop. Charlie ambled along beside her, with Walker behind him.

Perfect.

Sliding under the fence, Wayne ran, doubled-over, toward the bulkhead. He knew it wouldn't be locked. On a previous occasion, he had checked out the house and yard. No one had been around to hear Walker baying his indignation at a stranger snooping around.

Wayne tiptoed down the five steps of the bulkhead. It was dark crossing the cellar, but he knew the way. Once he had even spent the night. However, the proximity to the other people and the dogs' noisy attitudes had made for a nerve-wracking experience. It was better to be in the loft, but being able to fill his empty belly made taking the chance worth it.

Pausing for only a moment, Wayne tiptoed up the staircase into the kitchen. Once inside, he pushed a nosy cat away with his toe, then advanced to the table. A plate with three hot dogs left to cool lay near the edge. Inside the refrigerator was a still-warm half container of macaroni and vegetable American chop suey.

He heard Katie speaking outside, and a creaking board on the porch hinted at movement. Grabbing the container and the hot dogs off the plate, Wayne sprinted for the cellar door, fumbling with the old-fashioned latch and dropping one of the hot dogs in his haste. There was no time to retrieve it now.

* * *

The yard was lit in the satisfying glow Vermont afternoons offered after a busy day. Katie stepped back out onto the porch to find Rick leaning on an upright. As she walked up, he stepped to the edge of the top stair and gracefully cast out an imaginary fishing line. Used to his idiosyncrasies, she ignored him.

"Seems to me," he said, reeling in, "you were a mite quiet during the talk about the barn the other afternoon. What was chewing at you?"

"How do you mean?"

Rick jerked the make-believe jig, drew back, and cast again. "The look on your face was downright terrifying. I think it even put those guys from Morrisville off their feed."

Katie exhaled. Rick knew what the problem was. The same one that had weighed on her since she'd returned to this berg after ten years gone. "Come on, Rick. I'm working a job and a half. You're working, even Ruth is doing her bit. And now we've got Charlie's rent coming in, too. How is it we still don't have two nickels to rub together?"

"Yeah, I know all that." Rick reeled in, dancing the jig only he could see for the bottom fish. He knew the bass—real or imaginary—couldn't resist it. "But here's what I think. You're so busy looking toward the horizon, you can't see all the good pieces stacking up like cordwood. You walked into a hell of a mess. You didn't have a chance to see it coming. But you got it souped out. We do a little here, a little there, we've got friends to help, and even though you often have a piss poor attitude, I've gotta admit, you're a heck of a cook."

Katie hmphed and looked away, but was drawn back by Rick's silence.

He turned to look her straight in the eyes. "I know you don't want to see some bulldozer come in and shove the barn down. You and Fred, you're all about the soil, the land, and what's set on it right here. Let's hear what these guys have to say. No matter what comes out of it, we'll have a roof, food, and heat here in the house when the winter comes. It can't be all that bad. Course, we could do with finding homes for some of the kitten overload."

Katie looked beyond Rick into the yard. Marlie still giggled and rolled around on the ground with a couple of the babies. They all looked in her direction as she baby-talked to the kittens. Then Katie headed back inside. Solomon waited at her knee until the door was two inches wide, then thrust his nose in the opening and rushed to where he knew the hot dog lay on the floor.

Katie was just in time to see the end of the red wiener disappear. The empty plate was testimony to a theft.

"Solomon! Bad dog!" She grabbed the dog's collar and dragged him out onto the porch. She reported his indiscretion to Rick and left the old man to dole out appropriate punishment.

In the cellar, Wayne sat on the bulkhead steps. He could flee from here if needed, but it was safer to wait until the house quieted down for the night. Besides, it was wicked hot outside, and down here, cool and still.

Using his fingers, he scooped and slurped up the chop suey until it was half gone. He'd save the rest for breakfast. Even cold, it would be better than what he had stashed.

He heard a snuffle at the cellar door at the top of the steps and a lone woof from Walker, but a human voice shushed the dog.

Wayne sat still and silent. He was good at that.

Chapter Four

Katie left for work in the morning feeling tired and heat-hungover, with nothing resolved regarding the barn repairs. At break time, she realized her lunch bag was still on the counter, and Rick had taken a load of feed in the opposite direction.

Then, like Cinderella's fairy godmother, and Marlie, with a wide smile on her face, came through the door of Baldwin's Feed and Hardware. She held Katie's forgotten lunch bag high above her head. The deputy's plan was to leave early to swing down and see her grandmother in Williamsburg before she returned to Irasberg. The feed store was on her way, so she'd offered to make the drop on her way out of town.

Before Marlie could say a word, or Katie could acknowledge her friend, a woman stepped up to the register. "Oh. My. God. Katelyn Took. Is that really you?" she bawled out in a saccharine-laced voice.

Katie's head snapped up, and she took in the very blond, extremely teased and sprayed hair. Then the half-a-size-too-small pencil skirt, watered silk jacket, and pointy three-inch heels.

"Hi, Meredith." Katie's voice went flat. Here was a blast from the past that could have stayed buried away deep.

The other woman took a stance, zeroing in on Katie. Right hand on hip, foot forward, left forefinger pointing with the bright red-orange polish the same shade as her heavily coated lips.

"I haven't seen you in *forever*." It sounded like a quote from an old California beach movie.

Katie didn't bite. Instead, she offered her own observation. "I've never seen you in here before, Meredith. We don't usually get folks all dressed up like corporate, buying feed."

The other woman's shoulders pinched together as she issued a shrill giggle, followed by a short, very unladylike snort. "I only came in today because my boys need some things for their summer project. My au pair was supposed to pick the order up, but the boys had shots this morning and don't feel well enough to be out traipsing around."

"Sensitive, are they?" Katie asked, eyes searching to fix on anything other than Meredith.

A tiny frown flitted across the woman's face as she perceived the snub. "You haven't changed, have you?" she asked. The friendly, chatty tone had been replaced by a more pointed one.

"Oh, yeah, I have," said Katie. "I've matured."

The inference was plain. Meredith's smile was gone. "Is the order ready?"

Katie picked up her pre-order list. "Let's see. Meredith Coombs?"

"Block," said the blonde. "Mrs. Avery Block. You know, the assistant district attorney?"

Ignoring the other woman's attempt at name-dropping to raise her status, Katie re-checked her list. "I have an order for M.B. Block ready for pick-up in building three. If you pull around out back, they'll show you where to back in."

"Around back?" It was clear from Meredith's tone she wasn't used to being told to fetch for herself.

"Yes, Meredith. This is a feed store. We don't walk orders out to your car. It's called cash and carry." Then, before the woman could think of a retort, Katie added, "It was nice seeing you. Have a good day. Who's next, please?"

The blonde stomped across the wooden floor towards the exit hard enough to break the heel off one of her designer shoes. Shoving Marlie out of the way with no recognition, she headed out to a Pontiac parked in the walkway.

"Are you insane?" Marlie hissed when she got over to Katie's cash register. "You're supposed to keep a low profile. That doesn't mean you should pick a fight with Meredith Block."

"Come on, Marlie." Katie rolled her eyes. "It's Cheerleader Meredith.

What do you think she'll do, beat me up with her pom-pom? It's not like we ever got along way back then."

"Katie, even in high school, Meredith was trouble. Head cheerleader, president of the drama club, principal's daughter. Remember all that? Well, she grew up and married some football jock from Rice High School who went to law school. They may be divorced, but he's still a hotshot. And she's a paralegal in your lawyer's office."

Katie bit her bottom lip. Marlie might have a point.

"I'm going to spend the day with my grandmother, then head back north. Friday night, I'll be a little late calling. Okay?"

There were too many people around for Marlie to say anything else. Katie nodded. With one last look, Marlie was gone.

"What's that blonde got a pair of?" asked Davidson, the twenty-year-old cashier.

"Huh?" Katie asked.

"She said her pair was supposed to pick her order up."

"You dummy." Katie laughed. "Au pair. It's a fancy name for a live-in babysitter who watches her kids when she's not around."

"A babysitter?"

"That's right."

"Phfft. Why didn't she just say so?" the young man asked.

"Because that wouldn't be prissy enough for Meredith Coombs Block."

It didn't take Katie long to forget about Meredith. They had nothing in common, and probably wouldn't cross paths again.

Meredith, however, couldn't stop herself from whipping her waspish tongue at the guys in building three who were loading the trunk of her blue convertible. She pulled up to the exit, looked back at the loading dock in her rearview mirror, and saw that they still laughed at her. Seeing red, she fishtailed out into the street.

Back at her house, a large, bright-white colonial which sat behind a cedar barrier on the high side of US Route 116, Meredith ordered Danielle, the au pair, to empty the items the building number three guys had loaded into her car.

"And you better pick up the pace if you haven't got the boys packed yet," Meredith sniped. "You have to get them to their father's house in South Burlington by six. They're flying out to Michigan tonight."

"Yes, Mrs. Block," said Danielle. "I'll have them there in time."

The two Coombs-Block boys were booked to go on vacation to a wilderness camp with their father. Danielle would not accompany them, but she, too, had scheduled a two-week holiday away from her employer. Her suitcase was packed, every last bit of her personal property already stowed in her vehicle.

"When do you plan on getting this school project the boys were assigned done?" Meredith demanded.

The boys attended the Walter Penn Charter School in Williston. After an inappropriate practical joke misfired, the Carmelite Monks who ran the school ordered all four boys involved to construct two birdhouses each, to be donated to a local senior living center. Attorney Block had instructed the ex-Mrs. Block to see to it. Mrs. Block, in turn, had designated Danielle to make sure everything was attended to in a manner that would not provoke Mr. Block. The boys, seven and eight, refused to participate.

"As soon as I get back," said Danielle, pulling the first bird house kit out of the Pontiac's trunk.

To assure that the Carmelites wouldn't take offense at the use of build-it-yourself kits, Meredith had added sacks of birdseed and a large bird feeder to the order. The whole time Danielle worked to empty the car, pack for the boys from the list provided by Mr. Block, then load suitcases, sleeping bags, camping gear, and two irate boys who did not want to go camping, into her car, Meredith dogged the young woman's tracks. Besides taking the opportunity to direct the younger woman's every move, complain about her ex, and incite the boys' churlish behavior, she made additional demands that needed to be handled while Danielle was on vacation.

Once the boys were strapped into the car, Danielle took a deep breath and said, "I'm not ignoring you, Mrs. Block, but I'm not going to be in town while I'm on vacation. I'm leaving tonight for, ah, North Carolina. There's nothing more I can do right now. And if I don't leave five minutes ago, I'll be late getting to Mr. Block's house."

Danielle drove away as Meredith sputtered on the deck. As soon as she was out of the driveway, she pulled the car over. With one arm on the back of the seat, she said, "One more whine out of either of you, and I'm telling your father how badly you and Mrs. Block badmouth his new wife. That's going to make for a lousy vacation for both of you. And if you think you can lie your way out of this one, I have it on tape."

Danielle didn't care how long her threat held the boys at bay. Even five minutes would be good. She had no intention of returning in two weeks. With a new job already lined up, and everything she owned in the back of her car, she was out of there. Her future awaited. It included a wedding ring, and she had big plans.

Back at the house, Meredith had switched from the classical radio channel she demanded the boys listen to. Now rock and roll blared through the house. She kicked off her arch-killing heels and pulled the cork from a tall bottle of white wine. She also looked forward to some downtime.

Starting tonight at eight, she planned to spend her time doing the Watusi with a new guy in town. Wine in hand, she stood in the wide picture window on the front of the house. She'd changed into a skimpy Hawaiian-print halter top and white short-shorts. Never for a minute did she consider that the oversized house high on the ridge, far on the other side of the valley, was the old stagecoach inn. Katie's home.

She reminded herself to tell the yard guy to mow the narrow strip of front lawn that they never used, then yanked the drapes shut. Someone knocked at her kitchen door. The mowing, her boys, and all her other problems vanished as her kitten mules skipped across the floor.

Chapter Five

Six days later, Marlie showed up at the house just before supper. It was unusual for her to leave work early, but she had left the upper region of the state, sure Katie would be happy to see her and that she would be welcomed.

However, her joy took a nosedive when Katie and Rick returned home from work. There seemed to be a lot of stress circling the dinner table. At least Marlie thought so. She knew the upcoming arrival of the first Harwood Architectural Renovators' team was sitting heavy on Katie's mind. Her friend wavered between, not wanting to talk about it at all to sharing the bare minimum of information, but she never gave up what was actually in her head.

Marlie rotated her two days off between the farm one week, and being with her grandmother in Williamsburg the next. It was clear something had happened at Katie's in the few days she'd been gone, but Marlie couldn't quite figure out what it was. She shook her head. It was too hot for everyone to have a temper tantrum. Baskets of fresh produce sat on the counters waiting to be cleaned and processed, and Ruth looked exhausted. Most of what she heard between her friends were sarcastic quips or gruff answers, which was unusual.

Marlie took another roll out of the basket in the middle of the table. She loved bread, and Katie made good biscuits. Ripping it open, exposing the flaky, buttery layers, steam and the heady, yeasty scent invaded her senses. It almost made her forget what was happening around her.

"Excuse me," she said, her knife applying a layer of Grace Dean's creamy butter, which melted on contact. "I can't follow your conversations and eat at the same time. I'm missing something that's going on here. You guys jumped from what the company that might be repairing the barn are getting ready to do, to…I don't know. Some complaint about town business." Unable to wait another second, she took a big bite of biscuit.

Damn, this is good. She groaned inwardly.

"And inquiring deputies have to know, right?" Rick laughed. Like Marlie, he had a biscuit in one hand and reached for the butter dish with the other. His eyebrows quirked up in Katie's direction.

Finished eating, Katie leaned back in her seat beside Marlie. Watching her people make inroads into all she had put on the table gave her a bit of peace she was unable to put into words. But it definitely made her happy. The rubbish they were talking about, however, did not. She ignored her friend's reference to Harwood Architectural.

"When I took on Gram's job as animal control officer with the town, no one mentioned I was supposed to attend monthly selectman's meetings. It took a few months for anybody to let me know. Needless to say, some of those political types weren't too impressed when I didn't show up. You would have thought somebody on the council would've notified me." Katie was obviously disgusted.

Marlie nodded. Before her stint as a guard at the Pennsylvania Women's Correctional Institute, she had been a sheriff's deputy in Parentville, so she was aware of how local politics worked. She felt a moment's chagrin. She had been here, known Katie, been falling in love with her, and attending the meetings was nothing she had thought to point out, even though she'd known that was a prerequisite. Before she could open her mouth and add her name to the list of guilty individuals, Rick spoke up.

"It was something we all missed the boat on. One afternoon, when I was having coffee with Chet down at the dump, he was grousing about how he had to get cleaned up to go to a meeting that night. I think I might have laughed at him, and he took it bad." Rick paused for a sip of coffee, half a biscuit still in hand. "Chet told me I'd be laughing out of the other side of my mouth when the town found a new animal control officer because Katie had pissed them old guys off by not showing up. Instead of telling Katie, who was pretty hot-headed at that time, I went to the meeting with Chet. When they called the attendance and got to Katie's name, I stood up and said I was her representative because she was on a call."

"Really?" asked Marlie. "Was that while I still worked here?"

Katie nodded.

"Yeah," said Rick. "But you two were trying to track down Irma's murderer. To be honest, I didn't even tell Katie what I was doing for a while. Anyway, after that, I just kept going. They got used to me being there in her stead. To be honest, I mostly just sat there, drank coffee, and ate their donuts. Me, Chet, a few others."

Marlie looked around the table. Charlie and Ruth nodded in agreement. So far, she hadn't heard anything that would create a lot of stress.

"What changed?" she asked.

Rick gave a resigned sigh. "At the annual town meeting this spring, there were several issues brought up regarding all the new developments around the area. Then there's the budget, and we're coming into an election year. Usually, there isn't a lot said about animal control. Most of the talk has to do with the school, expanding the fire department, putting on another sheriff's deputy because Angus is never going to be able to go out in the field with a weapon because he's blind as a bat. Then one of the newcomers that's running for a board seat stood up. Seems the animal control officer had been out to a house in his neighborhood a while ago to catch a raccoon that had moved into the chimney. He had some questions." Rick paused to take a bite of his cooling biscuit.

"What kind of questions could you have about something like that?" Marlie asked.

This time Katie spoke up. "He wanted to know how I was disposing of the remains."

"Don't you usually just let them go?" Marlie asked.

"This was a different type of case," said Katie. "What we caught was a full-grown male fisher cat. And he wanted a piece of us. Rick was there. He dispatched the animal. I had to go back later with another trap for the raccoon."

"It was all resolved, right?"

"Yes, but that's not the issue." Katie stood up and began clearing the table. "This guy from out of town wants to run for a selectman seat. He needed to come up with a platform that no one else was all over. Something he could make a big deal about and catch the voters' attention. He selected animal control. Among other things, he pointed out that I'm per diem, not on standard payroll. I pick up stray cats and have a facility for that. I also trap small nuisance wild animals and remove them. But the dog population just took a big jump, and I'm not equipped for that. Other than Walker, that is. Ivy left him to me, and I couldn't just send him to the pound in South Burlington."

Charlie finally added to the conversation. "Dang city folks moving out here where they got no right."

Marlie turned to the rotund truck driver. "Who is this guy? Does he have a solution?"

Katie answered. "His name is Gage Fernald, and he has money. He lives in one of those fancy big houses down near Rocky Ridge Golf Course. His idea is for the town to subcontract with one of the bigger cities for animal control. If there's a need, the town would make the call, and a dog catcher would be dispatched. It wouldn't matter what the call pertained to. Dogs, cats, marauding raccoons."

"How is that supposed to work?" Marlie asked. "The town office is only open Monday through Friday, from eight to five. People call at all hours. Not to mention, there wouldn't be any way of knowing when some twit from another town will show up to take care of the issue."

"Exactly what I pointed out," said Rick. "Not to mention it'd cost a bunch more."

Katie laid down plates of marble sheet cake with peanut butter frosting and chocolate chip scatterings. "So, my representative here told the selectmen I'm in the process of designing a place to hold loose dogs."

"You told them you were going to build dog houses?" Marlie's fork stopped midway to her mouth. "Here?"

Katie nodded for Rick to explain.

"I'm thinking when the repairs on the barn are done, we can convert some of the free stalls," he said.

Marlie smiled all around the table. "That sounds like a marvelous idea."

Katie's face didn't seem to agree.

"Or if we don't go for the barn repairs, we can just put in a couple of temporary hold box kennels," Rick continued.

"Which is going to cost a pretty penny," Katie retorted. "Not to mention, dogs in kennels are a lot of work."

Marlie decided this was the perfect place to lighten the mood with her news.

"So, speaking of political intervention. Did you know that Deputy Brad Boyd is taking two weeks' vacation?"

Deputy Dennis-Brad Boyd had been the senior deputy in the Parentville Sheriff's Office while Marlie was working there. Like his supervisor, he had a nose-stuck-in-the-air attitude and didn't believe a badge should hang on a woman's chest. Unlike Sheriff Lewis, Brad was a strict believer in always being attired in the smartly creased, never smudged gabardine uniform shirt and pants issued to sheriffs and deputies. With his highly polished shoes and military haircut, Brad went from scene to scene, treating victims and criminals with the same disdain. If it was possible, Katie disliked him even more than Lewis. She certainly distrusted him more.

Marlie continued, "One of the deputies who is on the same rotating slot as me was going to come over from the western side of the state to cover Brad's job. I heard he was good and really in demand by some of the larger offices." Finished with her cake, she neatly laid her fork across the middle of her plate. "Then Bennington got into the mix, looking to fill a more permanent position, and the hotshot accepted that. The commissioner had to assign somebody else. He suggested to Sheriff Lewis that they send somebody already familiar with the area, as there wouldn't be any time for familiarization."

Everyone was looking at Marlie. Katie had to remind herself to breathe.

"And?" Ruth asked when the younger woman paused.

"The commissioner asked me if I'd be willing to step up." Her words sped up as smiles broke out around the table. "I start a week from Saturday. For two weeks."

"And you'll stay here, right?" Ruth asked, saying the words Katie didn't dare to.

Pressing her lips together to numb the dread, Marlie said, "I know I have to stay locally, but I'm not sure how onboard Lewis was with the commissioner's decision. I don't want to rile him up." Her face flushed a dark red. "I guess what I'm saying is, if I stay here, I don't want him to be down on me because he isn't happy about it."

Katie cut in. "Stop beating around the bush. What you're saying is, you don't want him to know you're in this house because he and I don't get along."

Her voice was icy. Everybody noticed. Marlie crumbled up, feeling miserable. No one knew she and Katie were a couple. Being gay was practically a death wish in this town. The last thing she wanted to do was hurt Katie, but they both wanted her to work closer. This was an enormous chance.

"I'm sorry, Katie." The small, buxom woman shrank beneath the edge of the table. "I just don't know what to do. This is a chance for me to reopen the lines of communication. I don't want to stay in the Northeast Territory forever."

Now it was Katie's turn to feel miserable. She hadn't meant to sound gruff. It wasn't who she wanted to be to Marlie. The thought ran through her head for the umpteenth time that trying to exist here on the farm was bringing her down. Everyone knew her. This was a rural area with small-minded people.

"Let's see if we can work this out." Ruth reached out to touch Katie's arm. It was a soft anchor to keep her from getting up and leaving the table. "You need to find a place quickly, and you have one here. But you're right, if you ever want to move back to this area, you don't need Sheriff Lewis badmouthing you to every set of pants in the county. Right?"

Marlie nodded.

"Do you have to tell him exactly where you're staying?"

"Not really," Marlie said slowly, eyes on her plate.

"Well, it's only two weeks, and on your days off, you'll be real close to visit your grandmother," Ruth continued. "Only the five of us know, and if no one said a word, nobody else would find out. The issue would be if somebody asked specifically where you were. You shouldn't lie."

"Ruth has a point," said Rick. "There are a couple of bed-and-breakfasts in Charlotte. Basically, that's where you'd be staying here, at a bed-and-breakfast."

"It's a lie by omission," said Marlie. Her fingers tapped the table for a few seconds before she added, "But you know, I kind of like it!" Her frown did a quick flip.

"So, mum's the word," Katie smiled as well. "Right, Charlie?"

"Not going to go anywhere near Lewis." Charlie crossed his heart with two Boy Scout fingers. "Won't say a word to anybody."

Marlie and Ruth hammered out the details of Marlie's arrival and subsequent needs. Katie watched from the sink, dishcloth in hand, unaware that out in the chicken coop, Rick had a stern talk with Charlie about how they needed to keep the womenfolk safe. Driving the dump truck for the town, Charlie got around. His inability to keep quiet was always an issue.

* * *

When Marlie had gotten out of her car in the late afternoon two days before, still dressed in her deputy sheriff uniform, Wayne had watched from the loft. He had taken to lying on the floor where the crosswind from the two open loft windows cooled him. As long as he stayed low, no one would pick him out. Every time Walker started to bark and carry on, the old woman told him to shush.

No one was in the house in the mornings, and Wayne raided the refrigerator on a regular basis. When Ruth returned after the lunch hour, she mostly stayed inside. For Wayne, it was a win-win situation, until Marlie showed up. It wouldn't have mattered if she was as incompetent as Angus, the sight of her uniform sent shivers of fear up and down his entire body. While the two women were inside, he slunk out the pig door on the back of the barn and back across the orchard.

Best I get out of here, he thought. *It's a good thing I know where there's another hidey-hole out on Route 116.*

Chapter Six

"What did you decide about the barn?" Stan asked when Katie showed up at work the next morning.

His words made her heart skip a beat, and not in a happy way. Instead of getting into why it shouldn't happen, Katie told her boss what he wanted to hear.

"It sounds like a great idea, Stan," said Katie. "But it's a huge expense. We talked about it and we're going to let them come out, do their evaluation, and make a decision after that."

He waited a beat, then said, "If you try to do this alone, out of pocket, it'll never happen. If you don't do anything, you might as well buy five gallons of gas and a match. You're going to lose the building. It's not going to cost you anything to have them come out and evaluate the project. So, it's a good idea to let them do that. In the meantime, there's an office in the state house that deals with historical preservation. Contact them about the stagecoach inn, like Percy said. If they can't help you, maybe they know someone who can."

Katie nodded, which Stan took for agreement.

That evening, shortly after Marlie headed back north, an RV camper pulled in and parked down near where Myers was offloading the new Rent-A-Potty. The five men who piled out of the RV were the first crew from Harwood Architectural Restorations, two older ones and three guys in their mid to late twenties. Katie and Ruth watched from the pantry window.

"I hope you got enough stuff moved out of the barn so they can see what they're doing and not waste time," Katie said.

"Yeah, well, I hope Bonnie stays in her new pig yard and doesn't try to run them all off," Ruth quipped.

Rick and Charlie had moved the brand-new picnic table they had constructed down to the level area where the camper was parked. It would be handy for Steve's crew. While the women watched, one of the young guys hauled a hibachi out of the camper and set it on the end of the picnic table. Another guy lugged out a cooler, and the third set up the first of what would be four pup tents.

Rick sauntered down to speak with the guys. Solomon followed. While everyone was occupied, he took a leak against the back of the nearest tent.

"Oh, my," said Ruth, hand over her mouth.

Katie had a slightly ruder reaction.

* * *

Morning broke hot and sunny. It was barely mid-July, but there had already been days when it was sweltering before mid-morning. Ruth complained about the truck gardens going dry and how the produce had stopped growing as fast as it had overgrown weeks before. Davey Dean sat in the seat of the big John Deere in the early morning and late evening, spewing water from a holding tank towed behind. The duck pond was a slimy mess of muddy gunk and duckweed. The mallards stayed by the pond, but Splish and Splash, having lost their goslings to cash-paying new homes, wandered up to the house periodically. There, they chased cats, pinched people, and ran away from Bonnie.

* * *

Katie and Rick staggered in at the end of the day, glad for the slightly cooler house, even if the air was a tad bit stale and the nine original and seven newbie cats were shedding like leaves falling in October.

"Another kitten gone today," Ruth said. "Five to go, but I don't think the mother is ever going to be tame enough to re-home."

"So, she'll have to stay?" Katie asked. She checked in on the gray tiger mom. Separated from her kittens, who could now feed themselves and needed to be tamed, she crouched in the furthest corner beneath a sheltering cover. But Katie could still hear the hiss and see laid-back ears and exposed canines.

When she had trapped this feral mother and her kittens, the property owner had been adamant that, even after the adult female had been spayed, she was not to be released back there. The request was justified when Katie encountered the homeowner's two large and not-friendly dogs.

"Seriously?" Rick groaned. The new mother cat was a squealer, who spent each night grieving her imprisonment.

Ruth clattered a couple of pots together and changed the subject. "Them poor young guys working out in the heat. All they brought to eat was mostly just sandwich fixings and chips. I've been watching them all afternoon, cooling down with the hose."

Katie stood for a couple of minutes in the pantry window, watching the activity down near the camper. Finally, she slid the bottom pane up. "What are you guys eating down there?" she yelled out.

When the answer came back as hot dogs, she directed the men to get rinsed off and come in where it was cooler.

"I'll set up the fans," Rick said. "You figure out what you're going to be feeding that mess of empty bellies."

Having just eaten hot dogs themselves, Katie suggested the workers save theirs and put out the last of Sunday's baked beans, slices of cold ham, side bowls of macaroni salad, and bowls of Ruth's freshly canned vegetables. The men were all polite and even offered to wash dishes. After they left, Ruth tsk-tsked about the workers having to live out of pup tents while Rick napped on the sofa. Katie was willing to bet he was faking it.

She hauled one of the box fans upstairs and futilely pushed LG away. But like a small heating pad attached by Velcro, the semi-feral who had adopted the least likely human in the house tucked in warm and close. Out beyond, a coyote called. There was no answering yip of young, so dinner hadn't yet been provided.

Chapter Seven

The first group from Harwood Architectural left on Saturday. Katie was out on an animal call where a mama skunk and her adorable babies were killing the lawns in one of the developments. It seemed the city folk didn't see the humor in the perfect polka dots of yellow grass.

Three days later, a second group of workers from Harwood Architectural Renovators showed up. Wayne had returned to the haymow, but with the up-sweep in commotion, decided he needed to find a different place to stay. Fortunately, Jacob and Irene Hunt had closed up their house on Route 116 and were renting a cottage on Mallett's Bay for the summer. He'd watched them go from the woods behind Meredith's house next door.

* * *

Katie hadn't seen the new group, as they had arrived late the night before. There had been a big flux at her animal control officer job. New homeowners were coming home from work after leaving their dogs in the house all day. But instead of going out into the heat to walk them, or even hook them on the run, they opened their doors. The pets were allowed to run amok, doing their business in the yards of others. It seemed as though people used to keeping their dogs restrained and licensed while living in the city felt Parentville was too primitive for such consideration.

Katie was summoned to the selectmen's office for a meeting on the issue. Shortly after she arrived, Sheriff Lewis joined the meeting, as did the town clerk, Janice. She had been a friend of both Katie's mother and grandmother, and very helpful to Katie since her return.

When Lewis opened the adjoining doors between the sheriff's department and the town hall, Katie caught a glimpse of Deputy Brad headed out the other entrance to the sheriff's office. She was sure nearsighted Angus, with his thick coke-bottle glasses, was seated at the deputy's desk. His job was to wait for the phone to ring or file incident reports.

Janice pulled the door to the inner office closed. A hand reached out to stop her. A man of Katie's height, and perhaps a few years younger, entered. He looked pretty buff, but not in a country boy way. The town clerk made a face, but didn't say a word.

"My name is Gage Fernald," the man said. "I have a vested interest in these proceedings and wish to sit in for this meeting."

"Well, it's not a closed meeting," said Paul Wright, the selectman chair. "So, I guess you can, but there won't be any participation. How'd you know we were meeting today?"

Behind Fernald, Janice gave a small head shake. Fernald didn't answer the question, but Lewis spoke up.

"Let's get this done. I've got a packed schedule today."

Mr. Wright picked up a short page of notes and referred to them. "Even though the town placed notices in the Burlington Free Press, as well as an attached message with the tax bills, and posted around town, there are still a lot of complainers who call the town office. As well as the sheriff's office. We need to come up with a plan on how to handle the issue of loose dogs."

"As I mentioned to you before, Paul." Lewis was very familiar with the chairman, but didn't so much as acknowledge Katie. "These calls take up a lot of time. By the time a sheriff shows up, the evidence is gone."

Katie almost giggled at the idea of poop being referred to as evidence. Fernald inched from the door to a place in front of Janice, closer to Lewis.

"Isn't that the animal control officer's job?" he asked.

Katie had heard him give a little snicker when Lewis had answered Paul Wright, never giving Katie a chance to speak. Even now, Lewis's sideways glance slid over her like she was non-existent.

Mr. Wright held up his hand. "I said you have no participation." He turned to Lewis. "I've given this some thought since our initial conversation."

Huh. This was Katie's first hint that there had been a conversation between the sheriff's department and the town.

"The board and town clerk's office have come to an agreement that when a complaint comes into the town clerk's office—Katie will go out to verify the presence of poop. If the sheriff's department wants her to act, they can also go through us."

This time, a giggle was heard. But it came from Janice. Katie was sure the need for Lewis to go through Janice to get to her had to have been put in there by the town clerk. Even the corner of Mr. Wright's mouth lifted.

"Katie." Mr. Wright addressed her directly. "When Janice receives a call, she'll contact you and issue a chit. What your SOP will be is to contact the caller, verify the problem, and get a description of the dog, because you aren't going out unless a dog was seen. After that, you will contact the owner and deliver a copy of the ordinance. Janice will run you off some copies. That way, we have a record. If there's a repeat offense, the complaint will be forwarded to the sheriff's office for fining. Do you have any questions?"

Fernald made a noise that sounded like he had something to say, but he was ignored.

"Do I need to get the chit signed, like when I remove a nuisance animal? If the dog is still there, do I pick it up? Or just get the tag information to track down the owner? And how am I going to get paid for this?"

Again, Fernald cleared his throat. He definitely had something to say, but Mr. Wright refused to ask him what it was.

"You've got some blank chits, right? If you can get a signature, either at the dump site or from the dog owner, that would be good. Chain of evidence, and all that happy horse crap. I think it's a good idea to notate the tag information. As far as picking up the animal, we'll need further discussion. There's no time for that today."

"Do I have to clean up the mess?"

"Nope. The deal with the fee is pretty much why we're here. You get paid fifty dollars for trapping, removing, and relocating what could be a dangerous animal. Ain't no way the town is gonna pay that for scooping up a pile of crap." Mr. Wright sat back, both palms on his desk, eyes on Lewis.

"Every time the sheriff has to serve a notice, there's a twenty-five-dollar fee," Lewis said. "'Course for us, there's always a danger issue."

"Ever been bitten by a dog?" Katie asked. "That's pretty nasty."

"Excuse me," Janice interrupted. "My opinion is that Ms. Took should be paid fifteen dollars if she goes out and delivers the ordinance. No delivery, no fee. We could attach an addendum to the notice that the first warning is no fault, as in no citizen pays, but if there is a second incident, the dog owner will be charged both fees."

"Sounds good to me," said Mr. Wright. "Of course, it'll have to go through the selectmen's meeting on Thursday. How does it sound to you, Sheriff? Katie?"

Both Katie and Lewis nodded in agreement.

"Mr. Chairman." Fernald stepped forward.

"Meeting's adjourned." Mr. Wright ignored the interloper once again.

Janice left the office, with Katie right behind her. A jostle at her elbow caused her to turn, thinking it was Lewis. It turned out to be Gage Fernald, rushing toward the exit to the parking lot.

"Well," said Katie. "Must be supper's waiting, or he's got to get back to work."

"It's only four-thirty," said Janice. "Too early for supper, and he works in South Burlington. I bet he's not headed there."

Fernald's Volvo pulled out of the parking lot, headed north on US Route 116. He bypassed the turnoff on Shelbourne Road, which would take him toward the cul-de-sac where his split-level was located, and continued toward Saint George. No one knew his destination except himself.

Chapter Eight

The next day, Katie told Cindy Baldwin about the meeting at the town hall.

"What a load of BS," Cindy said. "Or maybe DS, dog sh… ah poop."

Davidson, who was eavesdropping, laughed behind his hand.

"When I have to take the critters out to someplace new is all due to loss of habitat," Katie said. "Forest critters and their families will show up in places which had always been safe for them before. Now, practically overnight, a house, a family, and pets are taking up their space. Old habits are hard to overcome. But wild animals that have to deal with domestic dogs face a different issue."

"I know, and now people complain about their neighbors being outside with shotguns and rifles. No wonder the sheriff's department is involved." Cindy picked up her stack of time cards, ready to return to the office. "We got a letter in the mail. I also saw a story in the Burlington Free Press about the law restricting the firing of guns in residential areas. Get ready, Katie. Both stories featured you as the animal control officer, and your contact information was right there."

Katie let out a frustrated groan. There was nothing she could do about the wild critters that wandered into new backyards except respond and react accordingly. She still wasn't sure what to do about the dogs. Cats were a handful by themselves.

Her head felt like it would explode from the continued internal barrage between the changes in her town job and the arrival of the men camped down near the barn. Every time she thought about them, she remembered the financial quote Steve had given. Pondering on it made her physically sick, but she couldn't get away from the issue due to Ruth's continual harping on how inadequate the pup-tents were. It was a constant reminder of what was going on. Now, with the newly raised thunderstorm warning, Ruth would be even louder. Even Marlie, who had arrived the evening before, offered an opinion. She sided with Ruth that the workmen should be moved inside.

"Don't look now, Katie," Davidson whispered. "But your new favorite customer is back."

Katie watched the back of Meredith's brassy blond head dip and swirl in the paint aisle.

"What's she doing?" Katie wondered aloud.

"Looks like spackle, primer, and a quart of latex," Davidson answered. "Yeah, and a package of assorted brushes. Here she comes."

Katie decided that retreat would be the better part of valor, at least for the next five minutes, and ducked into the office. While she waited for Meredith to pay up and leave, she confessed to Cindy that she was hiding.

"Did you get a good look at her?" Cindy guffawed. At the shake of Katie's head, her friend continued, "Besides the fact she dresses like a teenager, there's something else in the wind. I saw her in the grocery the other day, and she looked really rough. Eugenie told me she let her boys go on vacation with her ex-husband a couple of weeks ago, and now he won't bring them back. Poor girl. I can't imagine."

Katie had to admit that sounded bad. But in the back of her mind, she remembered high school Meredith. That girl was not one who should ever have children. Had she changed so much, or just gotten caught up in the expected lifestyle of a lawyer's wife?

Katie slid back in behind the cash register just in time to watch Meredith's car jerk out into traffic. A fist waved out the driver's window as an approaching car's horn blared in indignation. Once again, Katie shook her head, grateful that her encounters with Meredith was a rare phenomenon.

Chapter Nine

Meanwhile, up on the hill, guys crawled around under the barn and over heaps of muck that had to be fifteen to a hundred and fifty years old. Ruth happily pasted labels on jars of pickles, relish, and chutney, and kept the phone line tied up as she updated members of the Feral Cat Rescue Society about their upcoming fundraiser. All through the first-floor rooms, cats and the two dogs sprawled out in front of box fans. Drifts of fur rolled across the old hardwood floors like tumbleweed.

Large, high-ceilinged rooms with tall, narrow, nine-pane windows comprised the building, which had originally been a stagecoach inn. Four rooms up and four down, all dormitory style, with two fireplaces on each level. The kitchen was an add-on ell, which included the pantry and bathroom. On the first floor, the parlor room was situated at the front, and the two rooms on the back corner were kept closed and unused. They were far from the kitchen woodstove, and currently empty of furniture.

Long before Katie had moved in with her grandparents, the stagecoach shed had been converted to a garage. While she couch-surfed in Illinois, Grandma Irma had renovated that single car space into the cat room. Lined with commercial housing crates—three tall along two walls, with an isolation space and a maternity ward—it was currently at three-quarter-feline capacity.

The telephone cord allowed Ruth to travel only six feet from the wall-mounted unit, receiver tucked between her ear and shoulder. "No, I won't be able to get down there to help sort stuff out, Dorothea. You'll have to see to it," Ruth said. "Tonight, we're moving my bedroom downstairs to the small back room."

"Why is that?" The cackling question came over the phone line. "Are you too old to do stairs?"

It was on the tip of Ruth's tongue to explain that Marlie had suggested Ruth and Rick should have the lower bedroom and she'd take the upper room. Then she remembered that Marlie's stay needed to remain a secret.

"Twit," she said. "It'll be cooler downstairs. But there's stuff gotta be moved down, and stuff that's gotta go up."

Marlie's meager possessions had been stored in the empty parlor since she'd taken the job in Pennsylvania. Even now, back in Vermont, living in the rent-by-week motel room in Irasberg, she had little use for her household items. Fortunately, there was a bed among everything stacked there.

"Yeah, well, I still think it's cause you're a danged old fart," replied Dorothea.

*   *   *

Before Katie, Rick, and Charlie got home from work, Ruth had most of her smaller things downstairs and some of Marlie's up. The rest of the move took a little over half an hour, with even Charlie's help.

Though he was short and round, Charlie willingly did whatever Katie asked of him. He had come home from Vietnam with a lot of problems and found a job with the town driving their dump truck. But he'd still been a short-timer with sobriety when he'd become homeless the day the boardinghouse went up in flames. Katie offered him space in the house. There were rules, but he was grateful. They'd made it through the spring, and even she had been impressed at the change in the little man.

"Looking positively slim," Katie had told him when the heavy clothing of winter had been shed.

Everybody knew it had to do with his giving up alcohol. And possibly the interest of the Widow O'Brien, but no one said a word about that. There were a couple of times he'd tumbled off the wagon, but Katie was a recovered drinker herself and understood how it could happen.

As Rick and Charlie preceded her up the staircase with the bottom end of Marlie's headboard, Katie noticed again the difference in the little man's girth. His suspenders were barely keeping his pants up. With the big rolled cuffs and sagging waist, he looked like a clown. She turned back toward Ruth at the base of the stairs and nodded upward.

"I think, Ruth, it's time you helped Charlie walk his fingers through the Sears catalog."

"I kind of thought the same thing," the older woman said. "From here, he looks like a trip-and-fall accident, looking for a place to happen."

The women giggled, but Charlie, huffing and puffing to keep up with Rick, never noticed.

Chapter Ten

Wayne had found a friend in a town employee who had picked him up walking and offered a ride. Their meeting had happened earlier in the same morning Wayne left Katie's hay mow, knowing he wouldn't be able to return. He had snuck down out of the barn loft and circled around through the high brush, which edged the little meadow to the east of the house and along the LaPlatte brook's wandering curve.

Wayne had just visited the retired one-room schoolhouse turned farm stand, and the newer structure beside it, which the Deans had built, since he had discovered it weeks before. One building was full of used junk, and the other, which looked like a maple sugar shack, had shelves of canned vegetables, a fridge with cheese and small bottles of goat's milk, and a latched cabinet of day-old pastries. The latch kept raccoons and squirrels out, but not Wayne. He'd been careful not to take too much, but when the pickings were slim, that's where he'd go. Too bad the cash box was emptied on a daily basis.

The morning he'd left the barn, a customer had dropped in and picked out some goodies, leaving two dollars and fifteen cents in the till. He hated to steal, but he had a need for some new pants and the old biddy at the thrift store only accepted cash. Wayne took only what he needed, and with one dollar and fifteen cents in his pocket, two pint jars of green beans, and the last three slightly stale cupcakes, he'd just turned off Fire Lane 61 onto the road into Parentville when a fairly new but dusty pickup truck pulled alongside him.

"Are you broke down?" A heavy guy hung out the driver's window. "Do you need a lift in to the village?"

Wayne was so surprised and scared, his knees clenched together. "Nah, I'll be okay."

"Don't be a sap." The guy grinned. "I'm headed right that way. C'mon."

Wayne circled the truck, tucking the pint jars into his pants pockets. One rapped up against the change and brought a small trickle of sweat down the side of his face.

"You new here?" The driver shifted into first. "I'm Charlie. Those look like Grace Dean's cupcakes. Good, aren't they?"

"Would you like one?" Wayne croaked out and suddenly realized where he'd seen Charlie before.

"No. You enjoy them. I get to have all that stuff on a regular basis. What did you say your name was?"

"Wayne."

He could have kicked himself. This was no time to tell the truth. The truck pulled up to the stop sign at Main Street with the right-hand blinker on.

"Where'd you say you was going?" Charlie asked.

"Over to the church. But I'm good right here." Wayne reached for the doorknob.

The truck spun around the corner. "I'm going right past there," Charlie said. "And you're in luck 'cause you're a little early. Dorothea won't be inside for another fifteen minutes."

Charlie proceeded to pull into the lot, shut down the truck, and uncap his thermos. He produced a chipped mug from the glove compartment and half-filled it with milky sweet coffee.

"Here. This will help wash them cupcakes down." He handed the mug across the bench seat.

For the next ten minutes, Wayne sipped hot coffee and chowed down on cupcakes while Charlie provided a thumbnail sketch of his life. It wasn't until he began to talk about moving into the stagecoach house with Katie, Ruth, and Rick that Wayne's ears perked up. Charlie paused to take a breath, and Wayne opened his mouth to ask a question when a green sedan pulled in beside them and a very old woman clamored out.

"Here you go." Charlie cranked the key in the ignition. "Dorothea will help you right out. I gotta get on. That dump truck ain't gonna drive itself."

Charlie pulled away, Ellen unloaded Dorothea's bags and sacks for the day, and Wayne somehow got to lug them down the staircase into the basement thrift store. Even though the morning was warm and dry, he felt a chill below, heightened by the buzzing and blinking as the fluorescents near as old as their keeper struggled to come alive.

"How about you take this hook and open them windows up there?" Dorothea handed Wayne a six-foot pole with a brass knob and a catch on the end. The high windows, all on the parking lot side, were dusty, both within and without. "Let some fresh air in here," she said, pawing through the first of her bags.

And the heat, Wayne thought.

Once he had the windows the way she wanted, Wayne hustled through the men's clothing, finding a pair of worn jeans in the right size with a dollar price tag. He paid and was headed up the steps before Dorothea had her first cup of coffee poured. She watched him go, wondering who he was until the jangle of the telephone announced the first of her gossipy friends with news to spread.

Wayne tucked the jeans and pints into the knapsack he'd taken from the Hunt house. Inside were some of Jacob's shirts and socks. Too bad he hadn't gotten free pants, too. But Jacob was a big-bellied man, and Wayne was lean. He could have wrapped the cotton pants that hung in the closet around his waist twice. Hence the trip to Dorothea World.

Traffic had started to pick up. Wayne knew he stood out perched on the side of the street like this. Even as he considered the options for a temporary hiding place, one of the sheriff's cruisers roared past.

Wayne was good with cars. He knew this was the vehicle the showy deputy normally drove. Today, the deputy moved along faster than he should have been right in the middle of town. Wayne was close enough to catch a good look at Brad's face. He could see the big smile and the piece of paper the deputy was holding against the steering wheel.

A frown pulled down Wayne's mouth. It was clear Brad was trying to read and drive at the same time. That set up a scenario where an accident could happen, and with Wayne right there, he could get collared and end up back in jail.

Wayne cut behind the next three houses and ended up on the back side of the general store's parking lot. There was a tumbledown garage way at the back, lost in a growth of spruce saplings. The old sign that once identified the building as Beauregard's General Store leaned against the broken front doors. It had been replaced by a new neon sign announcing the establishment as In Town Market. Wayne had no way of knowing the flashy, out-of-place sign was a Band-Aid Tracy Beauregard had put in place to diminish the shame her ex had brought to the business. For him, it offered a place he could sit and hide without being inside the crumbling garage.

Dang, good thing this sucker is here, Wayne thought as he got settled in behind the old sign. *Probably holding the place up so it won't fall down on my head, and nobody would find me for years.*

Later, at the diesel rumble of a big truck, Wayne peeked around the corner. He watched Charlie climb down from the driver's seat. When the door slammed shut behind him, the words TOWN OF PARENTVILLE let Wayne know where his new friend worked. That was a good and a bad thing. Not only did he know where the one guy in town who had gotten a good, long look at him lived and worked, but it also meant Charlie could pop up almost anywhere.

Wayne leaned back on his pack and let out a long sigh. Another thing he'd have to watch for when he was out walking around. He stayed well-hidden near the garage for several hours, except for the one time he ventured into the store to use the restroom. And shoplift a Coke and a candy bar.

Eugenie was working behind the cash register. She was an easy mark. All he had to do was wait until some local busybody started talking. Then, while the veteran clerk was complaining about how useless all the young employees were, he walked casually out with the goods.

While most were home for their supper, he hiked back out to the Hunt property. The weekend was right around the corner, and he'd be safer where there was less activity. As he passed Meredith's house, he noticed her car was on the side of the driveway and the garage door was up. Wayne laughed to himself because he knew that meant she expected guy company. He circled the big patch of rhododendron Irene Hunt was so proud of and stepped onto the back porch. The window over the kitchen sink had been left unlocked, which provided him with an easy way to slip inside.

Chapter Eleven

Toward the end of the evening, when the moving at the former stagecoach inn was all done, and the residents relaxed with a slice of cake and a last cup of tea, Wayne parked his butt on the edge of Irene Hunt's spare bed. Up here on the second floor, he could see up and down the road, far out across the pasture, and if the curtains were open over at Meredith's big white house, right into the bathroom.

Wayne considered himself no different from any other red-blooded male. If he had a chance at a little peek-show, he'd take it. Granted, the blond prude over at the nearby house was really good at keeping her curtains closed. But lately during Wayne's brief visits to the Hunt house, there had been something different to watch than her continual screaming rants at the kids.

Wonder where those little brats are right now. They've been gone for a while.

He'd been down in the basement, rummaging through the freezer looking for something Irene wouldn't miss when she returned at the end of the summer, when he heard a car roar out of the garage of the next-door house, then screaming tires as it hit the road back toward town.

Wayne knew the guy had been there. The one who was the reason the blond parked her car off to the side and left the garage door open. Wayne had seen the dark Volvo sedan pull in before, and immediately heard the slam of the garage door as it was pulled down. At those times, every curtain in the house was shut tight. Usually, the only light on was in the big bedroom upstairs.

It was early for the car to be gone. A light had come on in the bathroom, and Wayne saw the blonde as she leaned on the sink, and peered into the mirror as she held a cloth to the side of her face. Even though she looked tousled and one spaghetti strap of her silk nightgown had slipped down her shoulder, she didn't look rosy. There was something brittle about the way she stood, hunched up as if the breeze from the open window felt icy. When she turned for just a moment in his direction, Wayne could have sworn the right side of her face, lit up by the double row of makeup lights, showed an angry red around her eye and cheek.

Down on the road, an old gray Chevy Impala with a lot more miles than it should have, but still running, coasted along in the same direction as the sedan. Marlie, with her suitcases and plastic-draped, freshly dry-cleaned uniforms, had pulled into town. She'd finished her last shift in the north country at four, and tomorrow morning, she would report in Parentville at seven. She was thrilled—and scared to death. Not because of the job. She knew how to do it, and she was good at it. But Sheriff Lewis was a whole other story. He hadn't been on her side the last time she was here. And she wasn't sure how he'd feel about her now.

Chapter Twelve

The Feral Cat Rescue Society had joined forces with the knitting group, though most of the same women belonged to both. They had taken to setting up a table at every fete, church gathering, or fundraising event that came along. Saturday, the Saint Jude Church Thrift Shop offered a dollar-a-bag sale. There was also a petting zoo that consisted of two baby goats and a litter of kittens in a cardboard box. The FCRS was set up between the thrift shop entrance and the barbecue grills. Katie slipped over during her lunch break at the feed store to see how the ladies had done so far, and if any of Mrs. Meyer's strudel was left.

Katie was in luck on the strudel. After paying for her sweet, she waited for a break in the action and addressed one of the women. "Hi, Eugenie," she said. "Has it been busy?"

"Sold out of brownies, Rice Krispie treats, and fudge," Ellen said before Eugenie had a chance to exhale her cigarette smoke and reply. "Over at the knitting table, they're about out of baby and toddler mittens on a string."

"How come you're up here and not downstairs helping your Aunt Dorothea in the thrift?" Katie asked Ellen. To her eye, business looked a little slow for extra people to just hang around.

"Needed some air. It's like a zoo down there." Ellen looked over her shoulder, then whispered conspiratorially, "I had to sneak out. Aunt Dorothea didn't want me to leave. If you're looking for Ruth, she stepped into the rectory for tea. The firemen are grilling hot dogs and hamburgers. I hope to get over there before they're all gone."

Katie considered the temptation of a hamburger herself, but when she looked over to where the volunteer firemen in t-shirts and jeans were grouped around the homemade grill, her yearning disappeared. Among the guys who sported farmer's tans and discreetly held beers was Gage Fernald. Wearing a short-sleeved dress shirt and pleated trousers, he held a longneck between two fingers like it might jump up and bite him. Katie saw the forced smile on his face and the self-conscious way the fire guys leaned away. If this was how Gage planned to fit in and raise his chances at a vote, she knew he would fail miserably.

Ellen had disappeared, so Katie turned towards Eugenie, who was now the bake sale salesperson. She missed seeing the man who had stepped aside so Ellen could run down the stairs into the church basement.

Wayne was in a hurry to leave, as Dorothea had him in her sights. But he wasn't in such a rush that he didn't look before he went.

As far as Dorothea, she'd cocked an eyebrow when Wayne had come down the stairs and she recognized him. The man was a lot cleaner than the last time she'd seen him. He'd even shaved. Not only that, but he had money to spend. She watched him pick out another pair of pants, a couple of t-shirts, and a blanket.

"Got yourself a place here in town?" she asked, with a nod toward the blanket.

Wayne stopped moving down the aisle. Only his eyes slid to the side. He didn't want her to be looking at him too closely. "No. I'm out the other way. You know, got a room." He laughed. "Still trying to get my bearings."

He laid down the ten-dollar bill he had taken from Irene Hunt's cookie jar. He hadn't expected there to be so many people at the thrift shop when he'd walked into town. He wanted to find what he needed in the thrift shop and get out of the place fast.

Dorothea scooped up the money, swiftly making change while she considered which one of her friends she could fix up with this guy. He had to be fifty, and she figured he had a job because he had money in his hand. Now that he was cleaned up, he wasn't too hard on the eyes.

Wayne folded the clothing, picked up a paper sack, and bagged his purchases while Dorothea counted out his change. He was itching to get out of there. Dorothea had a different idea.

"You know, sometimes I need a strong pair of hands here," she said. "Pay is merchandise or cash."

"We'll see." Wayne smiled, but didn't look directly at her. *As if*, he thought.

At the top of the stairs, he saw Katie just as he stepped out. Lowering his head, he shuffled away.

But intent on Eugenie, Katie didn't even notice him, or Ellen leaving either. Tentatively, she asked, "Eugenie, how's it going, working over at the store now that Christopher is gone?"

Though Ruth went to the mercantile regularly, Katie was leery of doing so. She had been the one who identified Christopher Beauregard as having murdered his brother George Jr. in a futile attempt to save the family business. Parentville was a small town, and New Englanders had long memories. It wasn't often she went somewhere in town and didn't feel eyes on her back.

"When I heard the store was going up for sale after Chris got busted, I freaked out," said Eugenie. "Arlo and I knew our livelihood was gonna take a nosedive. You could have knocked me over with a feather when Tracy stepped forward and said she and the boys were keeping the store." Eugenie leaned across the table. "She's got a brass set. I tell you what, she's a next-generation Dorothea. But mostly she's okay, except the days there's a hair across her butt."

Eugenie, tall and spare, had a laugh like a braying mule. Nearby, heads turned.

Katie took a quick look around, then headed back to her car, snack in hand. Ruth repeatedly told her she was too sensitive, but Katie knew that if attention was drawn to a group she was in, she became the focal point. That was why she helped put together the FCRS events, but never stood behind the table.

Phyllis Ames, their main benefactor, and Ruth were just coming out of the rectory as Katie passed it. Their heads together, neither spotted her, and she continued on, but she wondered what the two women were cooking up. Usually, it was something she'd get dragged into.

Wayne was aghast at the number of people who were in the parking lot. The burgers smelled delicious, but to walk into that group of men was out of the question. Being around Katie, even though she wouldn't know who he was, made him nervous. Once he was sure Katie wasn't just out of sight, but gone, Wayne hurried out to the street and past four houses to the In Town Market parking lot. Then he returned to his hiding place behind the old sign.

Back at the hardware store, Katie shared her strudel with Davidson. As the junior clerk and all-around shelf filler, he was always anxious to buddy up. He unwrapped the dessert and gushed his thanks.

This time, Katie decided to buck his annoyingly over-friendly facade. "Chill out, Davidson," she said. "It's a piece of strudel. I didn't ask you to the prom."

The young man stopped cold. Katie could almost see him shrivel up. Head bowed, he slowly removed the Saran Wrap. The tips of his ears were red, and so was the little she could see of his face.

With a groan to herself, Katie tried to clean up the mess she had just made of their working relationship. "So, Davidson. I know you have a girlfriend from the village, but are you from here?" She opened her cash drawer, facing up her paper money, with an occasional peek at her co-worker from the corner of her eye. "I don't mean to be nosy, but I never hear you say oh, that's my brother, uncle, dad's-wife's-sister's-cousin-in-law, you know?"

The twenty-year-old relaxed visibly. "Actually, I'm from over Richmond way. I have two brothers. They both work in Williston, and I tried. It's just that, well…" He frowned at the piece of strudel as if the sweet he had really wanted to eat a moment before would turn his stomach now. "To be honest, I'm a nervous driver. When I have to drive into the city, I get all shaky, kind of sick. Sometimes it's so bad, I have to turn around and go home." His voice petered out to a whisper.

"I know what you mean," Katie said.

"You do?" Davidson sounded surprised.

"Yeah." Katie grimaced. "But with me, the problem is that I open my big mouth before I consider what I want to say. It's like my weakness. Yours is traffic, mine is what comes out of my mouth."

"Are you kids working or what?" Stan came up and handed Katie the inventory tally sheets. "Davidson, is that strudel for you to eat or give away? I could help you out."

"Don't give it to him, Davidson," Katie said. "He already had a slice."

Moving away to focus on the items listed that she needed to find and count, she heard the crinkle of Saran Wrap as Davidson took his first big bite.

Chapter Thirteen

Wayne hadn't been the only one to keep track of the ladies at the Feral Cat Rescue Society table. From his place among the group of redneck grillers, Gabe had his eye on the women as well. Katie in particular. When he had first decided he wanted a place in local politics, and eventually on a state level, he'd been hard put to find anyone local who didn't have a brother, son, niece, or nephew in just about every seat. He wasn't averse to rubbing elbows with the rubes he thought were intellectually, financially, and socially beneath him in pursuit of a seat on the selectman's board. Unfortunately, Gage had a problem identifying an issue for his platform that somebody established in town didn't already address. He had come up with the idea of the animal control officer after a general gripe turned into a full-blown argument at the selectmen's meeting. Most of the people complaining were fellow transplants like himself and Amanda. The guys in this group were close to his age, some married to his wife's friends. They would be agreeable to supporting him, he was sure.

His wife, Amanda, had taken to small-town life quickly. She was already active in the community and well-liked. Today, she was down in the church basement with that sly old crab, Dorothea. Just the thought of the old woman made him shudder. She had a cold fish eye that looked right into his soul. Gabe knew the old woman saw through him like a clear glass of water. He had made the mistake of trying to recruit supporters by complaining about the animal control officer's rate of pay, but Dorothea had been within hearing range. She'd come down on him like a ton of bricks.

"If you'd been around any amount of time, Mr. Smarty," she'd said, "you'd know there ain't a danged other person who wanted that job. There are times the officer has to go out two, three times a day, all on the same chit. Then too, ain't no benefits, nor insurance. One bite by a danged rabid 'coon and every dang cent she's earned in a year is blown out the window."

There'd been a lot of heads that nodded in agreement. He felt his face getting red at the memory and blinked hard twice, a trick to keep the other side of the courtroom unaware that his thinking had gotten confused. Now it brought him back to where he stood in the smoke of a charcoal grill and inhaling the greasy stink of fried hamburger. He kept his bruised right hand, the knuckles still raw from the couple of punches he'd thrown in his pocket. He could feel the part in his hair sunburn.

"You're getting a little red-faced there," Amos, one of the farmers, said. "Best you get a hat."

Several men laughed. A short, slightly round elderly man wearing a well-seasoned John Deere bill cap walked up. He asked for two hamburgers, one with just ketchup and the other with the works. He paid with a five and told Amos to put the rest in the till. Then he headed straight out of the lot and across the street.

"I'm surprised you could understand a word he said," Gabe said, referring to the old man's heavy French accent. He ended with a guffaw, then realized several in the group frowned.

Amos, dressed in worn bib overalls and smelling slightly like moldy wood, tapped Gabe's arm with the top of his beer bottle. "That's Arthur Fortin. He's been here a long time. Kind of one of the pillars of the town. This church," Amos nodded toward Saint Jude's, "is his baby. He and his boys built it with their own hands." Then Amos turned away to sell hot dogs to a woman with two small girls and a teenage boy.

Gabe looked at the other guys. "Whoops. Faux pas," he said and grinned.

His statement was met with small smiles and hooded eyes. He knew he'd stepped into a pile of poop. Amanda had told him that all these people were interrelated, and he needed to be careful of what he said. Excusing himself, he walked over to the doorway that led down into the basement. Ellen had decided to make her getaway from Dorothea and almost collided with Gabe.

They danced around each other for a few seconds, then parted. Neither paid much attention to the other.

At the bottom of the steps, Gabe called to his wife, "Amanda, didn't you bring a chili setup for the hot dogs?"

His petite, dark-haired wife rushed past him. "I bet it's still in the car. C'mon, we'll get it." Halfway up the stairs, she called, "I'll be right back, Dorothea."

Once they were out in the sun, Gabe said, "Couldn't you find somebody other than that old witch to chum around with?"

Ellen, who was behind the mitten table, didn't turn, but her ears stretched wide.

Amanda swung around on her heel, hissing at Gabe. "You wanted me to find out how the land lay here so you could get into local politics. That old witch isn't a bad woman, and she's lived here her entire life. She sits on every committee going, and she knows *everybody*. If you don't make friends with her, she will, as she says, fry your bacon."

Ellen's lip twitched at Amanda's very accurate imitation of her great-aunt.

Gabe stood there, suddenly aware of how his wife had blossomed since they'd moved here. She never would have jumped on him like that before. Not here, not in the car, and not at home. When he had bragged to her about what he planned to do, he had believed her simple little mind was unable to grasp what he spoke of.

With the crockpot of chili and containers of chopped onion, green peppers, and grated cheese, he returned to the grill area, hoping his offering might mend some of the fences he'd broken down. Amos nodded and smiled with everyone else, but he had insider knowledge via his wife, Monique, as to how Gabe Fernald was a barb in Katie's side. No amount of cheddar would make up for that.

Chapter Fourteen

At supper, Katie told Rick about how she'd hurt Davidson's feelings. "The kid is a rookie. He's still so awkward, and I feel bad for him because I know some of the other guys make him the butt of their jokes."

"It's because he tries too hard." Rick scooped the turkey shepherd's pie onto his plate.

"Yeah," Katie agreed. But what she really wanted to know was how to help Gabe. She wasn't good at communicating with young human males. She hadn't been in high school, and her skills hadn't improved over time.

She lifted the top of the oval casserole dish off the table where it left a big steam mark. It was a beautiful piece. Clear glass with a fancy etched design, Ruth had found it among Irma's barn collection. Instead of taking it down to the Schoolhouse Thrift Store at the end of the road, she'd brought it to Katie. She didn't need more cookware, but the look of it gave her pleasure. Katie smiled as she admired the piece one more time. Belatedly, she realized Rick was still speaking.

"Say that again?"

"We need to move all the rest of the stuff out of the barn before construction starts."

"We don't know yet that there will be any construction," Katie snapped. "Besides, I thought all the junk was about gone. Where are we going to put any more of it?"

"It's not junk." Ruth defended the side-of-the-road, dump picked, and yard sale cleanup collection Irma had left behind.

Both Katie and Rick stared at the elderly woman.

"Okay," Ruth said with a sigh. "A lot of it was. But we weeded out and hauled away all the clothes and broken stuff. Remember? You and Rick took those stanchions from the barn and stuff that could go to the recycling."

Katie nodded. They had done everything they could think of to pull together funds to pay off Irma's debts. They still were. Things were better now, as far as the creditors were concerned. But back then, they hadn't considered the state of the house and barn. Just the bills.

It was getting old.

Charlie had sat there, steadily shoveling turkey, mashed potatoes, and butternut squash into his mouth while he listened. He lived here, but it wasn't his house. These people had taken him in, but they weren't really his family. The old veteran was never sure how much he should butt in. This time, however, it felt right. "You've got a tractor," he spoke up. "Borrow a hayrick from across the street. Ruth and her buddies could load it up during the day. You haul it down in the evening, then they unload it the next morning. I bet you could get it done over a few days."

"We can't stack that stuff on the ground. It'd take a mess of pallets," Rick said.

"Have you been out to the back side of the dump, near the burn heap? That's where companies drop the damaged ones. Chet takes them apart, makes solid ones, and sells them for fifty cents each." Charlie's grin showed yellow teeth. He had a few empty spaces.

Ruth peered speculatively over her milk glass at Charlie. She, Monique, and Cindy Baldwin's mother, Donna, all sold their wares at the schoolhouse and worked to keep the stand open during daylight hours. She continued to chew while considering Charlie's words. It would be hot and dirty work. And there was a good chance it would be difficult to get her lady friends to help. But Rick's friend Philip had an in with the football team.

"Hmm." She turned to look at her beau.

Suddenly, Rick knew there was a big target on his chest.

"It'll take a couple of big pans of lasagna," Ruth said.

"Really? Lasagna?" Katie groaned.

Ruth didn't really cook. Well, not meals anyway. So, every time she came up with an idea that required feeding people, Katie was her go-to.

Rick called Phil to see if they could get a few muscular guys to lift and haul, while Katie wrote up a grocery list of ingredients needed for lasagna and double chocolate chip cupcakes. Ruth hummed along, happy as could be, but on the sidelines, Marlie and Charlie were quiet as church mice. Marlie knew she wouldn't be available to cook or bake the next day because she was the county sheriff on duty. Charlie, however, could feel the muscles in his back already protesting. Maybe the Widow O'Brien would have something for him to do over at her place. He decided that, after church the next day, he'd offer her and her younger two kids a ride home.

Chapter Fifteen

Katie figured it would be at least two weeks after the second set of students left before Steve from Harwood Architectural Renovators would call. That would be time enough for her to think of a good reason to decline gracefully.

Instead, she walked into the farmhouse the next afternoon after work, ready to start putting together Ruth's lasagnas, and found the old woman talking on the phone.

Ruth handed her the receiver. "Man's been waiting on long distance 'bout two minutes for you to get out of the car."

"We'd like to drive over, sit down with you people and discuss our proposal," the owner of the salvage and repair company told Katie.

While he spoke, her stomach rolled. She wondered if she could get into the bathroom, vomit, and get back without him noticing her absence.

No. He'd probably hear me trip over the first three cats.

"When would you like to come?" she asked.

"The weather looks good tomorrow. I know it's a Sunday, but if you don't mind, we could drive over, arrive around ten-thirty or eleven. Myself, Percy, and the leads from the two groups."

He was congenial and enthusiastic. Katie thought she'd been prepared for the call, but before she could say no, agreed.

"Okay. I guess we'll see you then."

She turned away from the telephone, stomach clutching at the idea of a meet. *We'll be quick and fast,* she thought. *Ruth and Rick will be at church, so will Raymond Dean. It's too late to tell Stan. Marlie is working days. I just have to get rid of Charlie.*

Across the room, red as a lobster, Charlie was coming out of the bathroom. "I really like the shower Rick installed in the bathtub," he said. "Though I almost need a stepladder to get in and out of that old-fashioned tub."

The old claw-foot bathtub, with its reclining back, had received an overhaul when Rick changed the nozzle to include a shower pole and trip. The oval curtain rod hung from the ceiling, and with the creative use of two shower curtains, the farmhouse now boasted a modern amenity. Katie had refused to give up the comfort of the big tub, but Rick had come up with a way to make it work for all.

Charlie scurried across the floor, still speaking. "I gotta get my gear together. Tomorrow, I volunteered to help Mrs. O'Brien paint a couple of old dressers Dorothea found for her."

Whew, Katie thought. *One down.*

But her relief was short-lived, because as soon as Rick walked through the door moments later, he knew something was up. It was like he had a second sense when she didn't tell him everything.

"What's going on in here that has the air all sparking?" he asked.

"What are you talking about?" Katie pulled a pan of chicken croquettes out of the oven and put in the first lasagna to pre-bake. If Ruth hadn't been busy in the cat room with a new litter of kittens as well as a pregnant feral secured in the maternity pen, the old woman would have spoken of the phone call. But the need to bond with the newbies took all her attention.

"I know you're up to something. Even the cats are looking at you cross-eyed," Rick said. He sniffed the rich smell of tomato sauce and looked at the croquettes with disappointment.

Katie spun around, an eye out for the offending felines. As far as Rick was concerned, that consolidated her guilt. He helped Katie set the table, but the badgering began in earnest between the bites and chewing of their evening meal. Somewhere near the end of supper, Charlie released a loud, wet belch. To save himself from Ruth's scathing tongue, he jumped into the ongoing conversation regarding Katie's guilt. "Is this about the guy that called this afternoon?" he asked. "The one from the barn fixer-uppers?"

"Charlie!" Katie snapped at the rotund little man.

Suddenly doubly chagrined, Charlie folded his hands tightly together, beads of sweat popping out near his hairline. If he'd had a beer or a whiskey in front of him, he'd have gulped it down.

Katie could see it written plainly on his face.

Now she had two choices. She could 'fess up and apologize to him, or continue the ruse and hope that neither of them had a chance to sneak out and buy a bottle. She leaned across the table, tapping his arm with her finger.

"It's okay, Charlie. They would have eventually worn me down." She turned to Rick. "Yeah, Steve Libby called this afternoon. They have a plan, and he wants to set up a meeting."

Marlie, as oblivious to the undercurrent that ran between Katie and Rick as Charlie, asked, "So, when is it?"

Katie didn't say a word, but Ruth smiled benignly and said, "I'm sure you didn't waste the cost of a long-distance call by not coming up with a time that works for both of you."

"Maybe he'll send out the proposal," Rick said.

But Ruth had spent a few minutes talking to Steve earlier while he'd been on the phone. She was sure he wanted to present it to them in person. If Katie planned to keep this a secret, the old woman knew there was a reason. And it wasn't good. She laid down her fork and knife, but didn't take her eyes off her prey. "Katie?"

Katie threw her napkin down onto her plate. "They're coming tomorrow morning."

Ruth picked up her fork and turned back to her dinner. "Pity, Rick, you're going to miss Blanche's coffee cake at the social."

Katie glowered at the gray head bent over her plate. Everyone else wisely remained silent.

Meanwhile, out beyond the barn, a solitary figure crept through the orchard. There was every chance this wouldn't be a safe place for him anymore, but Wayne had an agenda and an empty stomach. Saturday was always a busy day at the farmhouse, even though both Katie and Rick worked. There were always others around—Ruth, Charlie, Monique, and lately, the sheriff's deputy. People constantly came and went from the house, plus work being done in the gardens and around the yard. The dogs, geese, and that big pig would be all hyped up.

It was a setup where he could get caught, and he avoided it. Sunday was the same, but different. Some of the residents were gone most of the morning, there being church and all. But the one woman, the tall, young one, had different habits. But she cooked. A lot.

Wayne had come to realize that Katie made up big batches of beans, stews, or soups that would supplement the residents' meals through the week. There were always a couple of loaves of homemade bread. Though Wayne didn't dare touch them, the yeast rolls were a different story. As were the cookies, brownies, and sheet cake.

Maybe, he thought as he ran bent over, ducking behind one ancient apple tree and then the other, *she'll make a big roasting pan of mac and cheese.*

He salivated at the thought. Gut instinct told him to stay away all weekend. But in the outside world, the pickings were slim. And here Katie made sure every man, woman, dog, and cat had a full belly.

Chapter Sixteen

Katie needed to change the subject and took the chance that Charlie wouldn't question why she asked about the mystery man he had picked up. She'd led off with Ruth's complaint that someone was pilfering from the thrift shop and farm stand.

"I keep good records," Ruth said. "I might not know exactly what's gone from the Sugarhouse, but I know when the dollars don't add up to what the inventory should show."

"Okay, we'll see if we can figure it out," said Katie. She had instigated the conversation during the after-dinner cleanup, while she washed and Charlie wiped dishes. "Have you seen that strange guy again, Charlie? Do you think he might have helped himself to some of the food? Or heaven forbid, the cash box?"

"Haven't seen hide nor hair," Charlie said, then added angrily, "If I caught somebody stealing down there, I'd thump 'em a good one."

Katie watched Charlie. Though she believed the rotund truck driver was totally honest, there was a tremor in his fingers that concerned her. It had nothing to do with the conversation, she suspected, but a lot to do with Charlie's sobriety. She herself had been sober for a couple of years, and still worked at it every day. For Charlie, it had only been months. She was familiar with the challenges of keeping on the top side, even with weekly AA meetings down at the mason's hall. There had been a time, back in Illinois, when she'd attended meetings practically every day. This was the time, as his friend, she knew she should step forward.

"Thursday, I won't be home for supper, Ruth," Katie said. "I'm going to the AA meeting at the church in Charlotte."

Ruth nodded, then blinked in surprise at Katie's next remark.

"I'll pick you up after work down at the end of the road, Charlie," Katie said. "You can go with me to the meeting. When we get done, we'll stop in at the diner for supper before we head home."

Charlie didn't move. There was a heavy silence in the kitchen that seemed to grow darker.

Marlie had just come out of the bathroom and quickly perceived what happened. She rushed forward.

"Cool!" she gushed. "They make the best cannoli! I'll give you some money, Charlie. You can pick up a half dozen so we can have a treat. Make sure you get some of the ones with crushed walnuts on the end." Pulling money out of her pocket, she held it out to him.

"Okay," he said, but still sounded a little guarded.

When Ruth left the room, and Katie and Marlie both turned to what they were doing, Charlie visibly relaxed.

"So just six, right?" he asked.

* * *

Katie was true to her word. When she pulled into the parking lot of the farm stand on Thursday, Charlie, who had left work a few minutes early to dash home to wash and change his shirt, was waiting. Not a word was spoken about the AA meeting.

After the addiction gathering, the two of them crossed the street to fill up on spaghetti and tennis ball-sized meatballs. When they returned home, Charlie proudly presented the box of sweets to Marlie.

"I could have scarfed them all down on the way home," he said. "They smelled that good."

Marlie opened the box and offered him the first cannoli.

Chapter Seventeen

Late the next afternoon, Marlie came in through the kitchen door, kicking her mud-encased shoes off. Her uniform was stained with dirt and pond slime. "Check this out!"

Ruth held up her hand, stopping the deputy's advance. "My heavens, what happened to you?"

"I got sent out into the Monkton Bog to look for some old guy. No one knew he had a moonshine still out there. His family thought he'd wandered off and got lost."

"You should pack a pair of boots in your cruiser," Ruth pointed out.

"Yes, ma'am. But look at this."

Marlie had a peck-sized paper bag, which she laid on the table and ripped open. Five hardcover books tumbled out.

"The Richmond Library was having a book sale. I stopped for a minute and bought these."

As fast as the books hit the table, Ruth scooped them and the bag up.

"Not on the table. They could have silverfish in them if they were packed up a while before the sale."

She put the lot in the bathtub, spraying a fine mist of Lysol over the books and shoving the bag into the wood stove. "We'll give the vermin a few minutes to vacate while you wash up."

"Or choke to death," said Katie, waving away the Lysol fumes. "Did you get dunked in the still?"

"No, but I might have gotten splashed a bit while I was breaking it up. Sheriff Lewis wouldn't get close enough to swing the ax."

"Of course he wouldn't," said Ruth. "Now, you've got about fifteen minutes to move them books and fill the tub."

Marlie took off running, dumping the books on the floor. Then she raced upstairs to her bedroom to get a change of clothes while the hot water pummeled the bubble bath into rose-scented clouds.

Later, after the table had been cleared, everyone except Charlie—who was more inclined to nap in front of the television than read—checked out the books. Marlie explained that the seller had bags already packed. "You paid a dollar and picked out the one you wanted. You couldn't look inside, so you got what you did," she said. Her bag held four older romance novels, and volume twenty-eight of the Harvard Classics, Five Foot Shelf of Books.

Ruth carried the books into the living room. When they had first emptied the storage room on the second floor, they had unearthed a three-shelf missionary bookcase. During Katie's youth, it had held a place downstairs, stuffed full of Poppa's *Field and Stream* magazines and Gram's Harlequin Romances. Katie had insisted that it be returned to the same spot. One of the two boxes she had brought home with her from out west had held books. She and Ruth had read all of them a couple of times already. They didn't take up a lot of space on the bookshelf. The rest of the shelves had become a resting place for cats, who made room by knocking Ruth's knick-knacks onto the floor.

"You're not going to be able to push these off," the old woman told the first of the inquisitive cats.

In small groups, and sometimes singularly, all the felines trailed in to check on any changes made to their accommodations. LG usually led the charge, stretched out to her maximum length, ears and nose pointed forward. In slow, stealthy steps, ready to bolt back the way she'd come if the books proved aggressive, she crept forward. Her long tail, with its bitsy white tip, extended straight behind her. She was almost there when Rick, seated five feet away, spit out a sharp, "Phftts." LG sprang up in the air two feet and back the way she'd come. Everyone laughed, a few with suppressed guilt.

LG made a second advance, this time without a verbal interruption from the humans. When she was sure the short stack was nothing, others of the feline persuasion followed suit. The dogs, however, weren't concerned at all. If it didn't smell like food or something disgusting to roll in, it wasn't worth their effort.

The last few cats climbed up on the shelf and found a place to nap. Katie pointed them out to Marlie. "Cat approved," she said.

Chapter Eighteen

Unsure how many she would have to feed for Sunday dinner; Katie had a pot of beans on the back of the stove and a butt ham in the oven. The night before, she'd been adamant that the four men from Harwood Architectural would show up, state their piece, and leave. But Ruth had a different idea. Then, while the old woman was spouting off about lunch and dessert, Rick made some telephone calls alerting the people he considered to be Katie's support staff that a meeting was going to happen.

Stan and Raymond Dean arrived a few minutes before the Harwood Architectural vehicle pulled in. Though she'd planned on patrolling near the farm around lunchtime, Marlie had taken a lunch pail to work that day. Charlie had taken Walker and gone to help Mrs. O'Brien paint.

Steve had three sets of plans and several Xerox copies of the proposal, which he passed around the table. "I wasn't sure how many I would need," he said.

Below stairs, Wayne was taken by surprise. He had expected the churchgoers to be gone, and had no idea new guys would show up until the cars started to pull in. He took refuge behind Rick's stack of wood projects, afraid to sneak back out. He could hear every word. The dogs were excited about the doings in the kitchen, and didn't pay the sneak in the cellar a bit of mind.

* * *

Steve introduced Luke Wyatt and Trevor Arsenault, students who had come and inspected the barn. Neither Stan nor Raymond had met the young men before.

Luke began with a discussion about the damage, how it had happened, and where it would go from there. Katie was surprised at the latitude the young man had been given. Then Steve clarified a few points, and she understood that this was part of their training.

Next, it was Trevor's turn. He was so soft-spoken, Katie had to lean forward to hear his words. Trevor was small and wiry, very different from Luke. At first, he seemed unsure, but when he warmed up to his subject, there was no doubt Trevor was the brains behind the plan.

"I drafted a few sketches to show you what we plan to do. It may be easier than trying to explain it." He laid a full piece of poster board on the table with diagrams of the one-hundred-sixty-foot barn from on high. One showed the collapsed end of the barn as it was now, and then three more showed a sketch of the barn on lifts and then the finished work. "We propose, rather than rebuilding the entire structure, that the barn be disassembled to this point, with a loss of about a third. After that, we jack the remainder up, replace the fill, and pour a solid new concrete pad. We would temporarily seal the end, use support jacks, and remove that section of the pad. New footings and a retaining wall would go in here. We'd use a conveyor to backfill both sides, remove the jacks, and rebuild the new end closure. This sketch shows access points."

Everyone except Katie leaned over the table. She quietly excused herself, went into the bathroom, and sat on the edge of the tub. She knew nothing about construction, but she could see this wouldn't be like replacing a lightbulb. Just the description and sketches took her breath away. Once sure she wouldn't be sick, she returned to the kitchen just in time to hear Rick's question.

"What's the estimate for time?" he asked.

"Dependent on weather, six months," said Luke.

If Stan hadn't looked up at Katie, a question in his eyes, she would have returned to the bathroom. But once seated, listening numbly to the team describe the process, she was awed by how much technical knowledge the disassembly involved.

"This is not a demolition," Trevor repeated. "We disassemble in such a manner that we can reuse as much as possible."

"This folder," Steve laid a large manila envelope on the table, "contains a list of what we expect to remove as far as the big beams. For the most part, they are hand-shaped or old mill-cut. There's a market for them. We are always respectful of these old timbers and barn boards. They are for you to sell. We've included a list of buyers we know of, and going rates. It'll take some phone work, but it's there if you want to do it."

Raymond, a farmer with intimate knowledge of barns, and Stan, who also carried practical experience, asked more questions. Rick jumped in periodically, but Katie remained silent, unable to come up with a single question that didn't involve money.

There was a sheet showing the different stages of the project, a materials list, and finally a cost analysis. All Katie saw was the bottom line. Beside her, Ruth bumped Katie's knee, then ran her hand over her face, changing her expression as she did so. The move let Katie know her thoughts could be easily read.

She licked her lips and asked, "How long do we have to consider this?"

Percy, who had been as silent as she had and watched her closely during the meeting, seemed to read her mind. "Shall we say two weeks? It will take time to get everything lined up. This project will go quicker and be cheaper if we get it done during the summer and fall, before the snow."

"Ham's done," Ruth said, and rose.

Luke and Trevor picked up their charts and reports, then moved out of the way while Katie and Ruth set the table for lunch. Rick stood at the end to carve the ham. Casually, he picked up the conversation.

"Steve, you said there would be eight here to work. Where do you plan to stay?"

"We've identified two motels. One on the other side of Charlotte, and one in Williston," Steve replied.

"A-huh. So, what's that by the week? Five nights' accommodations for eight men? Four rooms? Plus, their meals?"

The owner of Harwood had reclaimed his seat. He relaxed and said, "About that."

Stan sat near Rick. He had pulled out a tiny notebook. Katie knew him well enough to realize he was doing math. Sure enough, he wrote a number, his estimate of the cost large enough for Rick and Raymond across the table to read, then slipped the notebook back into his pocket. Raymond didn't react, but Stan's right eyebrow rose slightly.

"Here we go," Rick said, changing the subject. "Help yourself. Make sure you try Katie's biscuits. As usual, she's outdone herself."

He smiled across the corner of the table at Katie. There was a glitter in his eye that indicated he was scheming.

Raymond, who had already begged off from lunch, saying his family was expecting him, said goodbye. Charlie, who had expected to be gone for the entire meeting, was disappointed when Mrs. O'Brien had explained she had the church ladies coming that afternoon. He had returned home just in time to reclaim the extra seat and add his two cents on the quality of the chow.

Charlie's every word had an extra listener, yearning to join in the meal. Wayne had crept halfway up the staircase, drawn by the scent of the maple and brown sugar crusted ham.

Through the meal, the conversation traveled more to state and national happenings than the need of the barn behind the farmhouse. It wasn't until Katie started to pass out pieces of the marbled sheet cake that Rick dropped the bomb.

"If your men stay at a motel, besides the cost of that, plus food, you'll be traveling ten, fifteen miles one way, twice a day, right? What if you stayed here? Could we negotiate the cost you'd save?"

Kate spun around. "*Rick!* What are you saying?"

Wayne was as shocked at Rick's words as she was.

From the expression on Stan's face, Katie knew he'd been in on this scheme, and her temper rose fast. The four men from Harwood avoided looking at her as she stood with a slice of cake perilously close to sliding off the plate.

"We'd be willing to entertain a proposal."

"Good enough," said Rick. "Watch out, Katie. You're gonna waste good cake."

Stan left at the same time as the Harwood team. The men had no sooner pulled out of the drive when Katie rounded on Rick.

"What were you thinking?" she demanded.

"I didn't do anything more than open the door," he replied. "Think about it, Katie. There's that big dormitory room upstairs, and the small bedroom. Charlie can move down to the small parlor on this floor. It's only full of storage stuff, anyway."

"We've got one bathroom. And who is going to cook for these guys?"

"We can rent a port-a-potty and set up a couple of outdoor showers. You cook just fine."

Katie's jaw dropped. She thought she might throw up. Or cry. Maybe both.

Rick stood across the table, watching her with a steady gaze. Ruth came around and laid her hand on Katie's arm.

"We've got a couple of weeks to think about it, okay?"

Katie yanked her arm away and headed out the door. She stalked up Lover's Lane, sending Solomon and the cats that followed her running back home. After a short way, she crossed the duck pond meadow to the orchard.

Bypassing the family boneyard, she headed down to where the tall grass gave way to the sparkling water of the LaPlatte. She lay among the supple green shoots, trying to think about what had happened to her original plans, way back when she had come home to sell the farm and head for Hawaii. Instead, her exhausted brain closed down, and she slept.

A couple of hours later, she woke to the sun far in the west, and the air a bit chillier. On the wind, she heard Marlie calling her name. When she stood up, she spotted her friend standing on the boneyard's iron pipe fence.

"Here!" Katie called, waving.

Marlie met her halfway between the brook and the boneyard. She was still wearing her uniform and smelled of honest sweat. Snaking her arm around Katie's waist and tugging her close, she laid a soft kiss on her lover's arm.

"I heard you had a rough day," Marlie said. "What are you doing out here?"

Katie gave a hard laugh. "I took a walk, sat down, and fell asleep. It was nice in the sun." She paused, listening to the hay swish and the bugs sing to each other. "How much did you hear about what happened today?"

"Not much, really. Only that you'd been gone for a while. You know how Ruth is, the old worrywart."

"Definitely old." Katie giggled.

"Even the pig is worried about you."

As they walked along, Katie told Marlie about the meeting and Rick's big idea. They ended up standing at the broken end of the barn. Katie realized a few more boards had fallen off in the last rainstorm.

"What are you going to do?" Marlie asked.

"I don't know. But I'm not listening to Rick. Not tonight."

The two of them were unaware that a man had crawled out onto the unstable end of the barn as far as he dared to go. Wayne had stayed in the cellar after Katie left and Ruth and Rick cleaned up. Then the two older folks, still talking together, left to check on the garden Ruth and Monique had put in that spring, where the hired man's trailer had been. Forgetting Charlie was still around somewhere; Wayne had ventured up the stairs. The cats watched him raid the refrigerator and then cut a large section of cake onto a piece of waxed paper. The kitchen was mostly silent, and the dogs had gone with Rick. He considered a quick hot water wash, but that was when Charlie, asleep on the sofa, had given a loud snore.

Wayne ran back down into the cellar and out the bulkhead, barely looking to be sure the coast was clear.

Now he watched the two women, considering how friendly they were with each other. When Marlie turned, and he got a good look at her uniform, his face soured. She was the law, and he was on the run.

* * *

The next morning, everyone was up early, getting ready to go to work. Katie had spent most of the night thinking about what Rick had asked Steve from

75

Harwood about boarding the workers. She'd almost made the idea work in her mind, but then considered that at that moment she had talked herself into seeing only the best side of the proposal.

Rick debated if he should bring up the subject, but there wasn't time. Ruth and Marlie were afraid one of the others would bring it up. Only Charlie was oblivious.

Earlier, while Rick and the hounds had been outside, Wayne had crept back into the cellar. The bulkhead had been barred, but there was a low window in the east wall, where the coal chute had been placed back in the day. Now, the flip-open door was covered by a rectangle of plywood nailed securely in place. Wayne had retracted the nails until, from the outside, he could give one solid kick and knock the plywood in. Then he moved some of the stacked cord wood around so he'd have a quick place to hide if anyone came down the steps. With the wood furnace closed down for the summer, he figured there would be few visitors unless they were hauling canned goods down.

There wasn't a lot he could do about the dogs, and he knew the little hidey-hole wouldn't keep him safe from them. His nerves were stretched a little thin, but he was hungry again. There had been a lot of food out the day before. While rummaging, he'd seen two big pans of lasagna that hadn't been cut into yet.

The arrival of the carful of men the previous day, and their quick tour around the barn, had made Wayne extra nervous. And the conversation he'd overheard had made it clear he would have to find a different place to go, because the barn would be out.

It was obvious to him that the owners were considering repairs. Wayne had figured the dynamics of the family included the old couple, their daughter, maybe a brother, but the sheriff's deputy didn't fit in.

Not that it mattered. Just having a deputy walking around wasn't good.

Wayne looked up toward the underside of the first floor. Lately, the schedule in the house had been off. He wasn't always sure when it would be safe to be outside, or to raid the refrigerator.

The smell of yesterday's ham still lingered. Wayne's belly growled, but

Ruth hadn't left the house this morning. In fact, just after breakfast, two other cars had pulled in, and the old hens had sat around the table yammering for a couple of hours.

Finally, when he was sure all the old women were seated at the table, he slipped out of the bulkhead, cut through the barn, and exited toward the orchard. There was a shallow place to cross the brook beyond the last of the twisted apple trees. On the far side, still nervous about the woman who had watched him weeks before, Wayne walked downstream to the next cul-de-sac development. By the time he'd walked the six miles to the Hunt house, he was hot, tired, and thirsty.

At the top of the driveway, he came to an abrupt halt. A bronze Buick was parked behind the big rhododendron, backed up to the steps with the trunk open. Worse than that, some kind of barky spaniel was coming at him, ears flying.

Wayne turned tail and ran. At the edge of Route 116, he barely paused to check traffic before he ran across the paved surface and dove into the drainage ditch. It was soft, mucky, and stunk. To stay out of sight, he crawled on his hands and knees, dodging hopping frogs and long, orange slugs. Behind him, a man called the dog back.

There was no way to know if the man had seen him. But with the driveway to a small farmhouse less than three hundred feet to the south, there was only one way to go.

It wasn't until he came to a culvert that Wayne stopped to think. With years' worth of sand and rotten vegetation filling the bottom third, it was big, but not big enough for him to crawl through. He was soaked down to the skin. Though it was hot, he was shaking. Did he dare peek his head up and look around? Had the man called the sheriff?

Like an eel slithering out of a brook, Wayne shimmied on his belly up over the bank and into the cornfield. Once he was half a dozen rows in, he came to a place left for tractors to drive into the field. Finally, he was able to hunker down and inhale. The sun felt warm on his back. He stretched out along the narrow space between rows and succumbed to exhaustion. When Wayne woke, his clothes, at least on the top side, were dry and stiff.

The smell of swamp water gagged him, and biting flies had followed the stench to where he lay. Before his doze, he had decided there were only two choices as to where to go. He could hide behind the In Town Market. Or head back to the farm, maybe lie low in the orchard, and from there, scout out another place to hide.

The roads were busy. Farming was at its peak for the season. Out-of-state cars were everywhere. Now, with midday barely passed, he didn't dare walk exposed down the street. Instead, he crossed Route 116, leaving the cornfield for a thick patch of bull pine and feathery young spruce. Driven by the buzzing, biting insects, he wandered through the trees on a path that took him to a spot where he stood hidden in the gloom, watching as Jacob and Irene Hunt loaded the car with laundry baskets of clean and folded linens. And also, what looked like boxes of groceries. Jacob locked the door, loaded the dog, and the Buick pulled out.

Wayne hung around until nightfall, but the Hunts didn't return. At one point, he went over to Meredith's house, but her car was still parked alongside the deck. The garage door was open again.

"Chances are she's inside," he said to himself. "If she sees me, that bitch will definitely call the cops."

Back at the Hunts, he found the kitchen window locked. He wasn't above breaking out a pane of glass in the cellar window beneath the deck and crawling through the opening. A quick survey supported his suspicion that the old couple had come in, done laundry, and returned to their vacation rental. He followed their example and used the washer for everything, including the purloined backpack. Walking upstairs to the bathroom naked in the dark, he had a good laugh at what would happen if they returned at that moment.

After frying a small cubed steak from the freezer, Wayne spent the night sleeping in the spare bed. The window was open, allowing a breeze to waft in. It was the best night he'd had in a long time. Except maybe for the howling coyote noises, and the stink from the overflowing septic tank.

The next morning, he got up, made a pot of coffee, and stepped outside on the deck. Once again, the southerly breeze brought the reek of waste to him. It was bad, and somehow not right. Leaving the cup on the railing, Wayne crossed the drive, pushed his way through the cedars that separated the two houses, and skirted Meredith's deck. The boyfriend must have left in the night, and with the number of alcohol bottles on the deck, Meredith was probably still passed out. Still no sign of the kids. The shed out back might be a handy in-case-of-emergency hideout.

Circling the garage, he came to a place in the yard where the ground looked all torn up. He considered the septic tank might be beneath the sod right there, and animals were looking for access to the stink. There was a padlock on the shed door, a new shiny one. Unable to get in there, he decided to walk along the garage on the side away from the house to see if there was a hidey-hole there. Wrinkling his nose at the stink, he made the corner, looked back over his shoulder, and stepped into a wild and weedy spot. Right into something that was definitely not a clogged septic system.

The back door to Meredith's house was unlocked. A beige phone hung on the wall just inside the door. Barely aware he was putting his freedom in jeopardy, Wayne screamed at the man who answered the sheriff's phone. It seemed to take forever before it was understood that Lewis needed to be at Meredith's house right now.

Chapter Nineteen

The phone rang shortly after Katie got home from work, at exactly the time animal calls always came in. People came home from work, found a strange cat or dog in the yard, a possum hanging from the porch rafters, or a raccoon doing a service call in the trash can, and they dialed for instant gratification.

For a fleeting second, Katie considered again that this was why this wasn't one of those jobs where a homeowner could schedule an appointment. For as long as she'd covered Parentville Animal Control, the phone would ring, she'd grab her gear, and hit the road. If she was lucky, she'd only be out for a couple of hours.

"Hello," she said.

To her surprise, it was Marlie on the other end of the line. In a hushed and strained voice, Katie's best girl told her to go ahead with supper. The sheriff's office was on a call that would last for a while.

"What's going on?" Ruth asked when Katie relayed the message.

"Don't know," Katie admitted. "But I think she was calling from somewhere she wasn't supposed to use the telephone."

Charlie sat outside the kitchen door, taking off his muddy boots. He'd spent all day driving up and down Route 116, hauling sand and gravel from the Rene Fortin pit. The highway crew was shoring up a place on the east side of town, where the road was sinking into Monkton Bog. It was messy and full of mosquitoes. The only places on his body that didn't itch were the ones covered by mud.

He grunted at Katie's words. "Some old guy found a woman's body behind a woodpile. Marlie and Lewis are probably there. What's for eats? Smells like Spanish Rice."

He walked through the kitchen, headed toward the bathroom, and a wash-up. Every human head in the room followed his movements, mouths slightly ajar. Solomon and Walker followed, because a sweaty man was always a good stink. Old Tom, up on a chair near the table, scooped a healthy serving of rice onto the floor with one swipe. Silently, more cats converged, hoping to have the mess cleaned up before the dogs knew what was happening. Even though the dogs returned in a rush, only a few grains of rice remained scattered across the ancient linoleum.

Chapter Twenty

A light was burning in the living room when Marlie returned. From where Katie sat, she could see her friend's shoulders were bowed. The shuffle of dragging feet could only mean exhaustion.

"I kept you some supper," Katie said. "You can have a shower and something hot to eat before you sleep."

"I'm not hungry," Marlie said.

"Sure, you are. You're just too tired to realize it." Katie shushed Marlie towards the bathroom. "I got your cute purple cow PJs out. You'll sleep better after you get cleaned up and fed."

While the water ran and Marlie bathed, Katie set about making sure her friend's supper would be warm and flavorful. She moved around the kitchen, doing what was second nature and considering the other woman's state. Katie was sure there were times when being a deputy was downright hard for anybody. But knowing what Marlie had shared with her meant seeing a bigger picture—and not just the part where Marlie had been held back from becoming a full-time deputy by both Sheriff Lewis and his golden boy deputy, Dennis-Brad Boyd. Even though Marlie was now doing Brad's job, on her first tour here, both men had repeatedly referred to her as a clerk, demeaning her and her knowledge. The title had stuck in odd ways, as when folks came right out and asked how come Lewis had let her out from behind the desk.

Then there were the looks Marlie got when she showed up on police business. Short and buxom, with dark skin, people considered her Italian-American. Maybe even Native American. But the truth was that, of all her mama's children, Marlene was the only one whose father had been African-American. No one ever uttered a word, at least not that Katie knew of, but Marlie said she could see speculation in their eyes, and that she was judged by her mother's loose ways. It didn't help that she was a woman doing work in a field where normally only men went out onto the streets. She was smallish, of indiscriminate heritage in a region where most of the population could remember when their French parents had traveled down from Canada. Her mama was long gone. Her siblings, farmed out into foster care, had grown and moved on to places their history wasn't known. She had no family living in town to stand behind her.

Then there was what Geoffrey Ash had known. He was gone, now a guest of the State of Vermont's penal system, serving a life sentence for two murders. But what he'd said to her about knowing she was gay before his arrest had taken Marlie's safety away. No matter how careful she was now, she knew someone else might stumble on that same truth. She didn't date. When asked, she responded that going out with anyone local might compromise her career.

Katie didn't date either. She told people it was because she was still getting used to being back in town and had just come out of a bad breakup. They could only hope no one would consider two women friends were anything more.

Katie stirred the Spanish Rice and chicken she'd put together for supper. With all these thoughts swirling in her head, she was feeling as she had before that life would be simpler if she'd move on. But then there was Marlie.

The bathroom door opened.

Suck it up. Pulling her shoulders back, Katie turned with a half-smile in place.

"Eat a little," she coaxed. "Tell me what happened today, because you look ridden hard and put away wet."

"Is that something your poppa used to say?" Marlie asked. "Because your cowboy accent sucks."

Katie laughed aloud. LG took advantage of her preoccupation and jumped onto the table. Scooping the semi-feral off and dropping her back on the floor, Katie answered with a nod.

"If you don't start putting that food in your mouth, you're going to have a lap full of cats," she said. "They don't know why you're eating in the middle of the night, but they want some as well. Oh, and look at this, here come the hounds."

Marlie did her best, making it halfway through the meal. When she stopped, Katie slid the plate into the refrigerator, getting sullen looks from all the furbies in the room.

"We got called out to a report of a dead woman this afternoon."

Marlie stared at the door. She didn't want to say anything about the last few hours at all, but couldn't hold it inside.

"Down on Route 116, a little over halfway between the Mechanicsville Road and the turnoff to Saint George and Williston." Her eyes skittered toward Katie and away. "There's a big white colonial on the high side of the road, almost across from a small farm run by one of the younger Fortin boys." She waited for Katie to acknowledge she knew the place, but Katie didn't speak.

"Anyway, this guy living in the Saint George trailer park raises thirteen-inch beagles for hunting raccoons and the like. He had a couple he was working with, getting them ready for some night hunting. One of them took off. He was out looking for it and heard it baying. He said he came down off the ridge along the back of the property. There's a shed there, and a mess of fireplace wood dumped in a heap between that and the garage. The dog had found the body. It's been out there for a couple of days. A mess of scavengers worked it over. Good thing I hadn't eaten anything during the afternoon."

"I'm sorry you had to be there for that," Katie said gently.

Marlie's soulful brown eyes gazed into Katie's.

"It gets worse," she said. "It's someone we, or you, know. And you've had words with. Eventually, somebody is going to remember. You'll need to talk to Sheriff Lewis. The sooner the better."

Katie felt her breath catch. *Who,* she wondered.

Marlie's voice rose. "This is when he's going to find out I'm living here,

Katie. The woman was Meredith Block."

Katie sat for several minutes, stunned. Finally, she realized her mouth was open.

"Meredith? Why would anyone kill Meredith? What makes you think Lewis will want to talk to me?"

"Remember her coming into the feed store, all Missy Lawyer, with the holier-than-thou attitude? Well, I've heard people laughing about how you shut her down. Somebody is going to talk."

A voice from the doorway spoke. "Then Katie needs to go to Lewis's office right now. If he doesn't come here, and he doesn't specifically ask, there's no reason to tell him where you're staying."

Rick walked past both women and into the bathroom. They were silent until he came out.

"Tomorrow, you both go to work like normal. Marlie, just do your job. Katie, gossip is going to show up at the store. If it comes in the morning, at noon, you go to the sheriff's office. If not, then after work. While you're there, ask Janice if you need to have a permit to rent out a room. She'll probably think you're talking about Charlie, but don't mention any names."

"No," said Marlie. "We're getting too deep into this."

"Marlie, your two weeks in Parentville are half done. Keep your nose out of the shit, and your yap shut from gossiping."

Both women were stunned. Easy come, easy go. Rick rarely came off as short. A few moments later, they heard his feet cross the bare wooden floor of the living room to the parlor-turned-bedroom he shared with Ruth.

"Go to bed," Katie said. "I'll get Ruth over to Grace's early tomorrow. If you don't need to be out of here before then, wait for her and Charlie to leave in the morning before you come down."

Marlie went up the stairs. She didn't have a good feeling about this at all.

Chapter Twenty-One

Rick had been dead on. No sooner had the doors to the store opened when both men and women started to gather in groups as they collected their feed and hardware needs, all the gossip was about the mess down on Route 116.

"How is it so many people seem to know what's going on this fast?" Katie asked Stan. Even Davidson knew more facts than she did.

"You're kidding, right?" he asked. "Sheriff Lewis called in the medical examiner. When that went out over the CB radios, every volunteer firefighter for fifty miles was alerted. Hell, after that, the party lines were burning up. Mine included."

At her frowning look, he shrugged. "Half my guys wanted to know if they should respond. The other half begged off in case I would send some of them out."

"Did you?" she asked. "Send them out?"

"Lewis needed a couple of people for traffic duty. You know, to keep the cars moving and stop the rubberneckers from pulling off to the side and climbing the banks. I've got a couple of guys who really need the extra few dollars. Those were the ones I sent, because if I threaten to ignore them the next time for not doing a job as ordered, they behave."

"You didn't call out Charlie," she pointed out.

Stan blushed a little and lowered his voice. "I know Marlie is staying out there with you people. I figured it would be bad enough if only one of you had seen the mess out at the Block house. That, and he's got a big mouth."

Katie cocked an eyebrow. She was concerned Stan might know about her relationship with Marlie. Then, too, she wanted to rehab Charlie. If he stuck to his old habits, the time she'd invested was lost. Stan read the look as a question about how he had handled the situation at the house on U.S. Route 116. He didn't want to talk about it.

"I had to go, Katie. Rescue falls under my department." He turned away, shaking his head. "I don't ever want to see something like that again."

The next time Stan stepped out to the feed shed, Katie ducked into his office to use the phone.

"Janice," she said to the town clerk, "is Lewis in his office right now?"

"Nope. Haven't seen him at all today. Only Angus."

"Do me a favor? The next time he comes in, give me a call at the feed store, okay?" Katie asked.

"Will do. Did you hear about the goings on?"

"I did," said Katie.

She said goodbye before Janice could say more. Back out on the floor, she collared Davidson.

"I'm waiting on a call," she said. "When it comes in, I'm going to have to take my lunch and go out, okay?" She didn't bother to explain that it wouldn't be an animal call.

"Sure," he said. "I've got you covered."

Over an hour later, the phone rang, and Stan came out to tell her Janice was on the line. When she told him she'd been called out, he let her go, summoning one of the feed shed guys inside until she returned. She probably should have felt guilty for not being up front with her boss, but she was more concerned about how the conversation would go with Lewis.

The sheriff's office was in the same building as the town hall, once a high school. Katie walked in through the entrance on the side. Angus held up his hand to stop her, but she walked over and rapped on Lewis's door. Marlie opened it, nodded, and left without a word. Katie kept her eyes forward and her face blank.

"Sheriff," she said. "I need to talk to you for a minute."

He opened his mouth, a frown in place.

"It's about Meredith Block," Katie said.

Lewis waved her inside. There were others out there with Angus. Katie closed the door and jumped in before he had a chance to get started.

"I heard this morning at work that Meredith Block might have passed away under suspicious circumstances." She didn't add what the gossip was. "I know you're going to hear that she and I had a conversation at the feed store that ended badly." Katie laid a handwritten page on the desk in front of him. "I took a few minutes to write out what happened there for you. Everyone who was on site is listed on the bottom."

She didn't add that she'd skipped Marlie's name or let him know she had actually written her memory of the event during the sleepless hours of the night. "Do you want to read it over in case you have any questions before I leave?" she asked.

"Why did you do this, Katie?" Lewis scanned the page.

"To be honest, because you and I haven't had a good history. I figured this time, I'd be up front with you. Maybe save you a little time, who knows? Create some goodwill." She was close enough to reach out and touch the doorknob.

Lewis laid the page on the blotter. "You know I'm going to be talking to these people, right?"

"I wouldn't expect you to do anything else," she said.

He nodded, and Katie's hand twisted the doorknob. It was only as she walked out that she realized the townspeople in the outer office included Corporal Derrick from the state police, whom she had met previously, an older couple clinging to each other, and Gage Fernald. If she wasn't mistaken, he was stumping in the middle of somebody else's heartbreak.

Chapter Twenty-Two

It wouldn't have mattered if Katie had listened to Janice's gossip. There was no way through the rest of her workday that she could keep her ears buttoned up against the voices swirling around her.

"…beaten to a pulp…"

"…in the sun for days…"

"…beyond recognition…"

When it was time to punch out and go home, Katie welcomed the chance to lock the doors. Even then, she dawdled until most of the other employees were gone and the area around the time clock was deserted.

"Taking your time today," Stan said from behind her.

"Waiting for the gossiping horde to disband," she replied.

A resounding click freed her from feed store duty.

"Do you mind me asking what's happening out at the barn?" Stan asked.

Katie's previous anger that he and Rick had conspired behind her back rose again, causing a dull pain in her head and a flash in her eye.

"What? You and Rick aren't planning all my hours and minutes anymore?" she asked heatedly.

Stan looked away for a moment, rubbing his hand over his eyes. "I knew you weren't going to like Rick jumping out like that without talking to you. Before you tear him a new one, you should know I was the one who raised the idea. But it came from Cindy." He went back into the office, returning in half a minute with a paper-clipped stack of papers. "My wife left this for you. She said to fill out all that you could, and she'd help you with the rest. Even if you don't use it now, you're going to need it soon enough." He looked decidedly uncomfortable as he thrust the papers toward Katie. "You and Cindy need to get together and talk it out." He walked toward the rear door, key in hand. As he stepped aside to allow Katie to precede him, he added, "I'll have Cindy give you a call."

Katie sat in the car, looking over the paperwork Cindy had left. Most of the pages were bank loan applications, but there was a detailed note telling Katie what else she needed to gather.

The ride home was a laborious effort, as her shoulders were up around her ears. Katie half expected to find Cindy—her friend, cohort, and the boss's wife—sitting at her kitchen table. Instead, she found Ruth up to her ears in young lettuce and spinach. The old woman's front was dripping wet as she washed produce in the sink. From the slump of her shoulders, Katie knew Ruth would be having an early night.

"Another banner day in the garden?" she asked.

"This will be the end of the leaf lettuce and baby spinach for the season," Ruth explained. "I've got little cukes, radishes, shallots, and cherry tomatoes."

"Sounds like a salad," Katie said. "How about if I crispy fry up some chicken chunks, make a honey mustard dressing, and we have that for supper?"

"Sounds good to me," Rick said, coming in the back door. "Where's the list for dropping off?"

Among the village residents, Ruth and Grace had regular customers. When they had made the decision, the previous afternoon, to make up a "bag" salad, they got on the phone, set up deliveries, and made a few extra bags for the farm stand as well. Rick and Charlie returned as Marlie pulled into the yard, and the last of the crispy chicken nuggets came out of the deep fryer.

Marlie, looking as spent as Ruth, had suffered no loss of appetite and dug in with relish. When Katie waved her away for cleanup, Marlie resisted.

"I need to do something normal. Sheriff Lewis and I spent all day questioning Meredith's family and her supposedly good friends. Mostly, they weren't a lot of help because they were asking questions. You know, they just wanted to know what the sheriff's department had uncovered. My brain is mashed potatoes."

Marlie stood beside Katie as she wiped dishes, wishing there was no one else in the house. That Katie could hold her tight, and she could cry, or scream, or just sit quietly if that would help. Though she wasn't speaking in a full whisper, she still kept her voice down. From the TV in the living room, they could hear Captain Pierce making a move on Margaret Houlihan.

"There was so much happening everywhere we went today, Katie. If I hadn't been keeping a scorecard, I swear I'd never be able to keep everything straight." Marlie folded the dish towel into a perfectly edged rectangle. "The parents were horribly distraught. The sister called her something they won't be repeating in the eulogy. The ex-husband was furious, like we or maybe even Meredith was creating chaos in his careful little world. None of her friends seemed to know anything about what she'd been doing the last three months. Oh, and get this, the au pair has just disappeared."

Katie gulped. "You don't think her body is going to turn up next, do you?"

"Oh, my God! I hope not." Marlie pulled out a chair and sat with her head in her hands. "Tomorrow, the children are going to be questioned. And we're going out to talk to the guy who owned the dog. He was pretty evasive when we were trying to talk to him. I asked where the dog was, and he said it had run off again."

"You'd better get some sleep, then," Katie said, "or you'll be too tired to keep up."

Marlie laughed into her palms. "It's my day off. I'm going to lie among the vegetables while Ruth and Monique hoe around me."

The phone rang. It was still daylight. An animal call might not be a bad thing right about then, Katie thought. She'd take Marlie for a ride. Instead, the deep voice on the phone asked to speak with Deputy Foster. Katie held the telephone receiver out to Marlie.

"Some gent wants to speak with the Deputy," she said softly.

Marlie's eyes held onto Katie's as she answered, "Foster."

Even as the conversation went on, their gazes were locked. Katie saw nervous fear, maybe annoyance, then confusion. Marlie's answers were short, sharing nothing about what the other person was saying. Rick drifted into the room and stood beside Katie. Drawn by the tension radiating from everyone else, Ruth peeked around from behind him. Marlie finally said goodbye and stood to hang the handset on its chrome bed.

"I have good news and bad." She sounded choked, as though her throat were too dry for words. "I won't be able to help you tomorrow, Ruth. I have to work. And probably for the next several days as well."

"That's the bad news, right?" Rick asked.

Marlie nodded. "Yeah. That was the unit commander. It seems Brad has taken a job with a different police service. I'm going to stay here until a permanent selection is made for the job slot."

"Are you kidding?" Katie shouted.

But Marlie, overcome with the stress of the day, her supervisor's words regarding her responsibilities to the open case, and the vague innuendo about her future, could only shake her head. Bright tears shone in her eyes.

Ruth danced across the room.

"Woo hoo!" she shouted, grabbing Marlie's arms as she went by and swinging them both around. "We're never going to let you go! You belong here with us now."

Suddenly, Marlie was laughing with Ruth, and they both clamored for ice cream to celebrate. At the mention of the cool, sweet dessert, Charlie's voice added to the fray. Not to be left behind, Walker and Solomon howled and barked. There wasn't a cat to be seen, as all of those still free in the house for the evening had darted away, looking for a place to hide from all the ruckus.

As Rick returned the stack of empty bowls to the kitchen half an hour later, the two long, one short ring of the telephone party line let them know another call was coming up Fire Lane 61, passing the Dean household as it headed toward its final destination.

"Katie. Telephone." Rick handed her the receiver as they met in the doorway between the kitchen and the living room.

"This is Katie," she said.

"Miss Took?" an unknown female asked. "This is Steffie Frith. I'm a realtor with Deven's Agency. We used to be Ash. You might have heard of us?"

Katie didn't bother to explain she knew the reason the Deven's Agency had been able to buy out Ash Investments and Insurance. Thanks to a boost from her, Geoffrey Ash was currently a guest of the federal prison system.

"Yes," she said.

"Well, we have a dilemma. I was given your name as a person who might be able to help us with an extermination issue," Ms. Frith said.

"I don't know who gave you my name," Katie said. "But I don't have anything to do with exterminations. I don't know anything about bug control."

"Oh, pardon me. Poor choice of words. What we actually are looking for is someone to extract some unwanted animals. Let me explain. This agency recently listed a piece of property on Franklin Road. It's an old, very dilapidated set of buildings. The owners moved out in the spring, and we submitted our plans for developing the property for single-family homes."

Steffie Frith spoke as though she expected an instant song of praise. Though Katie was all for families having their own homes, she was not impressed with the loss of farmlands to structures that were built cheaply and fast. They were springing up everywhere in the fields and pastureland surrounding the village.

"It seems," Steffie continued, "that the previous residents had a number of wild cats living in their barn. When we proposed to demolish the structure, the neighbors voiced their concerns and stepped forward, represented by the Society for the Prevention of Cruelty to Animals. The SPCA has put a court hold on all construction on the site until the cats can be removed. The town and county have been notified."

"Okay," said Katie. "So, you know you're dealing with feral cats, right? Not wild bobcats?"

"Oh, right. But I've seen these cats, and believe me, they are wild."

"The term for domestic cats who aren't tame is feral. How do I figure in this picture? I work for the town. They haven't sent me any kind of notice. And to be honest, this feels like a farm issue or for the SPCA, not a town problem. This is a lot of cats, not what I usually handle."

Katie felt a moment of shame. Throughout the conversation, the woman's tone had been condescending. She didn't really know Steffie, but she'd been letting the other woman's attitude guide her own response.

"I've had several lengthy conversations with the people at the SPCA, as well as with Doctor Nguyen at Valley Wide Veterinary Service," Steffie explained. "They will be working as the point of contact for the Society. Doctor Nguyen suggested you might be of assistance. I contacted the town. We came to an agreement that this issue would be contractual between you and The Deven's Agency. That's why I'm calling you. We'd like to hire you, at the same rate you get from the town, to trap and remove the *feral* cats from the Franklin Road property. You will have thirty days. I can have a courier deliver the contract tomorrow. Once it's signed, you can start immediately."

"What am I supposed to do with these cats after I have them trapped?" Katie asked.

"According to Doctor Nguyen, you will deliver them to her. She will process them; make sure they're healthy, give shots, that sort of thing, before they transfer to the SPCA facility."

"How many cats are we talking about?" Katie asked.

"Thirty-six."

Katie tried to picture that many cats in one room in her mind. Taking a breath, she tried to sound calmer than she felt. "Ah-huh. I'll tell you what, I'll think this through over the night and get back to you tomorrow.".

"All right." Steffie did not sound pleased at the delay, but she provided her contact information.

In the living room, the television still played. Ruth stitched buttons in place for Dorothea's thrift shop, and Rick read the paper. Katie stood at the edge of the braided rug, relaying the telephone conversation.

"First thing," Rick said, cutting off Ruth's clucking about acquiring more kittens, "you better check with the town and see if this is all on the up and up."

Katie returned to the Harvest Gold telephone and dialed Janice's home number. The town office had been closed for a couple of hours, but Janice, like Dorothea, had her thumb on the pulse of the village.

"Yes. I sat in on that conversation. Most of it was pretty clear," Janice said. "The SPCA wants the cats safely removed. Thirty days doesn't sound very long, but I suppose you could do it. That Frith woman wanted to make the town responsible, but Paul Wright said no. He also told them that he expected you to be paid at the same rate or better than the town pays you. I thought that was very kind of him. You might want to check with the veterinarian. It seems to me there's a bit more on that end. Anyway, it's up to you."

Paul Wright was the chairman of the selectmen's board. In the village of Parentville, he was the last word.

"That was nice of Paul. You're sure if I take this job, it won't affect how I'm working with the town?" Katie asked.

"Absolutely not."

Though Janice was willing to continue the conversation, Katie signed off. It was too late to call Doctor Nguyen's office, and Katie had to be at work by eight the next morning. In the living room, she went straight over to Ruth.

"Ruth, I need you to call Doctor Ronnie's office tomorrow and get all the information on this. You're good at ferreting out details. Let them know this Frith woman was a little vague. When you have it all sorted out, I'll decide if I want to do it. I told Steffie Frith I'd call her back tomorrow, so I need you to call early."

"Then should I call you?" Ruth asked.

"No. Stan will be working in the office. I don't want to disturb him. I'll call you from the payphone on my break," Katie said.

"That's going to make me late down in the cheese room. I told Grace I'd be there tomorrow," Ruth said.

Katie grabbed her upper lip with her teeth. After a moment, she said, "Okay. I'll call you by eight-thirty. Why don't you call Grace right now and tell her that you're going to be five or ten minutes late?"

Ruth laid aside her sewing, making sure it was in a place the cats wouldn't try to investigate as soon as she left.

Rick folded up the paper. "You only have eight traps. That includes the ones that were donated and we repaired." They could hear Ruth on the phone in the kitchen. He took advantage of his elderly sweetie's absence to whisper to Katie, "Whatever you do, don't let Ruth see those kittens. She'll go soft, and we'll be buried again. We've got enough to move along now."

When Ruth returned, Rick shut his mouth and sat back.

"I'll drive over there in the morning to have a look," Katie said. "After that, I'll talk to Ruth and let Steffie know. If I'm going to take this, I think eight traps will be enough to start with. If not, there's a list on the refrigerator of folks who have live traps I can borrow."

Marlie was lying on the braided rug at Katie's feet. She had collected all the ginger kittens and was playing with them, trying to decide which one to give to her grandmother. "You know, this realtor woman might be good at selling houses, but she might not have the ability to look at the feral situation and actually see what's going on."

"How's that?" Katie asked, smiling down at her best friend's head.

"You don't know if a neighbor told her there were thirty-six cats, or if she counted them while she was on the property. Even if she actually saw that many, you know, there are more hidden in the barn. What's going to happen to those?"

"If it looks like more, I'll drop a word with Janice. She might want to alert the SPCA."

Rick nodded. "Good plan."

"How are you going to get all those cats from the farm to the vet's office?" Ruth asked. "We don't have carriers for that."

"It depends on how wild they are. I may not be able to handle them to transfer them from a live trap to a carrier. If I need carriers, you can make some calls."

Ruth picked her sewing back up, and Marlie held a kitten up for inspection.

"I'm going to take this one for my grandmother," she said. The bright orange and creamy white kitten struggled to get back to his littermates. "I'll call him Creamsicle."

"That's a good name," Ruth said. "Check the chart in the cat room. I believe he goes to Doctor Ronnie to be neutered next week. Then, maybe a week later, he'll be ready to travel to his new home."

"Did you hear that, Creamsicle?" Marlie nuzzled the little ball of fur. "We're going to pack your bags to meet your new mama."

All the humans in the room smiled, except Charlie snoring in the easy chair.

Chapter Twenty-Three

Katie made the stop at the farm on Franklin Road the next morning. Just as Marlie and Rick had predicted, there was evidence of many, many cats.

The morning was bright. The sun warmed the grass. Grasshoppers and other insects were active. She could see them from the driveway, as well as several cats hunting the big bugs for breakfast. It seemed everywhere she looked, a cat was sitting, lying, or bathing.

"I didn't count them," she told Ruth when she called. "But I bet there's twice thirty-six."

"Doctor Ronnie said she's dealing with the SPCA, not Steffie Frith. But that's where your money is going to come from, and it's separate from what the vet will get. The deal is, you trap them and drop them off at the clinic. She gives them a physical, first shots, spays or neuters, and when the cats are ready to travel, you're the one who will drive them to the SPCA center in South Burlington."

"Well, there's an important piece of information I didn't get." Katie frowned.

"Dropping them off will be daily," Ruth said. "But it didn't sound like transporting them would be. Depends on their health. Don't forget, Rick and I, or Marlie, even Charlie, can drop off, too."

Katie spent the morning considering Steffie Frith's offer. It was a big hunk of money. In the end, she called Steffie, who had the courier at Baldwin's by ten o'clock. Katie signed the contract with Stan as a witness, and the courier left.

"When do you start?" Stan asked.

"I'll pick up eight or so cans of mackerel at the general store on my way home. I'll load the traps and set them up in the morning. Mackerel stinks so bad there's not a cat, raccoon, or skunk in the country that can ignore it. On the way home, I'll stop and spring them. I don't want a cat stuck in a live trap overnight. There's no way of knowing what else is out there prowling around."

* * *

Katie spent the rest of the morning trying to figure out the best way to handle the Devin's Agency's job. The money would be welcomed. The barn was going to take a lot, but how much time was going to be tied up? By the time her lunch break came around, she was crawling out of her own skull. She decided to take a little ride and calm down.

Two hundred feet beyond Meredith Block's house, Katie pulled over, parking in the narrow space between the tarred road and the ditch. She watched in her rearview mirror as traffic approached. She was here with no idea what to expect, but totally knowing she had no business interfering.

A milk tanker roared by at fifty miles an hour, so close the suck and blow of his wind draft rocked her truck. Fingers on the door handle, she waited for the next car, which was quickly over the hill and gone. No one else was approaching.

Without a second's thought, Katie was outside. Head lowered and fists thrust into her pockets, she hotfooted back toward the drive.

She was all the way around the mailbox before another car passed. Katie listened. The wheels didn't slow. No horn blew. Leaning into the slight incline, each step she took pressed her foot hard into the gravel. By the time the drive leveled out beside the house, stress had her panting. Ahead of her stood a detached two-car garage.

The side door was unlocked. The Pontiac convertible was gone. Marlie had said forensics hauled it away. Katie saw kids' bikes, a workbench with hand tools, cans of paint, and dust.

Pulling the garage door shut behind her, Katie considered the house. What if the same careless person who'd left the garage unsecured had been responsible for the house?

She crossed the drive. From her back pocket, she pulled out a pair of yellow Platex gloves, the same type Ruth used for washing dishes. Katie always carried a pair in the glove compartment. Some animal calls were messy. The kitchen door was locked, as was the sliding glass door on the patio and the bulkhead. Last, but most nerve-racking of all, there was the heavy wood and glass front door.

From the top of the broad fieldstone steps, Katie had a clear view of Route 116, the farm, and the acreage beyond. She felt herself shiver all the way down to inside her work boots. If she could see, then she could be seen.

Fighting the urge to run for cover, she peered in the windows, being careful not to touch anything. Even with the Platex gloves between her and the glass, she was aware of the road dust that filtered up this far. A finger here, a palm there, would leave a record. She shuffled her feet over the area she had walked on. Hopefully, some sharp-eyed investigator wouldn't notice the ground had been disturbed.

This fairly new house, maybe only eight or ten years old, had wide, bold windows. She didn't touch any of them to test for a lock, nor did she lean too close to the glass. Where the cellar windows rose a few feet from the ground, Katie stooped and peered, poking them with a stick. None tilted inwards.

"I'd never get my fat butt through that anyway," she grunted, rising to her feet.

In the distance, she heard the baying of beagles. Had they heard her sniffing around, or was something else happening in their yard? Something more pleasant than the stink of a decomposing neighbor?

"Get to it," she muttered, forcing her feet to move.

Crossing the backyard at an angle brought her to the back of the garage. Beyond a grape arbor lined with rose bushes, she saw the toolshed, and beside it, a jumbled stack of split firewood. The grass was a little long here, but not raggy, though the lawns in the front had missed at least two mowings.

She didn't have to worry about leaving a trail here. Every blade of grass or twig or weed left from the shearing blades of the mower had been trampled down, beaten and broken, by many footsteps after the discovery of the body. Katie looked over the confusion of footprints in the dust and dirt, wondering which tramplings had been Marlie's.

The two circles of fluttering pink and yellow police tape were still in place, except for one long piece along the far side. That bit had broken loose, but caught in the vagaries of wind, it was now entangled in milkweed and wild heather stalks lining the outside of the orchard. Far past the expanse of back lawn were three ancient apple trees. The blossoming had finished weeks before, and small, hard balls of pitted green fruit were now making their appearance.

Before Katie stepped over the outer rim of tape, she turned to study the yard and house. From where she stood, she could see the furthest corner and outer edge of the last window on the second floor. Trees she had walked by without noticing shielded the eye from where she stood.

Katie sidestepped to her left, keeping her gaze on the house while remaining outside the ribbons. After only a few steps, the garage created a screen, obliterating her view of everything beyond.

She turned away from the house, knees up against a second strand of ribbon. Here was the area of most concern. Leaning as far forward as possible, Katie was perplexed by what she had been told and by what she saw. The ground within the inner circle looked soft enough to retain tracks. Katie leaned further, the ribbon bowing with the pressure of her knees. She tilted a bit more. One. Last…

"What the hell are you doing here? Get off my land," a strident voice behind her demanded.

Unable to hold back, Katie, who had gotten caught up in what she was doing, unmindful of the area outside her focus, leapt forward, breaking the ribbon. She fell to her hands and knees in the soft soil and leaf litter.

Oh no. She had been so intent on what she'd been doing that she hadn't heard the small Chevy pull up in front of the garage. Swinging around, she faced a woman five inches shorter than herself, but with a strong, square countenance that brooked no argument. At the woman's feet was a bouquet of pink and yellow flowers, discarded for a thick, nasty-looking branch. Capable, sun-browned hands had a firm grip on the wood.

"Did you hear me?" the woman demanded. "I don't need any thrill seekers up here, slinking around. Get out."

Katie held up her hands, staying slightly crouched so she wouldn't tower over the woman, possibly creating more stress. Her mind whirled. *What* was she doing? "I'm Katelyn Took," she said. "I live here in the village. I'm not trying to trespass on your privacy. My friend works with the local sheriff's office. I was asked to just take a look to see if fresh eyes would, you know, give a different perspective."

That last line was a definite lie. Not a little one, but a whopper that had slid smoothly from between her lips.

The woman didn't move. She sniffed, not seeking a bad smell coming off of Katie. Rather it was a tell that she was considering the information, and her thought process was changing.

"Give me one good reason that nose-up-his-arse sheriff would send you up here?"

"It wasn't the sheriff who sent me." Katie straightened slightly, but kept her hand raised to shoulder height. "I have several friends in law enforcement. I don't know why any of them would ask me, but my grandmother was killed on our farm a few years back, and I helped find her killer."

"The way I heard it," the woman said, tossing the branch to the side, "it wasn't that you helped. More like you got it done. Go ahead. Put your hands down before they go numb."

Katie dropped her hands and moved out of the circle. Not directly towards the woman, but so that she was on the other side, closer to the small shed.

"I'm Brittany Giles. Meredith was my sister. If you want to look around, go ahead. I think the cops are all done here."

"Thank you," Katie said. "I can't imagine how it must hurt to have lost your sister. I'm so sorry."

Brittany picked up the bouquet. Though Katie expected her to step up towards the inner yellow taped circle, the woman skirted it and headed further behind the garage, keeping close to the building.

Katie followed. To her surprise, several feet into the wildflower and weed growth, they came to a second yellow circle. Like the first, this one was trampled, inside and out.

"I don't understand," said Katie. "What's this?"

Brittany opened the bouquet, and leaning over the tape, tossed flowers out a few at a time until most of the area was covered. When she turned back to Katie, her eyes were filled with tears. Blinking them back and wiping a tissue under the red tip of her nose, she seemed less threatening than before.

"What exactly did your law enforcement friend tell you?" Brittany asked.

"Only that a body had been found up here, identified as Meredith, and that foul play was suspected," said Katie. "The idea was for me to come to my own conclusions."

"Ah-huh. Well, to make it easier for you, I'll tell you that this is where Meredith's body was actually found, out here in the trash. The other place you saw, where the ground was all churned up, is where the fight happened. The pathologist said she might have struggled to try to save herself. That's what that was." Brittany squeezed by Katie. "Go ahead. Look around. Take your time. I'll be in the house. I have a lot to do there. As long as you're here, you might as well have a look in there as well."

"Thanks, I'll be right in," Katie said.

After Brittany was gone, Katie edged closer, slipping beneath the ribbon. She didn't see anything that might be construed as stains on either the ground or the eight-inch clapboard slabs covering the outbuilding. But there was a difference in the crushed growth here than in the area between the woodpile and the shed.

This is definitely where Merdith's body must have been lying.

Here in the smaller, more compacted area, the stalks were so crushed and broken down that they had started to blacken. But the discoloration seemed to be more than what should be found from such a short time. Katie gazed down the length of the garage, toward the front. It wasn't wasted on her that the side door was on this side, twenty or so feet away on the other side of the wild growth.

Among the rest of the battered down vegetation were bulked out spaces, probably from the forensic team's equipment being hauled in and dropped. There were also paths where Edward Richardson, the pathologist from Montpelier, and his crew had tried to stay within the same footsteps. There, a few stalks were trying to right themselves. Others, too damaged to do so, hadn't yet started to decay.

Katie backtracked to the first circle, turning slowly to look in all directions. On the far side, facing northeast and the back of the garage, she saw a narrow, slightly recessed door tucked into the edge of the building at the corner. She hadn't noticed the secondary entrance when she was inside the two-car structure earlier. She made a mental note to check it out later.

There was little else to see, but when Katie returned to the beribboned area in the open field, she approached it differently than she had before. Instead of trying to picture the placement of Meredith's body, she hunkered down and paid more attention to the disturbances in the soil.

Left for days, the uneven patches had taken on the same hue as the rest of the field. But now that she knew what to look for, Katie could see the raised divots, the scuffed places where vegetation had been pushed out from its root base. Or maybe pulled out by the handful, then dropped as Meredith's hand reached ahead, seeking another grip.

It's like a football field after a game, she thought. *Or the fairgrounds when we went to the horse pulling.*

She couldn't tell if the area had been disturbed by one or more people. Or how big the feet that had sunk into the soil and kicked up the turf might have been. But she was willing to bet Edward, or perhaps Corinne Cox, his assistant, would know.

Again, she circled both the inner and outer ribbons, viewing from all vantage points. On the far side, the remains of the orchard were behind her. The sun felt warm on her back, inviting her to face into it, and be gentled.

It was a siren call she could not deny. Standing still, face uplifted, and eyes closed, she let the heat bring up a sheen of sweat. When she became uncomfortable, she looked back over the orchard and realized the smooth expanse was dotted with tufts of wildflowers. Buttercup, daisies, some very wilted Indian paintbrush. Not a lot of raised vegetation, but randomly left across the mowed area.

No accounting for people's habits, she thought, shaking her head at the messy plantings.

Katie moved toward the spot where the mowing stopped. Walking the perimeter turned up several game trails, but no places that raised any questions. Believing she had seen all that was there, she followed the line of paving stones back toward the house.

At the front corner of the garage, Katie went around to the side door she'd entered earlier. Once inside, she crossed to the back corner and realized the reason she hadn't noticed the second door previously was because it was hidden behind a tall steel cabinet with double doors. Bikes leaned on the side; cardboard boxes were stacked in front.

Standing directly before the cabinet, she noticed a conspicuously empty spot to the side. It seemed an oddity considering the stack of junk before her, and drew her over.

The dust on the rest of the garage floor was absent in this area. Three-by-three feet, half the size of the cabinet. Squatting, Katie ran her fingers over the concrete, feeling the thin rows of scoring where the heavy cabinet had been pushed sideways to block the door. She stood and tried to push the cabinet, then put her shoulder against it and set her feet. A more solid shove made no difference.

She cracked the cabinet open, revealing paint cans and more tools. A woman wouldn't have been able to shove this aside by herself, even a few inches. Loaded as it was, a single man wouldn't have been able to, either.

Katie considered the floor again. The cabinet hadn't been moved long before. The floor was still relatively clear of debris.

Why? she wondered.

* * *

"Come in," Brittany called when Katie tapped on the kitchen door of Meredith's house.

105

Inside, Katie found the room in the first throes of moving. There were half-filled boxes stacked on the floor, some taped shut and marked "Kitchen." The refrigerator doors were open. The unit had been shut off and emptied. Cabinets were open, counters stacked with refrigerator contents, other foodstuff in boxes, and a large trash bag open and half filled. A quick peek showed more refrigerator contents. Brittany, small trash can in hand, waved Katie to follow.

"I don't have a lot of time today," Brittany said. "Do you mind following me as I go?"

"Not at all," said Katie. "Is there something I can do to help?"

"Yeah, you could tell me what to do with all this sh…stuff Meredith collected."

Stepping into the first open doorway down the hall, a half bath in shades of blue, Brittany yanked open the medicine cabinet. Reading medicine bottle labels aloud, she left some on the counter and tossed the rest into the trash can.

"With the police gone, it seems I'm going to be the one packing everything." Brittany gave a half-hearted shrug. "My dad asked me if I'd get the personal stuff out of the way. My mom isn't strong enough to do this. I didn't think walking in here would be so hard, though. My brother and I are several years older than Meredith. She was my sister, but as a person, she wasn't my favorite."

The woman set the trash can down, leaning on her hands over the sink. The silence lasted long enough to make Katie nervous. Then Brittany opened the under-sink cabinet and started again. She hadn't pulled much out before she sat back on her heels, idle hands on her lap, as she looked toward the hallway leading to the bedrooms.

"I'm supposed to pack the boys' stuff first, but I can't seem to go into their bedrooms right now. Poor kids. Maybe tomorrow."

Brittany went quiet again.

"I'm sure it's hard for you." Katie cleared her throat. "I mean, knowing your nephews will be leaving their home."

Brittany snorted. "You're kidding, right? Those obnoxious brats won't be missed by me at all. My folks will suffer some, I'm sure. But to be honest, they're way too old to be stuck for hours with kids who have no idea how to behave. Meredith used to do that, let them run wild. She and Avery were divorced a few years back. He has the kids two weeks, then she does. When she realized her social life was going to disappear as soon as her wedding vows did, she reworked her job credentials. She had made it as far as paralegal before dragging Avery to the altar. She went back to that after the divorce and started taking more legal classes."

She got to her feet, dusting her hands off. "My problem right now is more about the senseless horror of the whole thing. Why? I don't understand. Is this about Meredith, or could it have been anyone in any of the houses on this road? I just don't understand why."

Putting the trash can by the door, Brittany opened the linen closet and pulled out more over-the-counter medications and old toothbrushes. Everything got dumped in the trash can. When another hot pink box flew by, Katie looked into the decorative plastic container, studying the contents.

"This is a lot of Benadryl," she said.

"Look around," said Brittany. "It's everywhere. In every room, on the window sills, in cupboards, closets, her car. Meredith didn't go anywhere, not even out to the yard, without it."

Katie looked up, ready to ask why, but Brittany blew out an exhausted "Meredith was allergic to bees. Specifically, paper wasps."

"Bees are bees," Katie said.

"Not so. Every species of bee, even subspecies, has different venom. You'd have to be an extreme case to be allergic to all bees."

"I didn't know that," said Katie.

"Yeah, Meredith was really paranoid about it. Did you notice all the buds were cut off the rose bushes, and the backyard and orchard are cut back real short? No flowers out there. All that was to discourage bees."

Katie's head turned toward the front of the house. "But out front, the lawn hasn't been mowed in a while."

"I don't know anything about that, except Meredith and the boys never used the front door. When she found out even bees a person isn't allergic to can suddenly become a danger, she started wearing long sleeves and pants all the time and stayed inside even more. Already being allergic to one species meant she was even more at risk."

They left the blue bathroom and went upstairs to the peach-and-cream full bath off the master bedroom. On the way, Brittany dropped the medicine bottles with the boys' names on them on the bed in the first boy bedroom. That one was all about rockets and robots. The other room across the hall was trucks and cars. Two different mindsets.

Ignoring the plethora of pink boxes in the second bathroom, Katie asked about Meredith's job and friends. Brittany, kneeling on the floor, digging stuff out from beneath the bottom-most shelf, sat back, frustrated.

"I don't mean to sound callous, but I didn't really know my own sister well. My brother lives in Virginia. He knew her even less. Your best bet for information would be my parents, and I have to ask you to give them some space. Meredith may not have been my first choice as a friend, but my parents loved her. My mom is taking this hard."

Katie nodded. She understood the shock and confusion the sudden, violent death of a family member could bring.

"If I can't help you," she said, "I'll leave you to it. You asked what to do with the material goods. Saint Jude's has a thrift shop for the needy. The church ladies might even come over and help you pack up."

Brittany nodded, but didn't look up. She still seemed bowed and beaten.

After a quick goodbye, Katie left. She was several steps down the driveway when a sheriff's department cruiser pulled in. It wasn't the new spit and polish model Sheriff Lewis drove, but an old Ford Crown Victoria, which had probably seen the last of the dinosaurs.

"What are you doing up here, Katie?" Marlie leaned out the window.

"How did you know I was here?"

"Are you kidding? You left that relic from a dump heap parked out in plain sight on the main road. I recognized it immediately, and I just knew you'd be up here," Marlie said.

"Were you coming up here?" Katie asked.

"Nope, I was just checking to see what you were doing," said Marlie.

Katie felt her ears get hot. "How about a cup of coffee from down at Beauregard's? I'll tell you why I'm here."

She kept walking down the drive and around onto Route 116, where she had left her truck. Marlie backed the cruiser out onto the main road and was long gone before Katie had her truck turned around. Though she hadn't expected to learn anything walking around Meredith Block's backyard, she had been pretty surprised when Brittany showed up. And while the other woman unloaded the pain in her chest, Katie had picked up some interesting facts.

In the parking lot of the general store, Marlie was leaning against the front fender of her car.

"On second thought," Marlie said before Katie opened the door to get out of the truck, "I don't have time for coffee. I'm on the clock right now. If you tell me something I might not be able to ignore later on, I'll have to rat you out to Lewis."

She bit her lip. There was a fine line between sharing with Katie and keeping true to the responsibilities she had sworn to uphold. Being a sheriff's deputy was important to Marlie. She had made a mistake once before, and she was just now crawling out from under the stigma of that. She wouldn't be taking another chance any too soon.

As Marlie left, Katie realized how long she had been gone from her own job. She ran into the store, grabbed the mackerel, and hightailed it back to Baldwin's. She punched in twenty minutes late. Stan was standing behind the cash register area as Nate left to return to the feed shed. His eyebrow was cocked up slightly, and Katie didn't want to explain where she had been, so she took evasive action.

"I've been down at Beauregard's, excuse me, the In Town Market, trying to negotiate a case of mackerel. I'm afraid I lost track of time," she said. "And no dice on a discount."

Stan's eyebrow moved up a fraction of an inch. Katie couldn't look him in the face. She busied herself getting her till ready for the afternoon.

"What are my chances of getting a case of cat food here at a discount rate?" she asked.

"Just like the kitty litter," he said. "Take what you need, put it on your tab, and Cindy will figure it out."

"Thanks, Stan." Katie felt a little heat in her cheeks at her lie.

Stan nodded and walked off.

"Katie, Mrs. Merle was here while you were gone," Davidson said. "Ruth told her about the feral cats. The fixed ones. Her barn cat disappeared, and she's looking for a replacement. She doesn't want one that will want to come into the house. I told her you'd give her a call."

She couldn't help smiling. "Thank you, Davidson. To be honest, I didn't have any idea how this would work with those real ferals. I even have a couple at home. I'll have Ruth give her a call tonight."

Proud that he'd helped, Davidson grinned happily.

Later, when Katie related Mrs. Merle's visit to Ruth and Rick, the elderly gentleman was quick to point out that Ruth should advertise that she had some unfriendly cats looking for a place. Ruth was quick to give him a swat.

* * *

Katie and Marlie had taken to walking down Fire Lane 61 late in the evening on the pretext of closing up the Schoolhouse Thrift and Sugarhouse Farm Stand. It didn't matter if the heat of the day was still oppressive, or even how tired they were. It was a few minutes after they were out of sight of both their home and the Deans', when they could be alone. There was hand holding, a little kissing, a tiny cuddle, whispers that had nothing to do with work, or fears of the future. Just them, together for a small space of time.

That night Katie plodded back up the hill behind Marlie, pushing her along, when her lover declared she was just too tired to take another step. To a casual observer, they appeared to be two friends clowning around in the dusty spaces between sheltering trees.

"Come on, Marlie," Katie coaxed. "You can do it."

"We could drive down to the farm stand. Maybe sit in the barn. It would be cooler. Or how about taking a walk down the lane and sitting on the stone wall?" Marlie's options included places where their tryst wouldn't

110

include a return trip up the hill.

"There's nothing in the barn. How long could we get away with going in there?" Katie asked. "We could go down the lane, or out into the orchard, but we'd still have to close up the farm stand. Come on, one more step."

They crested the last rise. Solomon and Bonnie lay among the lilac bushes where the moist soil cooled their bellies. Seeing the women, both animals got to their feet. With a grunt, the pig headed to her sty and bed. Solomon wagged his tail, which shook off bits of earth that clung to his belly. He waited for Katie and Marlie to come to him. They'd go into the house, he'd have a drink of water, maybe a snack, and they'd all go to bed.

Washed and then cooled by the box fan in the window, Katie lay on top of the sheets. LG was curled at her side, hot and unwilling to move. On the other side of the wall, Marlie had stopped moving around and settled in.

"Good night, my love," Katie whispered.

No one in the house, Marlie included, could hear her. But LG's purring response brought a smile to her face.

Maybe, Katie thought, *we could go out in the barn, up into the loft. Who would know?*

Chapter Twenty-Four

It didn't take Katie long to find good places to set up the live traps, but while she was in the barn, she found evidence of multiple litters of tiny kittens. Catching nursing mothers would be an issue.

"Rick's not going to like this," she told herself as she drove away. "I'll have to get Ruth out here Sunday morning to look for litters."

When she got to work, Katie's second set of customers was a pair of women who had come in independently. Apparently, they knew each other, because they were deep in conversation when it came their turn to pay. Even as Katie cashed one out, they kept up the chatter.

The first woman hung around until her friend had paid. Katie watched as they continued to talk out in the parking lot. One leaned on her car, but the other stood close, heads together. Their conversation had jumped from one topic to another, quick as droplets of water jumping off a hot skillet. Then Katie, who rarely paid attention to customer gossip, caught the word "convertible".

"...and that flashy car! What kind of responsible mother drives around with her two youngsters in the back of a convertible? She let them stand and jump around on the seat!" said the first woman.

"I don't know much about the children. They don't go to school here. Believe me, I've asked," the second responded. "I didn't want my boys around them. They're out of control, and the woman does nothing."

"Mr. Coombs was at the high school for years. I saw him one day down at the barbershop with the bigger boy. I don't know how the child didn't come away with his ears sheared off. He was so unruly."

Then another thought must have flittered through the brain of the first woman, because she started to gossip about Tracy Beauregard. The doings of the Beauregard clan weren't of interest to Katie, but so far, everyone in town seemed to think the Block boys were brats.

Katie remembered Mr. Coombs. Tall, angular, stern. But not unfair. She'd never considered him a threat, never heard him raise his voice. She remembered him in attendance at every sports game she'd gone to, male or female teams.

Just as Katie was about to go outside and ask the women if they knew Meredith personally, the pair separated and headed toward their own vehicle. Then Stan stepped out of the office. There had been a small delivery that morning, and he wanted either she or Davidson to mark product and stock shelves. Normally, Katie was quick to claim the job. It gave her a chance to move around and avoid chatty customers. But today she saw those same talkative people differently.

"You go ahead, Davidson," she said, to the young man's surprise. "There's a lot of new stuff on the shelves. You need to know what's out there."

Davidson's surprise turned to a nod of agreement.

He was so easy to manipulate. Katie felt a moment of shame, but then she dug out a notepad from under the shelf. If it was her intent to invite gossip, she needed to keep track of what people said. That is, if it worked.

Her first couple of forays made people look at her in shock, or because they knew of her other involvements in the past, edge away. It was clear she needed a different approach if she wanted to fish for information. So, she tempered her opening to include a reference to the church ladies.

"I hear," she said as she carefully lined up a customer's purchases to slow the checkout process down, "that the ladies from the church want to hold a fundraiser for the children of Meredith Block."

When asked about the date, Katie wrote herself a note to suggest the fundraiser to Ruth and Father Metevier.

She soon learned there were just as many people who got started talking about Meredith, and sometimes her parents, and couldn't shut up as those who shook their heads sadly and moved on.

At noon, she used the payphone to call the rectory. Father Metevier wasn't there, but Mrs. O'Brien took the message. She'd become an integral member of the church ladies, so Katie was sure that word would spread.

At the picnic table during her afternoon break, Katie went over her notes. There was duplicate information, but the repetition established the facts.

She hadn't heard one person say anything good about the boys. Meredith's parents were well thought of and fairly active in the community. She hadn't known Mrs. Coombs was once a tutor. Nobody seemed to know much about Avery, and references to Meredith went from "showy" to "kind" and "considerate".

Folks didn't want to talk evil about the dead.

* * *

Janice had called from the town office and left a message with Ruth. Rick often stopped at home while making afternoon deliveries. Ruth waited to give him messages for Katie instead of calling the feed store. Today, Rick brought the message back. Katie dropped a dime into the breakroom payphone and called the town office.

"I've got a dog complaint for you, Katie," Janice said.

"Okay, I'll go out, make sure the poop exists, ask the poopee if they saw the dog. Maybe they know who it belongs to. Then I'll go to the dog owner, issue a notice, and let you know the results." Katie said. "Right?"

"Yes. See if you can get a chit signed by both the complainant and the owner," Janice said. "Do you have a camera?"

"Kodak, Instamatic, twelve shot," Katie said before she hung up.

"So," Katie told Davidson ten minutes later. "Not only do I need a photograph of the offending dog, but I've got to take pictures of poop as well."

Davidson laid on the counter, rolling with laughter. When he started to choke, he ran off towards the breakroom.

"Is he okay?" the next customer asked.

"Yes," Katie said with a sigh. She couldn't imagine what kind of jokes

114

would rain down on her soon, but she doubted they'd be nice.

Business through the afternoon picked up. It was harder to hold a customer in front of her cash register long enough to be offered an opinion. On the few times the speaker lingered, everything she learned was already written on her notepad. At the end of the day, she ripped off the page and shoved it into her pocket. She planned on a conversation with Marlie that evening. It was time to head out to the Franklin Road farm to see what her first day as cat catcher extraordinaire had produced.

Chapter Twenty-Five

Katie had expected to catch a few cats. But when she pulled into the Franklin Road barnyard and looked around, she saw that every trap held a hissing, spitting feline. The safest way to handle them was to load the traps into the bed of the truck, tie a tarp over them, and drive straight to Valley Wide Veterinary. Doctor Nguyen had already been alerted when Katie decided to take the job.

Though the parking lot was mostly empty, Lois, the vet's assistant, stepped out and waved Katie around to the back entrance.

"Until we come up with a better plan, we'll use the cages in the isolation room," Lois said.

Katie hauled the traps inside while Lois expertly transferred the cats from the live traps into the treatment crates.

"A lot of half-grown cats here, Katie," Lois said. "I thought we were told they'd be adult cats."

"Yeah, I noticed that too. While you've got hold of them, Lois, check for nursing females. I noticed a bunch of tiny kittens. If there's a mother with small babies, I want to take her back."

Lois nodded. "It's been so hot lately that the breeding has slowed down. With any luck, most of the litters will be at least a few weeks old. I'll keep an eye out. Also, if you have a day that you won't come over, can you call so I'll know I can go home? Oh, and don't set out traps on Sunday. There won't be anybody here, okay? Doctor Ronnie left this note for you."

"I'm glad you told me about Sunday." Katie took the note.

Lois's words reminded Katie that there might be mornings when no one would be available to pick up and transfer the cats to the SPCA building in South Burlington. She'd need to come up with a schedule and talk to Doctor Ronnie about that.

Back in the car, she opened the folded note. Doctor Ronnie asked about a dog Katie might be told to collect. According to the vet, the woman had passed away, and the emergency contact, Avery Block, had no idea where the black cocker spaniel was.

Starting the engine, Katie told herself, *the deceased woman has to be Meredith. But I don't remember anything around the house or yard that would be for a dog.*

Instead of taking the Parentville/Charlotte Road home, she traveled slightly north and cut across the Shelbourne Road. This put her at the intersection north of town that would take her to Champlain Valley High School if she kept on straight. Instead, she turned left and drove halfway to Rocky Ridges Golf Course, slowing for the approach to Meredith Block's driveway. Instead of parking two hundred feet away where she would have to walk back, she pulled in, goosing the gas slightly so the truck slid up the small rise toward the garage.

Katie sat for a moment before she shut off the truck. The only sound was the hum and buzz of insects. Far off, a car approached on Route 116, but that didn't interest her.

Exiting the truck, she walked up to the kitchen door and turned the handle. The door was locked, but through the window, she saw household items stacked on every surface. No dog dishes or bags or cans of food.

With no intention of walking around the back of the garage to the find site, she circled the front to the garage door, all the while looking for evidence on the ground of a dog. This time, she found the side door to the garage had also been secured.

It was darker in the small building than in the house, but with her nose up against the glass, Katie could see two distinct stacks of trash bags, one on either side of the overhead door. The closest pile had items of trash stacked near the heap. The other pile held what looked like fuller, softer bags. Linens, pillows, or clothes, Katie guessed. But still no dog stuff, or a carrier or crate.

Backing slowly out of the driveway, with barely a glance over at Jacob and Irene Hunt's house, Katie wondered how she could learn more about Meredith. Brittany seemed the only answer, but maybe the ladies' church circle could help uncover a different source. She knew exactly how to get that line of questioning started.

"It's a shame, don't you think," she said to Ruth as the clock struck the half hour and the television shows changed on Channel 3, "that Meredith's sister has to carry all the burden of sorting out Meredith's life. Mr. Coombs is an academic. Useless. Mrs. Coombs had a stroke, so she's not well." Katie sighed. "Brittany lives all the way across the state. Over near Morrisville somewhere. She left here after high school for college, and never came back. To live, I mean. It really is a shame that her sister's death is the only reason she'd be here for any length of time."

She felt Ruth's attention switch from the television.

"That's a distance to come," the elder woman said. "You're right, it seems somebody ought to offer to help."

Katie stayed silent, eyes focused on the hijinks playing across the screen on Happy Days. Five minutes later, Ruth was up. The whirr of the telephone dial came from the kitchen. Katie smiled. It was a sure bet that Ruth would be back shortly to tell her what the church ladies had decided. She'd wait until the next day to ask Ruth if she would question her knitting group about any information they might have regarding Meredith. Father Metevier was another source to tap.

She'd handle Dorothea herself.

Chapter Twenty-Six

Katie's plan to show her notes to Marlie that night didn't come to fruition. Her friend dragged in at ten-fifteen, stumbling with exhaustion on the doorstep. Katie waited up, concerned they hadn't heard a word all evening. On those occasions when the deputy knew she would be delayed, Marlie had always found a way to get word to Katie or Ruth beforehand.

"Marlie," Katie began.

"Too tired." Marlie's eyes closed. A shuddering sigh made her entire body shake.

"Sit here," Katie ordered.

Katie rushed to turn on the shower. As the water heated, she helped Marlie out of her uniform and then left her in the bathroom to find pajamas and slippers.

"Towels and clean clothes on the sink," she said through the shower curtain.

From the refrigerator, she took out a bowl of chicken corn chowder. She heated up a serving in a small pan and added a slice of toast and tea.

Marlie ate silently. Katie was tempted to spill what she had done that day, but she could see Marlie was barely awake enough to lift the spoon. Any words would be wasted. When finished with the soup and toast, cup of tea in hand, Marlie climbed the stairs. Katie locked up and followed. She hoped this wouldn't develop into a regular event. She couldn't help but wonder what calamity might have kept the deputy out so late.

In the morning, Rick remarked that Marlie looked like she had panda eyes. The joke didn't lift the corners of Marlie's mouth at all.

"We were out interviewing people who have called in about Meredith Block," she said.

Katie looked up, hopefully.

"It was mostly stuff like somebody had seen her six weeks ago out at nine o'clock at night. One woman was concerned because she has school-age children, and so did Meredith. She was worried her children might be in danger." Marlie poured coffee into her thermos.

"Meredith's kids didn't even go to school here." Katie frowned.

"I know. But we have to check out every call." Marlie picked up her thermos and brown lunch bag, ready to go. "Angus had a stack of calls. Lewis passed them over to me."

"Was there any helpful information at all?" Rick asked.

"Just vague references to her boyfriend. Who we don't know anything about at all. Like that he existed or what his name is." Marlie waved goodbye and closed the door.

"It stands to reason," Rick said, picking up his own thermos and lunch, "that a young-and-good-looking woman like Meredith would have somebody in her life."

"But who?" Ruth asked.

Rick shrugged. "Don't know, but there's probably something in the house that will give Lewis a heads-up."

Katie nodded in agreement. If Lewis didn't find it, Brittany might.

At mid-morning, as Katie continued to gather scraps of information, Marlie popped into the store.

"Angus's stack of callers has about dwindled off," she said. "I've got to go over to the other side of Richmond for a drive-by mailbox amputation, actually four on the same road. I bet that movie with the guy who carries a big stick is responsible." She laughed. Katie was glad to see her friend had gotten her second wind.

"*Walking Tall*?" Katie asked, referring to the movie.

"Yes, that's the one." Marlie's radio crackled.

"By the way, I went by Meredith's and there's a moving van in the driveway. So, stuff must be happening over there."

The radio crackled again. "Gotta go," Marlie said with a sigh.

Once again, Katie was amazed at the sheriff's department's timing. It was like they knew when their deputies were doing something unofficial.

Ruth had mentioned last night that the church ladies were willing to help Brittany pack up her donations. Katie decided to drive straight out to Meredith's house on her lunch.

Just as Marlie had said, there was a moving van in the driveway. Katie got to the kitchen door just as two broad men muscled the center of a sectional sofa out. The jade-green fabric was napped. A very offensive color.

The truck said Datro Bros. The men could have been twins, right down to the red suspenders which barely held their work-worn blue twill Dickies up in the back. Somehow, two inches of belly was exposed in the front.

"S'cuse us," huffed the one on the far side.

His partner offered a grunt as he backed down the steps.

"Brittney?" Katie called.

"Upstairs."

Passing the living room, Katie noticed the last of the big furniture had been removed. But prior to that, the room hadn't been packed. Lamps, throw pillows, and bric-a-brac scattered around the room. Upstairs, the beds and dressers were gone from the boys' rooms, but everything else was still there, dumped on the floor. Brittany's head popped out of the primary bedroom.

"Oh, hi," she said. Then disappeared again.

"Ma'am?" the deep voice of one of the movers called from the first floor.

"Oh, for the love of ..." Brittany hurried into the hall, pushed past Katie, then raced down the stairs.

Katie followed, then stood aside as Brittany and the movers went from one first-floor room to another, checking items off the to-be-picked-up list. Finally, the men were gone. Brittany turned back to Katie.

"Sorry. I thought it would be easier once the furniture was gone. Look around. Does this look easier to you?"

Katie glanced around at all the heaps of household and personal items.

"Actually, no," she said.

"Thank God. I was worried I was losing my perspective."

Outside, they heard the squeal of brakes as the moving van inched backwards down the drive toward Route 116. Brittany backed up to the wall and slid down to the floor, forehead pressed against her knees. After a moment, Katie slid down next to her.

"What's going on?" she asked.

Even though Meredith had been her age, and Brittany, the older sister, was fifteen years older than Katie, she felt a kinship. Not necessarily through Meredith, but more in the manner they had both been thrown an eight ball. After a couple more seconds, Brittany raised her head. Though she wasn't crying, her eyes were red-rimmed and her skin splotchy.

"I'm sorry." She took a swipe at her eyes. "I barely know you, and I'm sitting here floundering."

"I tell you what," said Katie, "I have broad shoulders. Why don't you take advantage of them? Believe me, you can't touch what I have to carry around. And, I won't tell a soul. I promise."

Brittany gave her a watery smile. "You're such an innocent."

For just a moment, her eyes met Katie's. There was something in the look that caused Katie to bat her eyelashes. Then her breath caught. She held perfectly still. "Marlie," her lips whispered silently. That momentary glance left a guilty sting like a Band-Aid ripped free. She exhaled, and the feeling was gone. Katie shifted slightly and shrugged.

"Maybe." She didn't want to get involved in another person's private angst, but there had been that moment when Brittany's look had drawn her in. She felt the need to lighten the moment, extract herself. "So, the movers had an offensive odor?"

"I don't know. I didn't get close enough to find out." Brittany leaned back. Exhaustion had sapped the strength out of her muscles. "I thought I could get this done in a few days; you know? But it took two days to get just the boys' stuff packed and over to Avery's. Then when I showed up with the second load, he told me half of what I'd already brought could go back or to the dump."

"Phfft," said Katie.

"I know, right? I thought I was doing the good thing. I didn't make him come out here and pack it for himself. Then, before I could get any further, my mom took a bad turn, and Dad needed me there. The big furniture had been sold, and those guys were scheduled. I didn't have time to get everything out of the way before they arrived. Look at the mess, will you? The Realtor will be here on Monday. There's no way I can figure out what to do with all this stuff before then."

"Who scheduled the Realtor?" Katie asked.

"Avery," said Brittany. "The land is his, the house belongs to Dad. Once it's sold, they'll split the profit."

Katie looked around. "You know, if Sheriff Lewis hasn't released the scene. When you tell him a realtor will be here to dress the house for clients, he'll have a drop-down-dead fit." She didn't add the house should have probably been left alone as well.

"Are you joking?" Brittany groaned.

"Nope. If I were you, I'd call Avery and tell him he might want to check on that little bit of information. In the meantime, let's see what has to be done here." Katie got up and reached out a hand to help Brittany.

"Well, I got rid of all the food and garbage," said Brittany, "but the back of my car is still full of the boys' stuff. So, I can pack, but I have to go to the dump before I can do much more."

Katie stopped short. "Wait, the dump? Is it good stuff? What about the thrift shop?"

"They won't want the boys' clothes and toys." Brittany looked out the window. Backed up to the garage was a Jeep filled with boxes and bags.

"That's absolutely silly!"

Katie rode with Brittany back into town and to Saint Jude's parking lot. She told Brittany that she'd like a chance to speak with the other woman's parents. But held off that if they could find a time when Brittany wasn't all wound up about Meredith's house, Katie wanted to sit down with Brittany again as well.

"I think once the stress of handling the contents of the house has been cleaned up, it'll be easier for everyone to concentrate. That's what I need," said Katie. "Everyone to think clearly."

Brittany opened the tailgate of her Jeep, and the two women lugged the first load of boxes down into the church's basement. While Brittany apologized for showing up unexpectedly, Dorothea pawed through the boxes like it was Christmas. Katie stood aside and let the old woman have at it.

"I don't know how much you'd want to take," said Brittany.

"There's more?" Dorothea's head popped up out of the box she was going through. "And you're just standing here?"

Now Katie stepped forward. She didn't want to mention in front of Brittany about Ruth already being on board with finding help, so she explained to Dorothea about the small appliances, household goods, and tools in the garage. There was a sure chance that one of Dorothea's first calls would be to Ruth. The old women could sort it out then. While she and Brittany emptied the jeep, Dorothea dialed up her friends. Before they knew what was going on, the keeper of the old but good salon had lined up packers for the next day.

"They'll be there tomorrow morning at eight," Dorothea told Brittany. "You need to be there so's they don't take any personal stuff. Once they get it all together, we'll set up for some trucks to come and haul it out. Now get along, I got stuff to do here."

"Shouldn't we stay to help?" Brittany asked as she and Katie headed up the stairs for the last time.

"No, we'd only be in her way. I'm sure some of her old crony friends will be here pretty quickly."

"Katie!"

"Sorry, but she's seriously bossy. She yelps; they jump."

Both women were still giggling when they pulled into Meredith's yard. As they got out of the jeep, Brittany looked back down the road.

"Brittany," Katie said, when she remembered the question raised by Doctor Nguyen's note. "What happened to Meredith's dog?"

Brittany shrugged. Her eyes swept the yard.

"I didn't know Meredith had a dog. She didn't give it to my folks, which is what she normally does when she gets bored with something. Right now,

I'm going to call Avery. Then I'll get the family stuff out. I'll call you after tomorrow, okay? We can talk. And, thanks Katie."

"You're welcome."

Katie drove away, disappointed there wouldn't be a chance to pick Brittany's brain that afternoon. The dismissal had been clear, though not sharp. She wondered about Brittany's mother. Ruth wouldn't know, and probably not Dorothea either. But maybe Cindy would. She drove out of town, headed back to work. If Cindy didn't show up that afternoon to work on the books and time cards, Katie would give her a call later in the evening.

As it worked out, Cindy walked through the door half an hour later. She carried a big jug of icy lemonade in each hand.

"Afternoon refreshment," she said, pouring paper cups for the employees in the store, then directed Davidson to take the second jug out to the guys in the feed buildings.

Katie stood behind the register. The icy beverage trickled down her throat, sending delighted shivers down to the soles of her feet. "So good," she said with a sigh. "Where are the kids?"

"Home in air-conditioned comfort." Cindy poured herself a paper cup full before Stan took what was left in the container into the safety of his office. "She stayed home today, so they can have an afternoon nap party."

"Ingenious." Katie laughed.

After a few moments of silent bliss, Katie asked. "Cindy, what do you know about Meredith Block?"

"Actually, I don't really know anything. Up until Stan and I got married, I'd never even heard about her." Cindy pulled Davidson's stool over and sat down. "I didn't graduate high school here. After she, ah, passed, Stan and I were talking. As near as I can tell, she went to college in Burlington, got married, moved away, and then they moved back. Stan said he knew absolutely nothing about Avery, other than he's a lawyer. Never even met him. I was here when Meredith first came back. Her mother used to drag her to town functions. Church suppers, women's guild, you know, stuff like that. She was always really dressed up. Full makeup, heels." Cindy's shoulders hunched together, and she squirmed on her seat. "We kind of laughed at her. Not right to her face, but she probably read the vibes."

"Yeah, I get it." Katie's cheeks puffed out. "She didn't fit in."

"No, Katie, she didn't. But you know, she grew up here. She had to have had some inkling about what to expect. She was all about inviting some of the women over for cocktails. When she had a reason to get all dolled up and show up with snacks, they included shrimp, or little egg rolls, where we all brought brownies and chocolate chip cookies. I think sometimes, even her mother was embarrassed. Eventually, Mrs. Coombs left her to bring herself. I might have seen her two or three times at town functions. Never anything to do with the school. Other than that, I'd see her driving through town. Or at the store. I heard she got divorced and went back to work at a law firm in Burlington."

"I wonder why?" Katie mused.

"I heard Mrs. Coombs talking at the ladies' guild. She said Meredith didn't need to work, but missed the social interaction with her city friends even though she had several locally." Cindy slid off the stool, gathered her cup and time cards and left for the office, where she ordered Stan away so she could use the desk.

Katie waited on her next customer, wondering who Meredith's friends, local or city, might be.

* * *

Stan paused as he walked by. "Come in tomorrow dressed to go to the bank," he said. "Bring all the paperwork Cindy helped you fill out and the stuff she told you to get together to apply for a bank loan. Don't worry about your action plan. I'll bring that with me."

Katie stood stock still, gaping. "Stan, I'm not applying for a loan."

Stan sighed, cocked his head, and looked at Katie like he would one of his own children.

"Because you don't think you're worthy, or you don't have enough to offer, or they just won't like you?" he asked.

Katie's jaw tightened. Stan was her friend. Why was he saying aloud the

126

very thoughts that ran through her head? The things that hurt her?

Stan had long arms. He reached out across the open space and drew Katie towards him and away from the register area where anyone could hear.

"Listen to me," he said. "Three years ago, I didn't know you from Adam. I hired you because you had spunk and all but dared me not to. We share friends and some pretty bizarre behavior patterns." He smiled. "You, Katie, are totally worth it. You have done an amazing job in the short time that you've been here to correct your grandmother's errors. Cindy and I love you the same way Rick and Ruth do. We will do anything you ask. But right now, I'm telling you. Be ready tomorrow. You and I will walk into that bank, and when we're done, you'll be ready for the next big step."

He gave her shoulder a little shake and turned away. Which was a good thing because suddenly, Katie's lower lip was trembling.

"One more thing," he said, turning back, but focused on the pages he held.

Katie fought to get her face under control.

"You won't be able to ride with me," her boss continued, "because I have an appointment after. Be at the Howard Bank on the corner of South Winooski Avenue in Burlington at one. Nate will cover until you get back."

With his eyes on the papers in his hand, Stan didn't notice Katie's shocked expression. By the time she'd recovered enough to ask a question, he had left the building.

Chapter Twenty-Seven

The next afternoon, Katie walked into the bank lobby, but she didn't immediately see Stan. She stood in the middle of the floor, waiting for him to find her. A bank teller offered to help, but Katie just shook her head. When Stan finally exited an inner office, he motioned her toward him. Then he pushed her through the door while thrusting a few loose pages into her hand.

"Are you done filling out your loan application?" she asked

"I did that weeks ago. I just picked up the check for the expansion," Stan said, then gave her a little push forward.

"This is Katelyn Took," Stan said to the man behind the desk. "The employee I told you about. Katie, this is Karl Tanner. He'll help you from here." With a nod, Stan closed the door and was gone.

Mr. Tanner accepted Katie's manila envelope of forms and receipts, as well as the pages Stan had passed to her. While she sat nervously, fighting the urge to chew her fingernails, he looked over every page.

"This looks to be about everything we need," he said. "I must tell you, this action plan is quite concise. You did a very good job. I'm going to finish checking your references, then an inspector will come out and go over the property. He'll call you directly."

Katie waited, silently thanking Cindy and her business college education.

"Is there something else?" Mr. Tanner asked.

Realizing she had just been dismissed, Katie replied, "No. Thank you for your consideration."

On the sidewalk, she looked for Stan, but he was long gone. She saw a tiny park with a fountain kitty-corner to the bank, and beyond that, the back of a white marble building. The courthouse. She had been in there the previous year. Little bells went off in Katie's ears. Pulling the tiny notebook out of her pocket, she looked up the address for the law firm where Avery Block worked.

Once in the car, she did a drive-by, barely suppressing the urge to just walk in and ask for the guy. Instead of heading out of town, Katie drove around the block. This was where Meredith had worked as well. She had questions, and if she had been on the verge of ignoring them, a car exited the parking space right in front of the door. It was a sign.

"Hi." Katie smiled at the receptionist. "I'm Kaitlyn Took. I'm looking for Meredith Block."

Totally deadpan, and without any pause, the woman said, "Ms. Block is no longer employed at this agency."

"No?" Katie asked, with a confused frown. "Can you tell me where she is now?"

This time, the woman paled slightly, and her words came slower. "No. I'm sorry. I can't help you."

Of course not, Katie thought as she left. *Because you know Meredith's working days are over.*

She hadn't accomplished anything other than establishing that the legal world was aware of Meredith's demise. The authorities had no doubt already been here. A dictum had gone out. Like wagon trains of bygone eras, the lawyers would circle up and set their defenses so that Katie's usual questioning tactics wouldn't work on them.

She returned to the feed store to find Nate wrestling with the cash register tape. He was trying to weave the inner tape around all the spindles and through the printer.

"I've got this, Nate," she said.

"You'll get dirty. I can do this," he grunted.

"No, seriously. I've got it." Laughing, she pushed him aside.

Just as she closed the side of the machine, Arthur Fortin walked into the store carrying a paper bag, which he set on the counter in front of Katie.

When she didn't reach for it, he said, "Dorothea told me to bring this over and give it to you. Ellen found it in that stuff you brought the other day. She thinks it's personal and should be returned to the Coombs family."

"Thank you, Mr. Fortin," Katie said.

He was still right there, smiling, so she asked, "Is there something else?"

"No. Just that you look really nice today. I'll bet you've got a new boyfriend you're looking to impress."

Katie felt her cheeks pink. Mr. Fortin was a quiet, generous friend. But not the kind who normally passed out frivolous compliments.

"No boyfriend. Just the guy from the bank."

"Well," the five-foot-four-inch grandfather said, "If I was him, I'd lend you money."

A hoot of laughter erupted from Katie before she had a chance to suppress it. "You are a bad, bad man."

Mr. Fortin turned and headed toward the door, waving over his head, but she could see the tips of his ears were bright red. After his old sedan pulled out of the parking lot, she opened the bag and looked inside.

Lane Furniture in Williston gave every graduating high school girl in nearby areas a solid cedar mini hope chest. Not only was it a clever advertising ploy for soon-to-be-brides, but for many, it became a treasured keepsake. When Katie had returned from Illinois, her Lane chest was right on the dresser where she had left it. When she'd flipped the lid open and peered inside, she had shaken her head at the hidden treasures of an adolescent girl. A chewing gum wrapper rope, braided with Juicy Fruit and spearmint wrappers. The moon ring that always turned her finger green. School photographs of friends. A lock of hair from her dog, Flossy.

Lifting Meredith's box out of the paper bag, her finger stubbed against something attached to the bottom. Just like her own Lane chest, this one came with a simple skeleton key. Meredith had taped the one for this chest securely to the bottom.

Without hesitation, Katie pulled the key free and unlocked the chest. Inside were several small bundles wrapped in blue Kleenex and secured with rubber bands. Holding up the first bundle, Katie marveled at the way an individual's mind worked, developing little customs that made them happy. Like gift wrapping with blue tissues. But after she removed the rubber bands and tissue, she hesitated for a jaw-dropping moment.

There were two items wrapped in this tissue. The first was a business card. The second was a driver's license. The date was current. And the name on the license was Gage Fernald.

Stan had stepped out to the feed shed. Watching for his return to the store, Katie stretched the office telephone cord as far as it would go.

"Janice," she hissed into the receiver. "I've only got a sec. Listen, I need Deputy Foster to call me at Baldwins when she comes in. And I don't want Angus or Sheriff Lewis to know I'm looking for her. Got it?"

"I understand." Janice's voice had dropped to a whisper. "This is covert."

The line went dead. Katie hung up the phone and darted back out to her place behind the register. Davidson looked at her suspiciously.

"What are you doing?" he asked.

"Me? Nothing. Nothing at all."

She paused to clear her throat. She'd sounded quite shrill and guilty. As she straightened out the nearest endcap, Katie was well aware that Davidson watched her.

Katie waited nervously for Marlie's call. Instead of hearing from her friend, she saw Rick walk through the store on his way to drop off delivery receipts. She cornered him.

"How did it go at the bank?" he asked.

"All I did was drop off the paperwork. Mr. Tanner is going to check the references." Katie looked over her shoulder. This was no time for an eavesdropper.

"That's weird," Rick said. "Didn't he ask you about a down payment or talk about making payments? Anything like that?"

Katie wasn't concerned about what Mr. Tanner might have said to her, because she truly believed there was no way a bank was going to loan her money. "Nope, but listen to this. Stan told me he picked up a check for the expansion. It didn't sound like he was talking about the house. Do you think he meant the store?"

Rick shrugged. "If he did, he'll let us know in time."

That time was not long in coming. At four-thirty, the PA system called all available employees to meet in the loading area behind the main building.

"Before you hear a lot of gossip, I want to let you know about some changes that are going to be happening around here," Stan said.

A shiver ran down Katie's back as she immediately assumed he would announce that the store was being sold.

"Because of all the development happening in the area, we've decided to expand our product line to more hardware," Stan said, amid a murmur from those assembled. "We will add to the back side of this building and carry all the hardware stuff, contractors, or new homeowners might need. Chick Windows and Doors will have a kiosk with a display, and we'll have room for a few appliances. This expansion will add four jobs. Those working here have the first option. Construction will start soon. When I know more, I'll let you know."

Some of the workers circled the owner, asking questions. Katie, however, hustled back to her place in the store. Cindy stood beside her husband during his announcement. Leaving Stan, she followed Katie.

"I've got a script put together for you for when the bank inspector comes. I'll be over later this evening to explain it," Cindy said. "If you just read through it a few times, you should be good for your meeting."

She left to return to where Stan still answered questions. Davidson, who had been listening from inside, edged closer to Katie.

"Katie, does that mean we'll have different jobs now? I just learned all the feed and hardware stuff in here." His forehead furrowed in concern.

"I don't think you need to worry about your job, Davidson," she said. "But we'll probably have more to learn. Let's wait and see, okay? I like my job too. I don't want to change."

He nodded and turned to a woman who had walked up with supplies for a new cat. Katie hoped she had adopted one from Ruth. With the kittens, the count had gone up to sixteen between the cat room and the house.

Chapter Twenty-Eight

Ruth, Rick, and Charlie sat out on the front porch, enjoying the soft evening breeze. The storm had passed, and the heat had returned, but the scorching burn of days and days of intense temperatures had washed away.

Cindy had been as good as her word. She'd stopped in and dropped off the notes she'd made for Katie.

"I can't stay," Cindy said. "I told my mother I'd only be gone half an hour."

True to her word, she went out the door fifteen minutes later, leaving Katie inside the kitchen and seated at the far end of the table on guard against the return of one of the people seated outside. She had touched Marlie's arm, holding her back from following the others. Now, with the two of them seated, she took the Lane chest out of the paper bag.

"Look at this," she said softly, explaining how she had come to have the wooden box. "Every one of these bundles is the same. Look how they're wrapped. It's like some secret society handshake thingy."

"You mean ritualistic?" Marlie asked.

After watching as Katie pulled on the Platex gloves and carefully removed the elastic and opened it, she had to agree. It was like a piece of origami. The first bundle was lying open on the table. While Marlie examined it, Katie took the exact same steps to open the second and reveal its contents.

When she had all six of the bundles open, Katie spoke. "See, a business card, then this one has the driver's license, this one has a Saint Florian medal, and this one has a house key." She was exactly right. Each contained a business card and an item of personal property.

Marlie frowned, reaching toward the items, then pulling her hand back.

"Oh, darn it, Katie," she said. "You touched all this stuff? Fingerprints, remember?"

"I touched only the first bundle," Katie said. "The one that had Gage Fernald's card. That's it, just the card. When I saw what else was there, I put on a pair of gloves. This isn't just random stuff, Marlie. These are the kind of things that guys keep in their wallets."

"Business cards are easy to come by," Marlie pointed out.

"Yeah, but you know this other stuff isn't."

"I know. Oh, this is going to be so bad." Marlie wiped her hand over her forehead.

"No, it's not," Katie said. "First, you are out of it. I'm going to verify the box was Meredith's."

"How are you going to do that?" Marlie cut in.

"I'm going to go see Brittany. Verify it came from the house, and she put it in the stuff for the thrift." Katie wrapped the bundles back up. "I made a list of all of this, so I'll remember. Right after I talk to her, I'm taking this down to Sheriff Lewis. Ellen saw the box. I don't know if she looked in the bundles. Arthur Fortin brought the box to me. Brittany can verify where it came from, and it will be Lewis's problem."

"Really?" Marlie quirked an eyebrow. "You're going to give this to Lewis willingly?"

"Absolutely. He's going to want to contact all these people. Let's see what they have to say about how Meredith got this stuff."

Marlie sat back in the chair. "Ah-huh. So, I'm going to be out of it. How exactly are you going to know what all these men have to say?"

"Mm, I don't know. Idle gossip. Slip of the tongue. Pillow talk." Katie smiled at Marlie, sliding the box back into the paper bag.

* * *

After Marlie went outside, Katie called directory assistance and got the telephone number for Mr. and Mrs. Coombs. She wasn't sure exactly where Brittany lived, but she hoped they would share their elder daughter's number. To her surprise, Mr. Coombs asked her to hold the line, and a moment later, Brittany said hello.

Katie laughed. "I thought you'd gone home and figured I'd just call you there. It never occurred to me that you might still be at your parents' house."

"Yeah, it's a long ride and I have to be back here tomorrow morning, so we're having supper and an early night. I assume this isn't just a social call."

"Actually," said Katie, "it's kind of both. I wanted to make sure you were okay. I hated to leave you alone the other day. Besides that, one of the ladies found a Lane cedar chest in the things you dropped off from Meredith's. She thought it might be a personal item you would want back. I told her I'd ask. It had some tissues and stuff in it." She waited, barely able to take a breath deeper than her upper chest.

"Lane chest? One of those small wooden boxes we got at graduation?" Brittany asked.

"Yes," Katie said. "I've got mine on my dresser."

"I have one as well." There was a smile in Brittany's voice. "I almost remember seeing one in a bunch of stuff from Meredith's attic. There were so many boxes. But unless the chest has something with Meredith's personal information on it, we don't need it."

"I kind of looked the contents over," Katie confessed. "There was nothing inside related to Meredith."

"Then it's good to go. Thank you, Katie, for your help so I could get through all this," Brittany said softly.

"You're welcome. I'm sorry we met under such sad circumstances."

Brittany said goodbye, but related before she hung up that Katie had been right about the Realtor. Sheriff Lewis hadn't released the scene. Nothing more could happen with the sale of the property.

A short time later, while Katie and Marlie closed up the thrift shop and farm stand, Katie told her friend about the call.

"I guess Sheriff Lewis wasn't happy Brittany had been in there to pack and get rid of stuff, but he hadn't been clear on the day you guys got the initial call about what she could or couldn't do," Katie said.

"Yeah, that's part of his problem," Marlie said. "He just assumes everyone knows what he does, or they can read his mind."

"Well, that would be a short book," Katie said with a laugh.

"You are so bad," Marlie said. But she giggled as well, then asked, "What did Brittany say about the small cedar box? The Lane chest."

Katie slapped the heel of her right hand against her forehead. "Oh, my gosh! I totally forgot to ask." Her eyes darted to see if it looked like Marlie believed her.

"Are you for real?" Marlie asked. "That's why you called her, right? How did you forget to ask her?"

"I don't know. She was all upset about taking stuff out of the house and the realtor. She told me Avery Block came down on her, the jerk. Then she said her mom wasn't doing so well."

Katie looked down at the road ahead of her. The lie had flowed so glibly off her tongue. And it felt so wrong. But then, so did the idea she would have to share anything that might help Sheriff Martin Lewis. As usual, when stress mounted, she felt her lips purse, ready to suck a hit off a joint. Her right hand sent out a request for an icy cold beer.

Shake it off, she thought. *Tell Marlie the truth. If you want to be free, then don't hold this back.*

One step became three, then four, then more. Soon, the two of them were marching along, lost in their own thoughts, with Katie aware she had failed again.

Chapter Twenty-Nine

Ruth had a patience Katie lacked. Though Rick wasn't happy about it, the three of them drove in two vehicles over to the Franklin Road farm after church on Sunday. As they pulled in, Katie noticed that, from inside the house, two cats watched them through the glass.

"Crap," she said. "How long have they been in there?"

"I'm thinking," Rick said, "they have a way in and out. Neither looks like they haven't been fed. I'll check around the house, maybe walk over and talk to the neighbor."

Katie nodded and followed Ruth into the barn. They were met by the strong stench of cat urine. She had noticed it before when she'd come out to the property to look, and again when she'd set the traps. But now, with the sun beating down for several days in a row, the musty smell of the old barn had risen. And so had the cat smell. Katie had wondered if it was just because the cats didn't want to leave the security of the building. But both big doors on either end were wide open. With the growth of weeds around them, it appeared they hadn't been closed in years. Then, too, there were missing boards and holes in the roof. If a predator wanted in, there were a lot of options.

Or more likely, Katie thought with a sigh, there were just a lot of cats.

"Be careful where you walk, Ruth. I'm not sure how safe this place is."

Ruth nodded. With small steps, the old woman moved slowly ahead, bent at the waist, eyes alert for ground nests of kittens. Katie's attention was fixed more on the structure of the barn itself.

This was a low mow building, built more in the style of UK barns with their low ceilings. It covered more land than modern barns, too. There were long sloping hay mows barely ten feet high, instead of one's like hers, where the roof was thirty feet up from the mow floor. Amid the age-darkened, wide beams, the reflective glow from many sets of eyes looked back down at her.

"The number of cats I pick up each evening is starting to fall," Katie said to Ruth. "The first night was the only time I filled all the traps. I think on nights where I only get one, I'll bring the cat home instead of making the trip to the veterinary until I catch another." She scanned the upper hay mow again. "There are probably kittens up above, Ruth. They would be safer there from foxes and the like."

"Here's a nursery right here, Katie," Ruth whispered. "Looks like four kittens. What do you want me to do?"

"Don't touch them. Don't disturb the nest." Katie came over and took a peek. Tiny kittens, milky blue eyes open but still not mobile, teetered together in a heap. "We'll find a couple more nests, and tomorrow, when I set out the traps, I'll put the kittens inside the trap. With any luck, the mother cat will go inside and spring it."

They found one more nest of new babies, and another where the kittens were old enough to play together. Knowing these more agile kittens would spring the trap if placed inside, Katie opted to take them with her on this trip. She'd place a trap here the next day with the nesting material from the kittens.

Rick was not happy to see Ruth place the kittens in a cardboard box. But Katie explained why they had to, and why Ruth couldn't keep them. "These are SPCA kittens. We get paid for each one. As soon as they're big enough, they go to Doctor Ronnie. Ruth will call over there tomorrow, so the vet knows we took them. We also need clarification on how we should handle litters. I'll need to clean three traps so they don't smell like mackerel. If I'm going to put kittens inside to tempt the mama, I don't want some other cat in there on the lookout for the bait and have it find unfamiliar kittens."

"Bleach wash, then a good rinse," Rick said. "Don't start cooing, Ruth. They look four or five weeks old. So, they won't stay long."

Katie and Ruth were loading the box of kittens into Rick's truck when an older jeep pulled in. Katie recognized it as Brittany's and walked over before the other woman got out.

"I'm surprised to see you over here, Brittany," Katie said.

"Actually, I'm probably even more surprised to see you." Brittany looked over at the two trucks quizzically.

"I was hired to trap some cats here," Katie explained. It was on the tip of her tongue to ask why Brittany would drive around on the dirt road.

"I knew the property was up for sale," Brittany said. "But not that there was a cat issue. Is that Ruth Beauregard?" Brittany reached out the window to wave.

"Yes." Now Katie was really stumped. "How do you know Ruth?"

"Well, I take my mother over to that little thrift shop off the Parentville/Charlotte Road, and I saw her there. She was also among the women who came over to help me pack up Meredith's house," Brittany explained. Laughing, she added, "I think she was Dorothea's onsite manager. You warned me she was bossy. And when Ruth showed up, she got right on things and told everyone, even me, what to do."

Katie blushed at the thought Ruth would push herself into the position of job boss.

"Well, I'm still surprised to see you out here," Katie said.

"You didn't know my folks live just down the road?" Brittany asked.

Katie shook her head.

Brittany looked off toward the woods. A lone cat stalked grasshoppers along the tree line. Katie shifted from foot to foot while she waited. Finally, Brittany seemed to come to a decision. She looked back as Rick started his truck, ready to head home.

"Are you in a hurry?" Brittany asked. "Would you like to come over and talk to my folks now?"

It wasn't what she had expected to hear, but Katie nodded. "If they don't mind me being in work clothes."

They drove back the way Katie and Rick had driven in. On the left was a modest gray ranch with white trim and an attached garage. Brittany pulled up to the edge of the front porch, and Katie followed.

After Brittany introduced her parents to Katie, she motioned Katie to a seat near Mrs. Coombs, but Brittany remained standing.

"Katie owns that small farm stand you like to stop at, Mom," Brittany said in a gentle voice. "You know, the one next to the old schoolhouse that's filled with 'tiques?"

"Yes, of course…I know…the one." Mrs. Coombs' speech was slow, with only a slight slur.

Other than the left hand curled and cupped within the right, it was the first sign of the woman's recent stroke Katie had seen. There was a pause as Brittany stood there, one foot on the other, unsure how to go on. Katie didn't know how to help, but Mr. Coombs, who sat on the sofa, leaned forward. He took his wife's hands, separating one from the other.

"Nora. This young woman went to school with Meredith. They were friends."

His words startled Katie. She and Meredith had not been friends. As the principal and a school counselor, Mr. Coombs would have known that. Yet his words were a lie to his wife. With his and Katie's attention on the older woman, neither noticed when Brittany slipped out of the room.

"Meredith."

Mrs. Coombs breathed out her daughter's name, and Katie saw a decided change in the woman's facial expression. Before, she had been placid, unfocused, and a little dull. Now she looked directly at Katie with eyes filled with sorrow. Her bottom lip trembled slightly. With a sigh, her shoulders straightened.

"Brittany…brought you here…because of Meredith," said Mrs. Coombs.

Katie nodded slightly, then waited for Mrs. Coombs to finish her thought.

"She said you were…good with finding…the slithery little things…that lie under the rocks. The things…that might never see…the light of day."

The surprise on Katie's face at the older woman's choice of words must have shown, because Mr. Coombs let out a loud and very pleased laugh. Giving his wife's hand a hearty shake, he leaned back against the sofa cushions.

"Did you know my wife was at one time a college professor?" he asked. "Or that her specialty was not English prose, but poetry?"

"No, I didn't," Katie admitted.

"Yes, it's true. Lately, her manner of speech has gone back to reflecting that love of words." Mr. Coombs smiled fondly at his wife. "When I first met her, it drew me to her. A small thing, but a habit of speaking that has been gone for many years."

Mrs. Coombs's face pinked up.

If it were me sitting in front of someone new and he said that, I'd be embarrassed to tears, thought Katie. Out loud, she said, "It's so elegant, like rose gardens and gardenias."

"That's…very kind," said Mrs. Coombs. "But you are…here to help us… correct? What can we do?"

Brittany reappeared, offering coffee in cups with saucers, rather than the mugs Katie was used to. She also brought a little plate of Royal Dansk shortbread cookies.

"I'm not a detective," Katie told the group. "Or a cop, lawyer, or judge. I'm just basically nosy. I didn't know Meredith well back then, or really at all over the last ten years. A friend in the sheriff's office asked me to snoop around a little bit. I may not find anything, but it seems to me Meredith was on the move a lot. Somebody should know more than any of us have heard." She sighed. "I don't have a clue as to where to start, or even if I can help ease your pain."

Mrs. Coombs looked at her husband. He gazed out the multi-paned bay window, then slowly nodded.

"Meredith was always a difficult child," he said. "Don't get me wrong, I love both my girls. But Brittany and her brother were of an age and an inclination. Meredith, fourteen years younger, was like a yearling colt turned out on fresh grass for the first time. Always on the run, stopping short, and snorting at the wind."

He took his wife's hand again. "We were older, more set in our ways. Her friends had parents a decade behind us, so we didn't mix. To be honest, I don't think we ever really understood what Meredith was all about. And she never slowed down enough for us to figure it out."

"I…just thought…Meredith would…grow out of it," said Mrs. Coombs. "Be more like…Brittany."

"She remained living here in Parentville even after she got married," Katie said. "Can you tell me who her friends were? What did she do besides go to law school?"

This time, Mr. Coombs's laughter was a short, hard bark that lacked humor. "She didn't remain in Parentville because she wanted to. Avery owned that piece of land just outside of town. It had an old ranch-style house on it that was falling down on itself. They told us they planned to live there, but I offered to have a new house built. I think that offer was the start of the end for them, even though they were barely married."

"What do you mean?" Katie asked.

"Well, we—my wife and I—had talked about the offer of building them the new house early on, but then, sometime during the pre-wedding stages, I heard Brittany and Meredith arguing. It was about all the money and the foolish, expensive things Meredith wanted. Like, her reception had to be held at the clubhouse at the Burlington Country Club. Brittany spouted off about how it was just a show for Avery's friends, a theater act. Some hurtful barbs went back and forth, and just before Meredith stormed off, she said something like, well, she might just skip the whole wedding, anyway." He sighed. "We had already paid a lot of deposits, and we wouldn't get them back if she didn't go through with it."

Katie heard Brittany, who had started to leave the living room but only gotten as far as the hall, catch her breath.

So she didn't know her father heard her and Meredith argue, Katie thought.

"I don't mean to sound petty," Mr. Coombs went on. "But if there was a chance Meredith would bolt, I didn't want to put the new house offer on the table."

"It was the…smart choice," said Mrs. Coombs.

Katie had to agree.

"They were married about three months, and it was coming up on fall, before I said anything," said Mr. Coombs. "They jumped right on it. Packed up everything: bed, bag, and baggage. They moved to a rental house on North Avenue in Burlington. Do you know where that is?"

"Not really. I've heard of North Avenue, but I don't think I've ever been further than Burlington High School. Or maybe Saint Joseph's Orphanage."

"Hmm." Mr. Coombs stared out the window again. "They rented a nice split-level, way out on the far end of the avenue. Meredith was all about how the entire area was populated by other lawyers, big businessmen, people of that sort. They threw cocktail parties, barbecues. All the children went to private Catholic schools. Even though Meredith had been adamant about not having a child right away, she got pregnant immediately. Keeping up with the Joneses, I suspect. By June, when their house was finished and ready to be moved into, she didn't want to move back here. But Avery insisted, maybe because it was all brand new."

Katie could understand the allure of a new house with no problems, but why had Avery been so willing to leave his buddies? Maybe he was already messing around and had been indiscreet with the neighborhood wives?

"For the first couple of months, every time we drove past, there would be several cars in the driveway. Their first boy was born in July, right after that, Avery changed firms. It was a step up, but not with people Meredith knew."

"So, with the move out of the area where all his groupies lived, he wasn't hanging around with them anymore?" Katie asked.

"No. Avery said he would feel like Benedict Arnold swapping war stories with the enemy."

"And Meredith wasn't…vested deep enough with…her new friends…to hold on to them," Mrs. Coombs added.

Katie could guess what happened next.

"Instead of staying home with her son, Meredith traded in her own few years of college for a degree as a paralegal," Mr. Coombs explained. "Then she got pregnant again."

He pulled his hand free of his wife's. His agitation was apparent as he tapped his forefingers together and studied his shoes. Katie watched Mr. Coombs, but couldn't tell if he was upset because his daughter had gone to work and left her son at home, or because she'd had a second child.

"Meredith was so mad. My wife and I believed she would get rid of the baby. But Avery's mother was still alive then. *She* was thrilled. She took Meredith and Shawn, the bigger boy, to Disney for two weeks, bought her a new car, and paid for the nursery."

"Sh… Shawn was too young…for Disney."

Katie noticed Mrs. Coombs sounded more exhausted.

"I hate to take off on you," she said, rising to her feet. "But I have to get back to work. Could we speak again later? Maybe you could make a list of people you know of that Meredith chummed around with over the last few years? And clubs, stuff like that?"

"Of course."

Mr. Coombs had also gotten up. His wife lay back in the corner of the couch, the armrest and back supporting her. She looked as gray as feathery wood ash, her features sunken.

Katie said goodbye and left. Her own brain was on overload. She had always considered Meredith the *Cosmic Edition of Shallow* when she was younger. What she'd heard from the woman's family was a scheming backwash of that same idea, in an adult version.

Katie needed to sort all of this out before she got lost in a whirling rush that would take her down the drain to the sewer. She heard Brittany in the kitchen as she stepped out of the house, but left without a goodbye.

* * *

Back at the farmhouse, Katie inspected the area where Ruth had set the feisty feral babies up in a family-sized crate. After what she had seen over at the Franklin Road barn, she decided to call Amos Surette, Monique's husband and the man who had introduced her to Harwood Architectural Restoration, to let him know about the building and Steffie Firth's plan to rip it down. Katie remembered the owners of Harwood saying they worked to salvage old boards and beams with history. It would be a shame for the whole thing to be demolished and hauled off without giving them a heads up.

"I'll drive over there," he said. "Take a look at it."

Her call finished; Katie turned to Ruth. "You didn't tell me you went with the church ladies to help pack up Meredith's house the other day."

"I guess I assumed you'd know that," Ruth said honestly. "Both Grace and I went. We rode together." She laughed. "Grace said it was hard work, but a nice change from spending the morning in the truck garden."

Katie felt as if she should apologize to Ruth, though she was not sure why. Maybe because she felt as though something underhanded had happened. But in all honesty, she was often the one who did things in an off-the-wall manner. Before she could figure out what to say, Ruth spoke up.

"Darlene Hooper was one of the church ladies Dorothea roped in to help. While we were packing up, she remarked about Meredith's housekeeper, and how come Brittany didn't get her to join us." Ruth laughed again. "Darlene didn't know Brittany was right behind her. So, when Brittany spoke up and said she'd asked the housekeeper, but the woman said no because she'd already started a new job, Darlene about died of embarrassment."

Ruth was still chuckling as she set the table for dinner. Katie paused as she sliced the pork roast. Had Marlie mentioned a housekeeper? She couldn't remember. But if there was one, and Marlie knew the woman's name, Katie wanted to talk to her.

Chapter Thirty

Lately, it seemed to Katie that every meal came in shifts. Somebody was always late. But this afternoon, a few hours passed when they normally ate on a Sunday, all five members of the household were present, washed, and ready.

Katie sliced a second round off the roast. Ruth had asked her where she and Brittany had gone after they left the Franklin Road farm, which brought the conversation back to Meredith's death. Every set of eyes drifted in Marlie's direction. Without hesitation, she helped herself to another slice of pork roast and spoke.

"Things have slowed down on the investigation. Even the state police aren't on the phone all the time. Nothing has turned up. We've talked to most of the people, some a couple of times. Sheriff Lewis is really getting ugly about the guy who called in the scene at Meredith Block's house and then disappeared." Marlie paused with her fork above her plate, ready to dig in. "You should have heard Angus! Lewis said there was no way to figure out who the guy actually was. He lied to us, and no one on-site recognized him. Angus said we should just knock on doors. Can you imagine? We don't even have a photograph to show."

"Well," Ruth said, "he's right that a lot of people moved into the area that we don't know. And let's face it, some of them have yet to show up at any of the local businesses or at church. You should point out to Lewis that women and children can be excluded from the photo shoot."

"Yeah, like that won't get my head bit off." Marlie threw a green bean at Ruth's head, which was lowered as the old woman chuckled.

Charlie helped himself to a second scoop of mashed potatoes. "Seems like every time I get sent out in the dump truck, I have to talk to some different dude on the other end. Like the guy I picked up a few weeks ago. Never saw him before, never saw him again. And he was right here."

"He was right here? Where, Charlie?" Rick asked.

"Right down near the end of the road. He musta just come out of the farm stand because he had some of Grace's goods." Charlie poured gravy, unaware that everyone except Ruth was watching him. "He was afoot. I guess his vehicle must have been broke down. I let him out down at the church."

"And you didn't know this guy?" Marlie asked. "You picked up somebody you didn't know?"

Rick held his hand up to Marlie, stemming her questions. Ruth had been raving lately that goods had been taken and not paid for. If some bum had decided to walk in and help himself, Rick felt they should all be on the lookout.

"What did he look like, Charlie? Do you know his name?"

Charlie chewed and swallowed. "Course I asked his name. It was Wayne, easy to remember. You know, like the Duke. And he looked just like us. Like he worked for a living, not in some office off someplace else."

"Short? Red hair?" Rick persisted.

"No. About the same tall as Katie. He had brown hair. I remember because he didn't have on a hat. I thought that was peculiar, what with the sun lately and all. But you should ask Dorothea. She had him lugging a bunch of dropped off stuff down the stairs, so I'd say she knowed him."

"Doesn't sound like anybody I recognize," Rick said.

"See? I told you," Ruth said. "Too many people from away now."

When supper was finished, Rick volunteered for cleanup and drafted Charlie, who had been about to sneak away to take a nap.

"C'mon, Marlie." Katie grabbed the keys to her truck. "Let's get out of here before he changes his mind."

With a carefree laugh, Marlie followed her out to the truck. "Where are we going?"

"For a ride," Katie said.

As soon as they pulled up to the stop sign, Katie turned to Marlie.

"Did you know that Meredith had a housekeeper? How about a lawn guy?"

"Yes, to both," Marlie said, slowly. "Why?"

"I want to talk to them." There was no reason to beat around the bush, and Katie didn't want to be all day at this. "Do you know who they are?"

"The lawn guy has a company out of Williston. There were two men on the job. They usually showed up at Meredith's house around noon, and hadn't seen anyone on their last trip. One of the guys said they pulled up, saw the cruisers, and went to their next job."

Katie frowned. "The grass was pretty short, except for all the wildflowers. It seems to me they would have had to be there no more than a week before the murder."

Marlie shrugged. "Lewis had the one conversation with them and checked the company off his list."

"Okay, well, they won't be working on a Sunday. What about the housekeeper?"

"Agnes Berstable. Lives just over the line in Williston, on the Saint George Road."

Katie pulled out to the left.

Chapter Thirty-One

In any other part of the country, the Berstable house would have been classified as a bungalow. Here, people called it a camp. Small and square, two rooms and a bath, it was set right on the ground, with a sunken crawlspace. And, Katie was sure, a lot of spiders.

"Stay in the car," she directed Marlie.

But the sheriff's deputy was already closing the door behind her.

The whole front of the dwelling was side-by-side windows. The sills had been painted recently, but not well-scraped first, so the thick coat of whitewash looked rough. When Katie and Marlie were three steps away from the screen door, it opened, and a middle-aged woman stepped out. Behind her, a dog barked out a threat.

"Can I help you?" the woman asked.

"Mrs. Berstable? I'm Katie Took. I'm working with the Parentville Sheriff's Office in regard to a recent homicide. I'd like to ask you a few questions, please?"

Marlie, slightly behind Katie, stopped. That was an out-and-out lie. She was sorry now she hadn't stayed in the truck, as Katie had asked her to.

"Okay," Mrs. Berstable said. "I thought you might come out again. My conversation with the sheriff was pretty short. Let's sit over here in the shade, okay?"

Katie followed the woman to a group of Adirondack chairs near the tidy flower bed that edged the front of the house. Marlie lagged behind again, relieved that so far Mrs. Berstable hadn't seemed to recognize her. The yipping dog bounced against the screen door.

When the women were seated, Katie asked Mrs. Berstable to explain her job at the Block house.

"Basically, I came in daily, Monday through Friday, from eight-thirty until five. I'd clean, do laundry, prepare the evening meal. That could be tricky sometimes," the woman said. "Especially when Mrs. Block went back to work."

"Sounds like you've worked there for a while." Katie had studied Mrs. Berstable while she spoke. The older woman seemed to be suffering remorse, or maybe there were memories from working for Meredith that she would rather forget.

"Mr. Block hired me right after their second son was born. I was there for six years."

"So, after the Blocks' divorce, Mrs. Block kept you on?" Katie felt her back teeth rub together. The yipping-yapping of the dog scraped across her nerves.

Mrs. Berstable's breathing picked up. Her eyes drifted away from Katie. "To be honest, it was Mr. Block who kept me there. He paid me."

"That would mean Mr. Block was your actual employer, right? Did you often have conversations with him?"

"Four or five times a year, I might hear from him. He has a secretary who normally called if he wanted something done or changed. Then, of course, I saw Mrs. Block a couple of times a week."

"But not daily?"

"No. She'd already be gone to work, and maybe not return before I left. There was an au pair, Danielle, who I saw every day. Or Mrs. Block would leave me a note if she wanted something special."

"Even after the boys started school, Danielle was there all the time? What did she do when the boys were at school?"

Mrs. Berstable shrugged. "Danielle took care of all the boys' needs. She picked up after them, did their laundry, made sure they ate, took them to school, all of that. I was there for the house."

"Forty hours a week?"

"Not lately, no. Though I did do the grocery shopping and sometimes ran errands for Mrs. Block." Mrs. Berstable shifted in her seat.

"What did Danielle do all day, besides take care of the boys?" Katie asked.

"I really don't know. The boys went to school in Williston. She'd drive them. There were a lot of days she didn't come back until they did. We were friendly, but not friends." Mrs. Berstable gave a dry laugh. "I didn't ask her what she did, and she didn't ask me about my soap operas."

Katie looked around the yard, framing her next question. Her eyes lit on an ashtray on a small table between the two chairs. There were two different types of cigarette filters. This was a cramped house for two people. Would Mrs. Berstable have a regular guest? Was there a Mr. Berstable?

"Tell me about the boys," she asked.

Mrs. Berstable adjusted her seat again. "I'd rather not, but I'm sure you don't want to hear that." She looked toward the road and licked her lips. "The older one has some behavioral issue that I've never understood. And he's mean." Her face softened. "Alex, the little one just wants someone to love him. To be steady, like family. Mrs. Block only has time for her sons when she's not busy with anything else. And Danielle is too young to be much of a mother figure. I don't have any idea what the boys' lives are like with their father. But Alex is friendly, honest, and unfortunately, easily led by his brother. He's really a sweet child. He used to pick me wildflowers, but his mother didn't want them in the house. After that, he'd pull them out of the ground, roots and all, then plant them in the back lawn for me." She flicked her wrist. Meredith's children were now a closed subject.

Now Katie knew where the oddity of the wilted Indian paintbrushes came from.

"Last bit," Katie said. "Did you like working for Mrs. Block?"

"At first, yes. Then they got divorced, and things were tense. It was as if Mrs. Block was on trial and waiting to be judged and sentenced. I don't know how else to explain it. Maybe two years ago, the dynamics changed again. Mrs. Block's whole attitude took a complete turn. If nothing else, working there got even stranger. I told my husband I wasn't happy. He told me to find another job."

"Did he tell you not to help Brittany when she had to clear out the house?"

Katie asked.

"No. He drives over the road and is gone for long periods of time. He'll be back in a few days. I'd already found a new job before things got cleaned out. When Mrs. Block started to give me whole days off during the week while she...entertained...I seriously started looking around. I'd already given her my notice."

"Entertained?" It was the first time Marlie had spoken up.

Mrs. Berstable looked at Marlie for the first time. The housekeeper's eyes narrowed, but when her mind didn't come up with where she'd seen Marlie before, she moved on.

Just then, the screen door banged shut with a sharp snap. Both Katie and Marlie swung around. A curly black cocker spaniel ran towards them, long ears flapping and pink tongue sticking out. The dog ran right to Mrs. Berstable and leapt into her lap.

Katie didn't stop to think before she spoke. "That's Meredith's dog."

"It was." Mrs. Berstable wrapped her arms around the wiggling young dog, who was so happy to be out where the people were.

The older woman's defensive tone wasn't missed by Marlie.

"It's a nice dog." The deputy smiled. "Do you take care of him right now?"

Mrs. Berstable sighed. Eyes on the dog, hand caressing his shiny head, she spoke around a lump in her throat.

"Mrs. Block was given Curly when he was just a baby. She kept him for several months, but she didn't like him. The boys were all excited, but eventually they were done with him as well. One day, while I washed woodwork in the hall, I heard Mrs. Block tell Danielle to get rid of him. To take him over to the vet's and have him put down. Danielle argued they could find a home for him, but Mrs. Block wanted him gone that day. After she left, I told Danielle that I would take Curly with me. She helped me pack all of his stuff. I left Mrs. Block a note to tell her I didn't feel good and left early so she wouldn't come home and find out I had taken him. She wasn't good at sharing, even if it was something she didn't want."

"Why would she do that, just destroy the dog?" Katie asked.

"Curly was gifted to her by this man she was seeing." Mrs. Berstable's face went hard. "She had no right to go with him. When he dumped her, or she finished with him, the dog was just a reminder she didn't want. I knew she'd been dating someone. Danielle told me Mrs. Block would come home, change, and be gone until the early morning hours. *Lots* of nights. At that time, Mrs. Block still worked in the city. Then suddenly she was done. To be honest, the way she ranted the day she came home with a cardboard box of her stuff from the law office, I think she got fired."

Katie cut in. "Did you tell Sheriff Lewis all of this?"

"No. I didn't work it out in my mind until after that. At my new job, I'm more like a house sitter, so my employer's dogs won't be alone. I have lots of time to just think. And what I believe is that, among everything else, Mrs. Block was carrying on with at least one married man. At her home, during the day."

"At least one?"

Mrs. Berstable looked Katie straight in the eyes. "People—men—are all dirty in different ways. When you clean a bathroom or a bedroom, you can tell who was there. Especially if they sometimes forget to take all their underclothing."

* * *

"Well, that was interesting," Marlie said as she and Katie drove away.

"And you feel the need to share with Lewis?" Katie asked.

"Yes." Marlie sighed. "I just don't know how to tell him that you and I were sneaking around behind his back."

"You'll figure it out," Katie said, but she hoped Marlie would wait a while before she did.

"I know the next thing you want to know is about the outside workers," Marlie said. "The lawn guys are from Clearcut Landscaping. They won't be working today, and they go from place to place all day long. Sheriff Lewis talked to them on the telephone."

Katie's next day off was Tuesday. She mentally added a visit to her list of errands.

Chapter Thirty-Two

As usual, on her day off, Katie took care of the cat room chores and did some of the other cleaning around the farmhouse. With all the work they had this summer to keep up with the two extra gardens, Grace's second truck garden, and their own patch, housework had taken a slider. She ran the vacuum, took the cat beds outside for a good shake, and considered dusting. But before she started on that, she got the telephone number for Clearcut Landscaping and called their office.

Right beside the back door was one of her canvas totes. Inside was the paper-bag-wrapped Lane Chest. She could see it from where she stood, even though it was out of reach. A silent whisper called, demanding to know when she planned to deal with it. She didn't have an answer.

After once again identifying herself as working with the sheriff's department, Katie told the receptionist they wanted to verify the last time the property at the Block house had been mowed, and where those workers were today.

"We want to speak with them face to face. It can be as informal as a walk out and hello, or we can do this in a courtroom." Katie didn't know how a subpoena would work, but it sounded good.

"There's nobody here for me to ask," said the young woman on the other end of the telephone. "Everybody is out right now."

"That's okay. I have Judge Albee's telephone number right here," Katie said cheerfully.

The woman groaned. "Okay. I'm not sure exactly where the men will be at any particular time, but I can give you the addresses they're supposed to service today."

"Go ahead." Katie grabbed a pencil. "I'm ready."

Just before she left the house, a call came in from Doctor Veronica Nguyen's office, Valley Wide Veterinary. Some of the cats Katie had dropped off days earlier were ready to be transported to the SPCA facility in South Burlington. It was the opposite direction from where she was headed, but she told Lois that she would be out in a short while to pick them up.

The first place she drove past on the Monkton Road had been mowed, and the driveway looked recently raked. At the second place, one mower was already off the trailer, and being gassed up.

"Guys," Katie said as she stepped out of the truck. "I'm Kaitlyn Took, advisor with the Chittenden Valley Sheriff's Department. I've been sent out to get clarification on what happened at Meredith Block's house on the day you arrived, and the sheriff was there." She flashed her driver's license, then quickly pocketed it.

The thin guy with the gas tank looked over at her old pickup truck.

"Seriously?" he asked with a smirk.

Katie thought he might realize she was lying. Her face went hard, and she gave him a once-over. "Here or down at the sheriff's office," she said.

"Shut up, Gary." The other guy stepped forward. "I'm Les. We told our boss what happened. What else do you need?"

"How often were you scheduled to mow over at the Block house?" Katie asked.

Les shrugged. "We were supposed to work as needed. She only wanted us there on certain days. Like, once a week. But the lawns everywhere were growing fast, so we had to double our usual schedule. She didn't like that. We came up to the road, and all these cop cars blocked the area around the Blocks. Honestly, we had no idea what was going on, so we moved on down the list."

"You hadn't been there at all in the six days prior?" Katie asked.

"Nope."

"Did you see anything suspicious the last time you were there?" she asked.

"You mean, other than the naked broad sunning on the deck?" Gary asked with a leer.

"Shut up!" Les said. He turned back to Katie. "She wasn't naked. Just topless. And from the way she staggered around, she'd already had a few cocktails."

"What time was that?" Katie asked.

"I don't know. About eleven."

"In the morning? That's either pretty late or way too early." Katie felt her eyelids reel up and away, like a window blind snapped and released. A sudden and new view had been added to Meredith's life. Had Meredith still been under the influence from the night before, or had Mrs. Berstable's remark about a change in Meredith's behavior been because she knew her boss was a drunk?

"Yeah. Sorry. It happens." The guy's face reddened. Was he embarrassed at what he and his co-worker had just shared with her? Had her reaction been the reason Sheriff Lewis hadn't been given this information?

"Was Mrs. Block normally already gone to work when you got there?" Katie asked.

Les shrugged. "I kind of thought she had taken the summer off. You know, because of the kids. Or at least she wasn't working that day. Sometimes the other woman's car was there when we showed up. But not then."

"The other woman? The housekeeper or the au pair?"

Both guys shook their heads. They didn't know one from the other.

Katie thought about what she'd seen in the yard. The back lawn had been just at the point where it needed to be cut, but the front lawn was unkept.

"So, when you came the last time, you only mowed the backyard? Why not the front? It looked like it hadn't been cut in a couple of weeks."

"Bees," Gary said. "Well, actually, wasps. It was me on the mower a couple of weeks before, and they were all over me. Let me tell you, they are nasty."

"Yeah," Les said. "I left her a note saying we couldn't mow the front until the nest was found and they were eliminated."

"You left a note? So that day Mrs. Block wasn't home?"

"No," Les said. "We have a form we have to fill out." He reached into the truck and opened the glove compartment. "It looks like this. I filled it out and gave the top copy to the guy who was in the house. He said he'd give it to the owner when she got back."

Katie took a copy of the form, as well as the description of the guy. She turned to walk away, mulling over what she had written down about the man the two lawn guys had described. The description didn't match the one for the man Marlie and Lewis were looking for, the guy who supposedly had been out looking for his dog, found Meredith, and called the sheriff's office.

"Sheriff?" Les called out. When Katie didn't respond, he yelled louder. "Ma'am?"

Katie realized both calls were for her. She half-turned. "Sorry. I guess I was thinking. What can I do for you?"

"What's your name again? I mean, if we think of anything else, we can just call you at the sheriff's office." Les sounded sincere.

Katie's stomach dropped. "Yeah. That's fine. Ask for Marlie, I'm, ah, on the road a lot."

She drove away with sweat running down her back. She'd need to find somebody else to impersonate. Maybe Corinne?

Chapter Thirty-Three

Driving through the village, Katie passed Jill's Hair Salon and Barbershop. Sheriff Lewis's cruiser was parked out front. On the other side of the elementary school, and the opposite side of the street, was the retired high school, town office, and sheriff's department.

Katie pulled into the town office parking lot, made a loop, and drove back the way she'd come to Jill's salon. She had things to say to Sheriff Lewis, but meeting on his turf gave him an edge. Just the thought of it made her wince. Normally, she would avoid the man, even to the point where she would look in a different direction if she met him on the road.

There wasn't a front border on the wide sweep of gravel in front of the parking area at Jill's. The wooden frame house on Katie's approach side held three apartments, with Dorothea and Ellen's in the back on the ground floor, and she hoped the octogenarian was at the thrift shop, not home.

"All I need," Katie muttered to herself, "is that old busybody stepping out and asking what I'm up to. Her first call will be to Ruth, for cripe's sake."

She pulled in to park on the sweep so her vehicle would be in plain sight of anybody that drove past. It was safer that way, to be where the public could see her. Jill's customers, however, would have to step outside and around the building's corner to know Katie was there.

Less chance he can duck and run, she thought, though in truth it was more likely she'd run from the sheriff, then he'd hide from her.

Jill's was one of two salons in Parentville, with the other on the Mechanicsville Road at the far side of town. Exiting the truck, Katie leaned casually against the rear fender. Lewis's haircut wouldn't last longer than fifteen or twenty minutes. She could wait.

Lewis exited the small, single-story garage converted to a salon, vigorously dusting stray clippings off his shoulders. With the loss of the outer layer of his thick mat of hair, Lewis's hat was lower than usual on his ears. He was off the stoop and almost to his Crown Vic before he noticed Katie.

"Good morning," Katie said with a smile.

She wanted to sound friendly, not smug or snide, but the look on the sheriff's face told her he hadn't read her greeting that way. She gave up the effort and took a step forward.

"Martin."

He scowled.

"Sheriff Lewis." It was a small concession to give him his due, but she felt the teeth in the back of her mouth grate against the inside of her cheek. "If you have a moment, I'd like a word."

"Is it town business?" he asked. "I've got an office."

Katie ignored his curt tone and the inference that she needed to be inside those four walls to address him.

"If you mean about the dog catching thing, no. Though I will tell you, I've already been out on my first poop inspection."

He blinked. She tried not to smile.

"This is actually about Meredith Block's boyfriends," Katie said.

"Boyfriends?" Lewis drew out the "s." His left eyebrow quirked up, but just as quickly returned to a scowl.

"Yeah. it seems, or so I've heard, that Meredith got around."

Lewis had kept walking until he stood with his hand on the door handle of the cruiser. At Katie's words, he half-turned. Katie's original intent had been to dump what she knew on him, and make it his responsibility. But his stance, cold shoulder in her face, gave her pause. Her brief hesitation seemed to spark Lewis's interest.

"What do you know, Katie?" he asked.

The question, or command, loosened Katie's tongue.

"Rumor has it she had a couple of beaus," Katie said.

"Two?"

Lewis's snide smile told Katie that he was aware Meredith had been entertaining, but she wondered if he knew to what extent, or who.

"Six. At least at last count. She didn't seem ready to settle down. Maybe it was time for her to sow her wild oats."

Lewis removed his hand from the door handle. She saw the flare of his nostril and the question in the back of his eyes. He didn't like it when she had her nose in his business.

She kept talking. "No one seems to know a lot more than that. It wasn't like she brought them home to meet her folks. Maybe because she liked the married ones. Lawyers, firemen, and a couple of business wheelers and dealers." She shrugged. "That's all I've got. I mean, it's gossip. Maybe you already know."

"This is a small town, Katie. There are always eyes and ears around." Lewis opened the door to his vehicle. Obviously, their conversation was over.

She drove away, mentally giving herself a solid kick in the pants. She could have given it all up, the Lane chest and her guesses. Or kept her mouth shut. Instead, she'd dropped a spark next to a dried brush. And the road ahead was littered with blue Kleenex bundles.

Without stopping at home, Katie drove to Charlotte and Valley Wide Veterinary. Fortunately, Lois, who had the inside scoop on everything that happened with the cats picked up at the Franklin Road farm, was available.

"If you've kept a tally," she said to Katie, "you're probably aware we've almost reached the thirty-cat limit."

"Ruth told me," Katie answered. "There aren't so many half-grown cats or old ones lately, either. Maybe I've already caught most of them. But the healthy ones and maybe more litters are still out there. Have you noticed there are a lot of toms?"

Lois smiled. "That's because the males are basically lazy. Instead of hunting, they'll wait for a female to catch something, and then take it away from her. Opportunity feeders. Food left around fits their needs perfectly."

Katie nodded. "What am I supposed to do with the ones that are still in the barn after I reach the limit? What about the tiny kittens we've held back until they're big enough to spay or neuter?"

"Are we talking more than, like, ten?"

"The estimate is probably another thirty," said Katie.

"Ouch. I'll need to talk to Doctor Ronnie. She'll have to make some calls."

"Leave a message out at the house," Katie said. "The tear-down is scheduled in a couple of weeks. If they're still there, a lot of them will get hurt."

"Double ouch. I'm sure the doctor will make some calls, get an extension or something. Though I don't know what," Lois said.

Katie left comfortable in the knowledge that if anybody could put Stephie Firth in a position where she would have to ante up for a few more cats, it was Veronica Nguyen. The veterinarian was a petite transplant from India with a big heart for four-legged animals, and a short fuse for those with only two. She was also soft-spoken, like her Indian mother, but tenacious in the manner of her father's Vietnamese family.

Lois called ahead, alerting the receptionist at the SPCA compound that Katie was on route. By the time Katie got the last individual cat carrier unloaded, the occupant from the first had been confirmed and relocated into a more permanent domicile in a community cat room. Once she had all of her cat carriers reloaded, she was ready to go. At the end of the driveway, Katie had two choices. She could turn right on Dorset Street toward the interstate on-ramp. Or she could turn left and, after a short drive, be in Avery Block's new neighborhood.

Instead of the straight-run layout of streets in the city, Avery's neighborhood was made up of softly curved roads with small, branching cul-de-sacs. Lawns were well-manicured. There were granite curbs, a central mail hut, and several houses that had above-ground pools.

Not too shabby, Katie thought.

When she got to 42 Greenbough Lane, she slowed down and cruised past, eyes on the house. She almost missed seeing the woman who knelt in the flower garden. Across the street stood a house in the last stages of completion. Katie backed into the driveway, took a small spiral notebook out of the glove compartment, and walked over.

"Excuse me," she said. "I'm lost. Can you help me?"

The woman stood up. Medium height, blond, pretty, dressed in a sleeveless cotton blouse and Bermuda shorts. She had a softly rounded, fuller figure that would one day make a great grandma. As she stepped over the bags of mulch, the woman pulled off her gloves and smiled.

"Who are you looking for?" she asked.

"The name is Ida Javis," said Katie. "The address is 45 Greenbough Lane. But that house isn't finished yet."

"Hm." The woman looked up and down the street. "We've lived here for five years. I don't recognize that name, sorry. Maybe it's the new owners. I don't know who they are."

She and Katie studied the unfinished building. Katie took a chance on eyestrain as she peered at the blond woman, with her smoothly coffered French twist, out of the corner of her eye. The woman rubbed the fingers of her left hand over the angry red marks on her right. There were similar marks below her knees. With the number of rose bushes that lined the property, it would be easy for any amateur gardener who didn't wear long pants and sleeves to lose a fight with that many thorns.

"Well, thanks for the help, Mrs...ah?" Katie paused.

"Block." The woman smiled. "Allison Block."

Katie smiled as well, pleased to have so easily found Avery's second wife. "Thanks, again, Mrs. Block."

Katie crossed back to her truck. Mrs. Block had already returned to the flower bed. Katie's momentary exchange with Avery's second wife led her to believe that this woman was as different from Meredith as peas were from squash. She'd been all set to think the worst about Avery Block, who had dumped his wife for another woman. But after hearing so many negative things about Meredith, and then actually meeting this little dumpling of a woman, she had to wonder if he hadn't traded up.

Chapter Thirty-Four

From behind the kitchen table, Katie could look straight through the kitchen doorway to the front yard when the solid wood door was left open. That's the way it was this afternoon. She heard a car come up the rise on Fire Lane 61 and lifted her head from Irma's old sewing machine—just in time to see the old sheriff's cruiser slow as it turned into the drive.

"That's odd," she said to no one in particular.

That was the vehicle used by the deputies. Lewis saved the new Crown Vic for himself. But at the end of her day, Marlie drove her own car. Equally old, but still hers. Katie rose and went to the window, where she could see the vehicle and driver. It was Marlie.

Katie waited, sure that Marlie could see her, yet she stayed seated like a stiff cardboard cutout.

Concerned, Katie stepped out the kitchen door. That was when Marlie moved, eyes still on her girlfriend. When she stepped out of the cruiser, she planted her hat on her thick hair. Then, with the sheriff department's shield pinned on her chest between them, she held up her hand to stop Katie's advance.

"Stay right there, Katie," Marlie said.

Stunned at her friend's sharp tone, Katie did just that. Her toes inched ahead on their own accord, but basically, she didn't move forward.

"What's the matter?"

Her voice was choked as she imagined the worst that could have happened to her love. But her inner thoughts were nothing compared to what Marlie had to say.

"You told me, and I believed you like it was a promise, that you would take that box to Sheriff Lewis and give it to him." Marlie's words were brittle and seared with pain. "I believed you. I trusted you. Then, not twenty minutes ago, he told me you stopped him on the street and gave him some news by way of gossip. He asked if I'd heard it, and if it was me who gossiped about police matters."

"Wait, Marlie." Katie gave a little half smile. "I did go to see Lewis, but he was such a…"

"QUIET!" Marlie shouted. Then she swallowed hard, fighting for control. "I don't need your excuses. What I needed was to be able to trust you."

She paused. Katie's throat dried and seized. Words wouldn't come.

"He'll come for you, Katie. I didn't tell him, but he's not stupid. I heard him speak with Corporal Derrick. Sheriff Lewis is sure you know more than you've said. He's coming for you."

Marlie got in the car and backed out of the driveway. Behind Katie, the kitchen door opened.

"What was that all about?" Rick asked.

Katie shook her head, unable to speak. She was angry, confused, and scared all at the same time. On top of all that, she knew it was because she was in the wrong. But her fear was not so much that Lewis would show up on her doorstep as what she had done to her relationship with Marlie. Turning, she stepped around Rick, who stared down the road where dust still floated, and rushed through the kitchen to the pantry.

Between the antiquated freezer and the dusty window was the broken kitchen chair Katie sat in to watch out over the duck pond meadow. This time she didn't balance her butt on the split seat, but pulled out the paper bag she had tucked back against the wall. Then, pausing only to grab her keys, she jumped in her car and followed the fading cloud down the main road.

What have you done, girl? Rick wondered as he watched her speed away. He considered if he should follow. He would have done so in the past. But today it didn't feel right.

Once out of her car in the sheriff's parking lot, Katie hesitated. She had the bag tucked under her arm, but fear held her. Marlie's car was in the lot, which meant she was in the office. Katie didn't know if she could face her. There was another way in, through the town office, where Janice was a safe harbor. Katie swiveled, foot raised to take a step in that direction, but her grandfather spoke from the back side of her mind.

Step up. It takes a strong person to admit when they're wrong. We're strong people, Katie-girl. We always have been.

She felt the wet on her lashes brush the top of her cheek, but she headed straight toward the door beneath the *SHERIFF OFFICE* sign. Inside, Angus was seated at the reception desk. Across the room, Marlie was seated at another desk. Katie couldn't look at her friend, so she forced herself to walk toward the closed door of Lewis's office. Angus's butt half rose from his seat.

"Hold on," he said, attempting to stop Katie's advance.

She waved him aside and rapped her knuckles hard, twice, against the wood. Lewis jerked the six-panel door open.

She pushed past him. "I have something I need to show you."

Though she wanted to add if he wasn't going to be an ass, she held her tongue. He closed the door behind her, and she hesitated, of two minds about letting him shut it with just the two of them on this side. If it were open, Marlie could hear what she had to say. But with it closed, Marlie wouldn't witness Katie's humiliation.

Katie dropped the bag on the desk and pulled Ruth's yellow Playtex rubber gloves from her back pocket. Then she ripped the bag open.

Lewis started to speak, but she cut him off, unwilling to allow him to distract her.

"This is what I started to tell you about earlier," she said. "Just listen for a few minutes." Silently, she told him she wasn't the enemy, but once again, the words stayed tucked away. "Look at these bundles. See how they're wrapped? Like Christmas presents, or special secrets. This box came from Meredith Block's house."

Lewis opened his mouth again. But Katie laid her gloved hands on the box.

"For just a minute, listen. You need to have this. You're the sheriff, and I'm sure this is important. Brittany Coombs is Meredith Block's sister. This was among some things Brittany took from the house and donated to the thrift store. Ellen thought it was a personal item and gave it to me to return. When I asked, Brittany said it was junk. She didn't want it. I started to empty the box, but when I saw what it was, I put it all back. I tried to tell you this morning. Unfortunately, as usual, you and I started sparking, and I shut up. I've spent most of the day worried about this stuff. Now it's yours. You figure out what to do with it."

She opened the bundles. Just as Katie had, Lewis put on gloves. His brow furrowed as he examined the business cards and the personal items. Katie broke in on his thoughts.

"Meredith was messing around with all these guys. As near as I can tell, they're all married. She stole these bits from them, probably right out of their wallets. Either they were keepsakes for her, or she planned to blackmail them. I don't know."

He looked up. She didn't see hate or speculation, the type that might hint he believed she was right.

"Who did you tell about this?"

"You," she said. "Just now." She jumped past the fact she and Marlie had discussed this. "The family doesn't want it. That makes it public property. Now it's yours."

Katie removed the gloves and turned the doorknob. As she walked out, Lewis called, "Thank you, Katie."

She gave a nod so Lewis would know she'd heard, but continued toward the door and the sunshine from the window beyond. Her face flamed to the point her eyes watered. Without acknowledging Angus or Marlie, she left and made it to her car, all of five buildings away. At Arthur Fortin's house, Katie pulled into the yard, drove around the barn, and parked in front of the lower-level doors. Then she sobbed like her chest would split.

It didn't matter that she had done the right thing in the end. Along the way, she had destroyed her relationship with Marlie. It would never be the same, and it was her fault.

Chapter Thirty-Five

The heat wave continued, but today there was static in the air that raised the short hairs on the back of Katie's neck and sent shivers down her spine. She had worked all day with the pain of the evening before, still thick in her throat, causing her fingers to tremble. When Marlie had returned, it had been late. She'd come in, gone right in to take a bath, and then straight up to her room. Rick had asked if she was okay, and been told she needed to sleep. In the very early hours before any, including Katie, had risen, Marlie had left.

Earlier, Stan had asked Katie if she was feeling alright, or if she suffered from the heat.

Rick hurried in the back door and around the corner into Stan's office. A few moments later, he came back out with Stan right behind him.

"I'm out of here, Katie," Rick said. "This storm coming in is a bad one. Ruth just got hold of me and said the whole Dean family is out in the hayfields. They cut and baled the last three today, and have only got one picked up so far. They're never going to make it. If they don't save the hay, they won't pay the rent of the field for it."

Katie's heart sped up. She knew all about haying, and the tricks the weather could play. So much work, so much product, could be lost in a short time. Rick's words were clear. The loss of the hay would seriously hurt Katie's bottom line.

"Go ahead, Katie," Stan said. "Business is already slow. People are buttoning up."

She pulled her drawer, clocked out, and followed Rick through the village and on up Fire Lane 61. Once home, they hurried out to where two tractors pulled hayricks from either end of the second hayfield. Katie, Grace, and Ruth rolled eighty-five-pound bales into straight rows to make the pick-up faster and more efficient. Davey and Billy, Raymond Dean's young sons, drove the lumbering tractors with the help of wood blocks tied to the pedals. While Raymond Dean and Phil Carwell tossed bales up onto the ricks, Steve Dean and Rick stacked the load crisscrossed to hold the bales in place until there was no way to get the piles taller.

When a load was ready, one of the men took the tractor controls and maneuvered the awkward load over the rutted field and dirt road toward the barn. The rest of that team hung onto the side of the rick or tucked into narrow spaces between the bales for the ride. Once the rick was barnside of the loft conveyor was fired up, and one man dropped a bale into each slotted space. The other members worked in the loft, sliding the bales aside to where they were stacked higher and higher. That was cattle feed needed for the next winter season. To Katie, the stacks were created like the building of the pyramids, each block of hay in the right place to support its brothers as the pile grew thirty feet upward.

They were into the third field now. Charlie had joined the teams shortly before Raymond and Steve had to leave for the evening's milking. One hundred and forty-seven head of Holsteins needed their keepers' attention. It was dark, not due to the time of day, but because thick, black clouds rolled in so fast their shadows raced in front of the tractors. Even Marlie, when she pulled in after her shift, realized the need and hurried up to the hayfield to help.

A fat plop of wet hit Katie in the center of her forehead.

"We have to stop now!" Philip yelled over the wind. "If we don't get this load undercover, it's for naught."

"Phil!" Rick ran to where Philip climbed over the driver's seat. "There's no time to unload. Pull down to our barn. I'll cut across lots and get the big doors open. You can back the rick in there." With that, the elderly man took off at a run across the field.

The tractor rocked across the uneven ground. Ruth and Billy stood on the narrow deck that extended from underneath the driver's seat, holding on tight to the curved metal seat. Only a few dozen bales still lay around the field.

"Help me!" Katie yelled to Marlie over the wind. "If we get these stacked, the ones underneath will have a little protection. Bales are hard to dry out. These will have to be fed to the stock soon, before they spoil."

Together, the women made two big heaps. As they worked, the usual easy feeling between them that had disappeared slid back into place. Katie tried to apologize, but the wind tore the words away. Marlie stopped her, a finger against Katie's lips.

"This time, and this time only, you get a free pass," Marlie said. "You should have seen how excited Sheriff Lewis was to drag all those guys of Meredith's into the office."

The rain fell heavily by the time they finished. They had done all that was possible. Rainwater dripped from Katie's chin and hung like tiny bubbles in Marlie's thick hair.

"Marlie," Katie began.

The need was there again to explain and to beg forgiveness. Her fingers reached out, but she didn't dare touch. But Marlie also reached out. One fingertip lay against Katie's lips.

"Shush," she said. "Just shush, okay?"

Holding hands, they ran down Lovers' Lane, slipping in the clay mud, soaked to the skin, and squealing as lightning bolts lit the sky. It was exciting, scary, fun, and somehow intimate.

Supper was late, with PB&J, bologna, and cheese sandwiches, and hot mugs of tea. Rinsed and toweled off, dressed in PJs, and wrapped in blankets against a damp chill. Everyone laughed and talked.

Marlie told them about the doings that afternoon at the Sheriff's office, but refused to say anything about the interviews.

"A couple of the guys hadn't lived here longer than six months, and seemed to be irrelevant. There was one man named Anderson who was wicked nervous. The fireman is a lieutenant in Charlotte. He pulled into the driveway in this enormous red pickup truck. I know you've seen it around town, Katie. He hangs out with the local fire guys. And what an attitude. 'I'm a big shot. Look at me! How dare you…?' Angus about wet himself."

"So, you got nowhere with him?" Katie asked.

"No, he cooperated as soon as he figured out the only one intimidated was Angus, and he was irrelevant." Marlie reached for one last cookie. "There was one no-show, Gage Fernald. It seems he stayed in town because of a case he's the second chair on."

"Phfft!" Katie spat.

All five members of the household felt exhausted but exhilarated. The work had been hard, but the satisfaction of helping the Dean family carried the Took household on a giddy high until bed called.

Out in the barn, Wayne had left Jacob and Irene Hunt's house, sure they would return as soon as they heard of Meredith's death. He had returned to the only other haven he knew. Now, he ignored the noise of the full hay rick as it was pushed over the concrete floor.

Wayne was suffering. When the storm came up, his hiding spot on the collapsing side of the haymow had become a place of terror. Wind whipped through loose timbers. Boards slapped against each other. Lightning flashes darted in from unexpected directions.

He scuttled across the length of the mow to huddle against the far wall, wrapped tightly in his blanket, face pressed into the backpack. Each time the lightning flashed and thunder roared quick on its heels, the man cried out. He hated storms. *Hated* them. From the time he was a child, he had experienced uncontrollable fear.

Light flashes and rain continued to sweep in through the open mow doors on either side. He knew he could close them. But fear held him in a tight bundle. Wayne couldn't summon the strength to force himself to move away from his spot, even if it meant closing his demon outside.

Chapter Thirty-Six

At eight-thirty the next morning, right after Ruth had walked out the door and headed toward the cheese room, the telephone rang. "Seriously?" Katie asked the cats. "I take a day off and I get an animal call?"

But the caller wasn't an irate homeowner. Walter LaSalle, the property inspector for the bank, wanted to come by and look everything over, and he wanted to do it when Katie was there.

She explained that Tuesdays and Sundays were her days off, but that she had taken an extra day this week. After a short silence, he asked her if she would be available that afternoon if he could change up a different appointment. She agreed, and when the call ended, headed back into the cat room.

"Come on, you guys, cooperate. If this bank dude comes this afternoon, we need to get all these cat boxes freshened."

She let all the kittens lose, but kept most of the indoor cats penned. With extra snacks in their bowls, they were good. Old Tom and the other indoor-outdoor cats had been turned out first thing. Mr. LaSalle called back to say he would be there by twelve-thirty.

That only left Marlie, who was taking a nap upstairs, as a possible issue. With the addition of a new deputy to help out during the investigation, Sheriff Lewis had instigated nighttime patrols. It was an issue he had advocated for a while, but with Angus only in a clerical position, he and Marlie hadn't been able to cover day and night shifts on a regular basis. During the upcoming nighttime hours, Marlie would go on duty at ten and return at eight the next morning.

The last thing Katie wanted was to have Marlie come down while the inspector was there. She was sure her friend would have points to offer, and Katie was still on the fence about what she actually wanted for an outcome.

Mr. LaSalle pulled in promptly at twelve-thirty. Even though he told Katie to relax, her nerves fluttered. They went over the basics of her request. Then for the next hour, Katie walked him over the property, through the house, quietly avoiding Marlie's room. And then down to the farm stand, and into the barn, where she explained the repairs that were needed while he surveyed the damaged end.

"My position as the animal control officer has developed a need to house dogs for the short term. You know, either lost dogs or some who might be in violation of town ordinances. We plan to have a section of concrete poured out past the end of where the barn is. Then we'll put in chain-link outdoor pens and inside runs for up to four animals. It would be cheaper to have all the concrete poured at one time. There's already water pumped in, but we'll need heat, lighting, that kind of stuff. Eventually, we'd like to put in a floor separation in the mow, so we'll have two floors we can rent out."

"Who do you think you will find for renters?" Mr. LaSalle asked.

"There are, ah, a lot of artists and small, sort of cottage industries who are trying to get started. You know, small businesses without room who are looking for space," she said. "I recently had a conversation with a man who has eight employees. I have another meeting with him in two weeks. Light manufacturing."

Cindy had scripted what Katie should say, given her the bare bones.

"Make him understand you have a vision, Katie," Cindy had said. "You know, a grow plan."

She was sure she'd missed a lot of what she was supposed to say. When she felt like she was floundering, she offered to let Mr. LaSalle climb the ladder up into the mow. Lying on the floor overhead, Wayne knew his only escape would be to jump out of the mow window on the back, right into a big patch of burdock. But Mr. LaSalle said he was good and asked to see the final functionality report for the new well.

"What you propose is pretty ambitious," Mr. LaSalle said. "What if you don't get voted into the job again?"

"Then the next person will have to come up with this same type of facility." Katie smiled. "At least I have a head start."

Cindy had tutored her closely on what to say only days before.

Katie and Mr. LaSalle talked about the Mosher property she had inherited through her grandmother. The small tract was on the other side of the ridge and included the sand pit, rental property, and plans for a Christmas tree orchard. Mr. LaSalle said he wanted to drive over there to check it out.

"Would you like me to follow you over?" Katie asked.

"No, I'm good, but is there a road across the farm that's more direct?"

"There is, but it's up the lane. I don't think your sedan would handle the rocks or the creek well."

Mr. LaSalle laughed. "That's honest. So, you have a contract for a group that's ledge climbing on the ridge, right? How do they get there?"

"They come up the other side. The road needs a lot of work. It hasn't been a priority."

They shook hands, and the inspector left. Katie went back inside, thinking she'd said a lot more than she'd planned to and missed some of what she wanted to. She rubbed her sweaty palms on her jeans. Marlie was awake and had just placed the percolator on the stove.

"What's going on with all that?" Marlie asked.

"Remember when I said it would be a secret about what we planned to do up here? Well, not everyone got the memo. Mr. LaSalle had already heard gossip," Katie answered.

"Maybe it's something Stan said," Marlie replied.

Katie whipped around. Her eyes were hard. "Why would Stan say anything?" she demanded.

When Marlie spoke, her voice was low and soothing. "Stan could have said something to the banker. It might have been his hope to help you, Katie. I don't know how banks work, but it seems to me if the first guy got information that he thought the next person should have, he'd put it in his notes."

"Stan." Katie exhaled, sure that Marlie was right.

In the loft, Wayne had moved from bay window to bay window as he tracked Katie and Mr. LaSalle's progress. The last thing he wanted was for them to climb the ladder and discover his hidden place. The empty Tupperware container left from pilfered food lay on its side amid the other rubbish he had brought with him. He had eaten cold mashed potatoes and chicken croquettes, but like Rick, he had sniffed out the scent of the lasagna. He'd barely fought off the impulse to cut into the pan, which had been left to cool on the sideboard. But he'd taken a lot from Katie's kitchen over the past weeks. Soon, they would notice.

He crawled backward to the nest of hay and blanket and tried to sleep. But his thoughts returned over and over to a wish for a big, saucy slice of four-inch-tall lasagna, hot and filled with meat and cheese. His attempt to ignore the desire was futile.

Chapter Thirty-Seven

After Mr. LaSalle left and Marlie had gone on personal errands, Katie paced around the house for a while. She hadn't wanted to say anything to Marlie, and didn't dare open a conversation about the bank with any of her other friends. Confusion took her breath away and made her feel slightly nauseous.

"I know," she told the cats. "With all my heart, I want to save this place just the way Poppa and Gram left it. I know I do. But for crying out loud, that's a lot of money. In my entire life, I'll never see that much."

What she had accomplished in the short past was lost to her because of her fear of the future.

Katie grabbed a rag and the can of Pledge, but before she even got the furniture polish open, her intent to dust dissolved. The cats gave up following her, as did the dogs, yet she continued to pace from the living room through the kitchen to the cattery and back again. Each time she passed, all eyes followed her movements.

"This doesn't really mean anything. You fill out an application. They're required to come out and see what you really have to offer," Katie said. "Heck, the government probably pays them to report all the stuff you have that you don't pay taxes on."

She threw herself down on the sofa, which sent the cats asleep on the back, scooting for a safer perch.

"But it would be nice, you know? To be able to keep Poppa's barn right where it is for another hundred years. I mean, eventually it'll be somebody else's problem. I just hate to be the one to throw it down the tubes."

"Then what are you going to do about it?" a voice asked from beyond the screened kitchen door.

Katie jumped to her feet. Cindy stood on the porch, her young daughter in her arms.

"Ruth told us we could come over and play with the new kittens today," Cindy said. "Is she home yet? Or should we come back later?"

"No, she's not here, but come in."

Katie ran to push the door open. Cindy came in, and the cats went out. Solomon reached up a wet nose to touch Hope's leg, and the baby squealed.

Before Cindy had a chance to say so much as boo, Katie started to tell her about the investigator's visit.

"I wanted to tell you after he called," Katie said, "and maybe ask you to be here when he came out. Does that sound stupid? You know, like nuts?"

"Absolutely not." Cindy smiled. "You should have seen Stan when we had to sit down with the people from the bank about the loan for the feed store. He was a nervous wreck. They didn't come out to the store. Not that we know of, anyway. We were there for a couple of hours while they went over every piece of paperwork you could imagine. Stan will be so excited to hear that Mr. LaSalle has already been out. I can tell him, right?"

Katie nodded. The door opened behind them, and Ruth came in.

"Hello, hello! I thought I saw your car drive by," she said to Cindy. She reached for Hope's pudgy hand. "I need somebody to help me pat all the little kitties. Do you want to help?"

It only took a few minutes for the squealing and giggling in the living room to ramp up. Adult cats had their ears laid back while the kittens danced around with arched backs and tiny tails upright like exclamation points.

"Oh, my God! You two are so noisy!" Cindy exclaimed, as Ruth and Hope let out another peal of laughter.

Katie stepped out the kitchen door, and Cindy followed. Bonnie, who had found a good place to lie in the sun, jumped up and hurried over. She knew the kitchen door led to food.

"Oh, no you don't, Fat Girl. It's not suppertime yet." Katie pulled the door closed tight behind her and followed Cindy down the sloping lawn to the barn.

"It's a beautiful building," Cindy said.

"Yes, it is," Katie agreed with a sad sigh.

"Tell Mama what the problem is," Cindy said, with the same coaxing tone she used for her children.

Katie gave her a little shove. "You're a twit."

"I know. But seriously, what gives?"

"I don't know how banks work, but I do know that, as a general rule, you have to have something of your own to put into a project," said Katie.

By this time, she and Cindy had walked up to the big doors on the western side of the barn. Rick had left them thrown open. The stacked hayrick was still parked inside. Wayne, who had heard the women approach, had slipped down the ladder. When Katie and Cindy walked along one side of the rick deeper into the barn, Wayne planned to creep up the other side to the outdoors and slip away. But he wasn't above eavesdropping on his way.

"Let me guess." Cindy closed her eyes and waved her hands over an imaginary magic ball. "It is your desire to ask the mystics how one such as yourself acquires a down payment. Woo-ooo-oo."

In actuality, Katie was laying the groundwork to turn down Harwood Architectural on the basis that she couldn't get a loan and not let them talk her into another way of committing thousands of dollars. Cindy's words made her press her lips together as her mind searched for a suitable opening line.

"What you seem to continually forget, Katie," Cindy said, "is that you own the farm. Lock, stock, and barrel."

Wayne's jaw dropped. He'd thought the old man, Rick, was the owner.

"No. Gram borrowed money," Katie said.

"And I bet the way you three have been pulling at it, you're about caught up on all the arrears. Am I right?"

Rolling her eyes, Katie nodded. "But the note is still out there. It's not paid off yet."

"Not a problem. It can't possibly be as much as the property is worth," Cindy said.

CHAPTER THIRTY-SEVEN

"It doesn't earn anything by itself," said Katie. "It's not a working farm."

"Not in the sense of cows and corn," said Cindy. "But consider all the revenue it generates. And the fact that, four years ago, it didn't do any of that. You opened the sand pit, rented out the house lot in Charlotte, work two jobs, have boarders, all that. You told Mr. LaSalle what I said about renting out the work area in the barn, right? Okay, and how about the Christmas Tree farm? With any luck, there will be enough money in that note to buy at least some baby trees. Rick says the land is ready."

Katie opened her mouth, but Cindy wasn't done.

"There are the rock climbers, too. I know they haven't come often, but we can work on that. And last but not least, what about this deal with the cats? You know, where you go out and set up the live traps for the nasty-attitude woman from the Realtor's office? Yeah, I know about that. Ruth told my mother at the Feral Cat Society meeting. That's a lot of cats. Janice made sure you got top dollar. I hear there is a buyer for the property in the wings. Frith wants all those cats out fast. When you get that check, it should be earmarked for the restoration. Separate account. Show the bank you're serious. All that you do shows you're resourceful, committed, ready to step up. It will make a difference."

They had stopped at the bottom of the loft ladder. Squatting on the concrete floor across the barn, Wayne could hear every word. He couldn't believe all the stuff the new woman had said about what was happening around the farm. It was a wonder that he hadn't gotten caught by somebody yet.

"Do you want to go up?" Katie asked.

"Phfft, like you could stop me."

Cindy grasped an upper rung and was popping out onto the floor of the haymow before Katie could tell her to be careful. Over Wayne's head, he could hear the tap of Cindy's shoes, and only then realized he wouldn't be able to dart outside without the chance he would be seen. He headed deeper into the barn.

Across from the enclosed box stall, which had been Bonnie's home for a time, was a stack of the odds and ends that remained from Irma's collection of roadside pick up trash. Feed Bags were stashed near the back. Squeezing between the stacks, Wayne made his way into the little nest. Then, pushing Old Tom out of the way, he settled in.

Up in the loft, Cindy oohed and aahed at the enormous beams and the view from the mow windows. Katie sidled a little closer to the broken-down edge. A square of bright blue caught her eye. With small steps, she crept closer to find the attraction had been the lid of a Tupperware bowl. She also found half a dozen pint canning jars, a mound of hay, and a single sock. She picked up everything except the hay before she returned to where Cindy stood.

"This is so beautiful," her friend said. "Can you imagine a bedroom here with this view? What have you got there?"

"Just some leftover junk," Katie said. "Are you ready to go down? We won't squeeze past the hayrick. Right beside the ladder is the door to the milk room. Let's go through there, okay?"

"Sure. I'm ready for some lemonade, and I bet Ruth is ready for me to take Hope out of her hair."

They climbed down the ladder and left the barn. Twice, Katie nervously peeked over her shoulder. She and Cindy joined an impromptu tea party after they'd washed their hands, and Katie tucked away what she'd found.

* * *

"Does this look like a man's sock to you?" Katie asked her family group that night after supper.

The bag she'd used to hide the discovered goods lay ripped wide open on the table, the items inside spread on the brown paper.

"Where did you get this stuff?" Rick frowned at the dirty bowl.

"In the barn loft." Katie pointed to the Tupperware. "I saw this last in the refrigerator, filled with American Chop Suey. I thought Charlie had scarfed it all down during the middle of the night!"

"I didn't," declared Charlie.

"I know that now," said Katie. "Look at the jars. Every one of them has a handwritten tag that Ruth stuck on it this summer."

"Do you mean somebody not only stole food from the house, but is living out in our barn?" Ruth's voice grew shriller with every word.

"When I first came back here, I hung out in the loft," Katie said. "I swept the whole thing clean. Poppa said it was the best way to prevent a spontaneous combustion fire. Well, today I found a big stack of hay that looked like somebody was nesting in it. The only hay in the barn are the bales we brought in for Bonnie to sleep in. How did it get up in the loft?"

Rick started to rise from his seat, but Katie held up her hand.

"Whoever was there has to be gone by now, right? What we have to worry about is, not only did they steal food from the farm stand and camp out in the barn, but they walked right into the house and up to the refrigerator."

Both Ruth's and Charlie's jaws dropped.

"How many keys are there to the house?" Rick asked.

"There's an old skeleton key in the front door lock. It's been stuck there for years. And there's another one on the nail by the kitchen door," Katie said.

"What about the cat room door?"

"Two, I think," Ruth said. "It's a much newer lock. And there's the bulkhead."

"Okay," Rick said. "I'll go down and drop the bar on the bulkhead door. Tomorrow I'll have keys made up at the feed store so, everybody has one for the kitchen door. From now on, the doors are locked when we're gone. And at night."

"What about the windows, Rick?" Marlie asked. "It's too hot to keep them closed all the time."

"The only ones low enough are on the front porch, and maybe the one over the sink."

"We'll just have to close those when we're not here," Katie said.

"Is everybody on board with all this?" Rick asked.

When every head bobbed, he headed down the cellar steps. A few moments later, they heard the heavy wooden bar slam into place.

"That's a pretty frightening thought, that someone was here," Marlie said to

Katie when they were alone. "I think you need to consider stronger security measures. I'm not so worried about myself, as I am Ruth, and probably Charlie. You're not going to like this, but Sheriff Lewis needs to be notified. He may have some idea about how we can protect everyone here, and the people over on the Dean farm as well."

Katie shook her head sadly. "I don't remember a time in my whole life when those doors were locked. We can secure the house, the outbuildings and all the doors on the barn, but that leaves all the windows with no glass and the collapsed end still open. I'd think about getting a dog, but we've got Solomon."

When Rick came back upstairs, he headed over to the Dean farm to tell them about the uninvited guest. Grace directed him down to the farm stand where Raymond was hanging a set of cottage shelves for the canned goods. Made with a small lip on the front to hold plates so they wouldn't slide off, they would work similarly to secure canning jars.

Rick made the walk down and, tight-lipped, told Raymond what Katie had found.

"This isn't good," Raymond said.

The two men worked on the shelves together, while they discussed what other safety measures they could put into place. They were unaware that the interloper sat against the back wall outside, listening to their every word.

After Katie and Cindy had left, Wayne climbed the ladder and was able to tell immediately that things had been removed. Knowing Katie and possibly the woman deputy would soon return, he had snuck out the back of the barn and traveled toward the brook until he came to the boneyard. Then he had deviated toward the Sugarhouse. Now he was in a dither, as he tried to decide where to go. He only half-listened to Rick and Raymond until Rick spoke up about the barn renovations.

"We've tried to figure out where we can nickel and dime to save on the cost. Percy pointed out there's cleanup that needs to be done before work actually starts. Stuff to be picked up and shoveled away. Percy said it will be cheaper for us to do the work than to pay them. None of it is stuff we can't do, and it will save a couple of days of labor. Isaac will come out whenever

I'm ready. I plan to post a notice here and at the feed store for another laborer." He walked out of the Sugarhouse, turned the key in the lock for the Schoolhouse Thrift, and tucked the key behind the outside lamp. "Two men, three or four days. What do you think a fair wage would be?"

The two farmers headed up the hill. One carried the toolbox, the other lugged the saw. Both were intent on Rick's question. Behind them, crouched in the weeds, Wayne smiled across the lot at the old-fashioned oil lamp.

Chapter Thirty-Eight

Ruth had called Baldwin's Feed and Hardware and caught Katie five minutes before she clocked out. An animal call had come into the farmhouse.

It was Stan who provided directions for Katie to the address. "It's down near Monkton Bog. There are two ways in. This side is quicker. Go back through the village and out up along the Mechanicsville Road. That way isn't as rough."

Rick, who had just pulled in with the delivery truck, told her he would check the cat traps. Katie opted for quick, but as her teeth jarred together on the washboard dirt road, she wondered at her choice. When the fallen-down mailbox came into view, she was more than glad to have reached her destination.

The short drive ended at a stately, two-and-a-half-story brick house with double chimneys and a carriage house behind. It was easy to tell the place hadn't received any real TLC in a while, but it was still stunning. The wide front door was centered between two tall windows. The brickwork was solid. But the beautiful house still had an empty, lonely look.

Katie had to knock the tension out of her knees when she climbed out of the truck. She saw a car with New York plates in the yard, and a middle-aged couple in jeans, plaid shirts, and work boots seated on the wide granite step-up.

"Hi, I'm Katie Took, animal control. This is quite a house! I grew up around here, and I don't remember ever seeing it before." Katie had walked halfway up the gravel approach. She expected to be directed to the carriage house and paused.

"Built in 1820." The woman beamed. "I can't believe we were lucky enough to find it, and I can't wait to live here."

"Harrison Minor." The man stepped forward and extended his hand. "This is my wife, Deb. Why don't you step inside, and we'll show you why we called."

Katie winced internally. What kind of damage had a raccoon or squirrels done inside this lovely house? She wasn't four steps inside when she realized that, even though the outside needed a small amount of work, the interior was a mess. Not to mention the murky, vinegary smell. Her nose wrinkled, and Deb Minor noticed.

"I know. I've got all the windows open. But every time we close the house to go home, we come back to the same smell." She led the way to the wide staircase and started up.

"The whole interior has to be gutted," Harrison said. "We've done a lot of the demolition by ourselves and had started on the first floor. This morning, Deb decided she wanted to poke the bear on the upper floor."

At the top of the staircase, they crossed the hall and entered one of the rear bedrooms. Other than a pile of pulled-down wallpaper in the center of the floor, there wasn't anything to see. However, there was a noticeable increase in the smell. Deb pointed to the back corner of the outer side wall.

"The wallpaper was warped, kind of slipping off the wall, so I pulled at it. And when it came down, the plaster was all gunked up." She bit her lip, then added, "I was so surprised I yelled down the stairs to Harry."

"I was on my way up, and Deb almost plowed me over," Harry said. "When she yelled, something overhead began to move around. I didn't check, but I think some animal is up in the attic."

Katie kicked at the pile of crumpled wallpaper. It was evident it had gotten wet multiple times, and the staining told her it wasn't rainwater. She walked over to the wall, leaned in, and took a deep sniff that made her yank her head back fast.

"This is urine, or something maybe a little messier," she said, face tilted toward the ceiling.

At that moment, a chunk of the horsehair plaster fell from the corner, smashing into bits on the floor. The echo from the crash in the empty room had the same effect as Deb's loud call: a flurry of movement, then a rush of squeaking calls from above. With a little squeal of her own, Deb rushed to the top of the staircase, ready to dash downward.

"Whatever it is, it's not just one," Katie said. "How do you get up there?"

"There's a narrow staircase. The door is in the bedroom across the hall," Harry said.

Katie went out to the truck and returned with a net and a flashlight. She'd also pulled on her knee-high barn boots.

"Okay, let's have a little look-see. Deb, maybe you should stay down here. I'm not sure what we'll find, but we may want to have fewer of us if we have to get out fast."

Deb nodded and retreated to the top of the staircase. Harry pulled open the attic door, and the smell, which had already been pretty nasty in the warm, closed-up house, was enough now to make Katie gag. She motioned Harry behind her, switched on her flashlight, and slowly advanced upward. Two-thirds of the way up, they encountered a slick residue that Katie believed at first was a decomposing animal. Flies, maggots, and what looked like the waving tentacles of tiny worms became visible in the light's beam.

"No further for you," she said to Harry.

Katie planted her booted foot firmly so she wouldn't slip and went all the way up until her head breached the floor. Her flashlight beam showed an attic filled with boxes, trunks, and furniture. All of it was covered with several inches of the same shiny, slimy residue. Then her commercial-grade flashlight swept the roof, and the rafters came alive.

"BATS!" she yelped.

She turned and ran solidly into Harry, who had ignored her request for him to stay behind and followed her up. Both slipped on the stairs. This was no place to fall down. Katie put her hand on the wall and immediately yanked it away. The slime was thick there as well.

"MOVE!" she yelled. "MOVE!"

Harry had also touched the walls, and like Katie, was terrified by what his hand had encountered. They were almost to the bedroom door when Katie saw Deb, frozen in place by Katie's scream.

"Downstairs, Deb," Harry ordered. "Now!"

His wife turned and fled. It wasn't until they were all outside that Katie took a breath.

"Not my best moment," she said grimly.

Deb was pale and shaking. "What happened?"

"Bats." Harry tried to laugh. "More bats than I've seen in my whole life."

"How do we get them out of there?" Deb turned to look at Katie. Her husband followed suit.

"Okay," Katie said. "Here's the deal. I don't do exterminations. One bat I can catch, or at least get outside. This is out of my league. You can't gas them for multiple reasons, one of which is they're probably protected. That gunk you saw slide down behind the wallpaper, and that the stairs are covered with, as well as everything in the attic? That's bat poop. Tons of bat poop."

"Now what?" Deb turned to her husband with tears in her eyes. He could only shake his head.

"Even if you get up there and scare them off, they'll come back," Katie said. "They've been living up there for years. I mean, like since the dinosaurs."

"Or maybe 1821," Deb said tremulously.

Katie had to smile. "Yeah, probably then."

"How did they get in?"

"I'll bet if you get out a couple of lawn chairs and sit here about dusk, you'll see them come out, like a rising cloud. You'll hear them flap and squeak."

Deb huddled closer to Harry.

"They won't hurt you. To be honest, living this close to the bog with all those mosquitoes, you want the bats. Just maybe not in your house. They can get through really tiny openings, like around the chimneys. If you can see a light shine through, they can squeeze inside," Katie explained.

"I guess that just goes to show you, even when you think you've found all the bad, there might still be a worm in the core." Harry sighed. "We planned to pull down all the horsehair plaster and lathe, then start with the electric and plumbing on the first floor. But now maybe we need to have the roof taken off this year instead."

"Bats migrate," said Katie. "In another two and a half, three months, they'll pack their little suitcases and go. If you start to get ready now, that's probably when you should have the roof done. I believe it'll take you a while to find somebody to excavate all that bat crap. I don't think you'll want to carry it through the house."

Deb made a face. There was no running water in the house, but there was an outside spigot attached to the wellhead.

"Can you recommend somebody?" Harry asked as they washed their hands and rinsed off their boots.

"I can't, but I'll ask around. If you decide to keep working in the house, maybe you should wear masks."

Harry nodded, then pulled out his wallet. "What do I owe you?"

"Nothing. The town pays me. I just need you to sign my chit so they know I answered the call."

As Katie drove away, she could see in her rearview mirror that the couple had turned to look back inside through the open front door.

"I don't know about you guys," Katie told the couple as they disappeared from view, "but I really need a hot bath. And I really hope you can find somebody to clean that mess up."

The road out hadn't improved during her house call. Lost in thought as Katie considered who might know about bat removal, she wasn't aware of a particularly deep pothole until the front end of her truck fell into it.

Even though the front wheels rolled out just as the rear tires rolled in, the truck continued forward a few feet. The vehicle had developed a roar from the undercarriage. Then Katie saw the exhaust system, which had been connected beneath the truck's rusty frame, had been pulled off the manifold and lay wrinkled and twisted twenty feet behind her in the dust. She braked sharply and stared at it for a few minutes with the hope the assembly would crawl over and reattach itself.

Katie loaded the metal pipe system in the back of her truck, then spent a few moments with her forehead against the tailgate, wondering for the umpteenth time why she was still in the state of Vermont.

* * *

The supper hour traffic had dwindled away. Katie continued north on Route 116, cringing every time she saw a head turn toward the noise her truck was making. She had a stop to make on her way home and refused to be deterred by a mechanical problem. Just past Meredith Block's house, she started to look for the place the fireman had hidden his truck. It wasn't hard to find.

With her pickup hidden in the cornstalks, Katie followed the path Meredith's boyfriend had described, crossing the road and through the conifers. At one point, she turned off the path too early and ended up in Jacob and Irene Hunt's backyard. But eventually she found her way to the three knurled apple trees.

Katie crept ahead toward Meredith's house, eyes alert to catch every detail. Though she couldn't see Route 116, she heard the occasional car pass by. The dusty smell of overgrown hay, chirp of birds, and buzz and whir of insects filled her senses. Suddenly, half a dozen wasps dive-bombed her.

Ducking, trying vainly not to swat, Katie ran out of their range. Or they let her go, as she had proven not to be a danger. Not inclined to take a second chance with the stingers, Katie headed down the driveway and up the side of the road when she left. She had seen the route the boyfriend had described and verified his story. Breaking into the house or the garage would only get her in trouble, so she curbed her curiosity and walked away.

As she passed Hunt's house, she considered that it looked like no one was home, but it didn't feel that way. She smirked at her own imagination, but kept on. When she drove back on her way to the farm, she missed seeing the thin man who had stepped outside, beer bottle in hand.

Chapter Thirty-Nine

For the next few days, the missing tailpipe and exhaust on Katie's pickup raised a lot of attention. No matter where she drove, heads turned. Rick, Ruth, and Stan all pointed out that if Marlie didn't write her a ticket, Sheriff Lewis would. An appointment was scheduled for Phil's Garage, with arrangements made so Katie wouldn't have to walk the ten miles home after she dropped it off.

It was a nice morning. Warm, but not as hot as it had been. Even with all the pieces of her life vying for her attention, Katie focused on the need to get the truck repaired and the resulting bill paid. A smooth, warm breeze wafted in through the window, Katie continued her drive straight through the village. Past the general store, the turnoff to the Mechanicsville Road, the creamery, and suddenly, the fire station was on the right.

Barely larger than a tall two-car garage, the building housed the town's two fire trucks: a water tanker and an equipment truck. An ell added while Katie had lived in Illinois housed the rescue ambulance. There were several pickups and a few cars in the dirt parking area, including the oversized one Marlie had told her belonged to the fire lieutenant from Charlotte. Katie slowed down, then realized that the volunteers weren't out at a fire. This was a meeting, an oddity for a weekday morning. The big doors were open, the fire trucks had been pulled out, and folding chairs filled the interior space. That meant the firefighters were participating in a training class.

Katie blew the horn as she passed. The few men who stood in the open doorway turned to wave. One man, dressed in trousers instead of blue jeans, was Gage Fernald. Katie winced. It seemed lately, now that she knew who he was, and that he intended to make her life miserable, the guy was everywhere she looked.

Marlie showed up at Phil's Garage to pick up Katie. The truck would be having a sleepover, but at least it was repairable. Katie opened the passenger door of Marlie's private vehicle and paused.

"Am I supposed to ride with you while you're in uniform?" she asked.

"It's okay." Marlie waved her in. "I'm off duty, and my weapon and utility belt are locked in the trunk." When Katie was strapped in, Marlie asked, "How about if we share a treat and drive over to A&W for lunch?"

"Cool! I haven't been there in years."

The closest A&W Root Beer was in Essex Junction, two blocks from Essex Five Corners. They drove through Saint George and the southeastern tip of Williston to the power plant bridge in Essex. Though Essex Junction had changed a lot in ten years, the tiny red and white diner with the big, frothy mug of root beer that hung over the entrance hadn't.

The carhop brought them Michigan hot dogs, stacked high with chili and chopped onions and tall steins of ice-cold soda. Sixties rock and roll blasted out of the speakers as people pulled in, snacked up, and drove away. Marlie waved the carhop over to take their tray just as her service radio went off, alerting local officers that a knock and cuff with a warrant needed backup.

"Assistance required," said the dispatcher. "Additional suspects on property."

The address was given as the Cloverleaf Motel, 97 Pearl Street, Essex Junction. Marlie and Katie both looked directly to their left.

"For crying out loud," said Marlie, keying the mike on her radio. "Deputy Sheriff Marlene Foster, responding. ETA, one minute."

Katie laid her hand on Marlie's arm. "You said you were off duty. Besides, this is Essex."

"It doesn't work the same way for the sheriff's office as it does for city cops," Marlie said as she shifted the car into reverse, backed up twenty feet, turned, and pulled directly into the Cloverleaf parking lot.

"Stay in the car," she told Katie.

Katie watched as Marlie snapped on her utility belt and advanced to where the local police department vehicle was parked. A fairly young patrolman guided a much larger man in cuffs from the building and into the back of the cruiser. Katie could see the sweat circles on the officer's dark blue uniform shirt. If that big guy was reacting nervously about what he was doing, did that mean Marlie was walking into danger? Her stomach clenched, and the taste of chili and onions rose. Against the building, an officer kept an older, also sweaty, man in place. Katie assumed he was the motel owner because there were no restraints visible.

Marlie unclipped the strap that held her weapon in the holster and advanced out of Katie's sight. Maybe four minutes later, she came back into view, pushing a second bear of a man in front of her, also in cuffs. Even to Katie's eyes, it was obvious these two were brothers. Same size, coloring, and florid, bushy beards.

The prisoner was a lot heavier than Marlie, and Katie felt a stab of apprehension in her chest. However, the deputy competently passed the prisoner off to the patrolman, who held the man in place against the cruiser. Sirens approached, indicating reinforcements were on the way. That's when Katie realized Marlie had gone back into the motel room.

On the A&W side of the motel, the building was two stories, white, and covered with road dirt. Definitely a little seedy. On Katie's end, further from the soda shop, it was easy to tell the eight rooms had been converted to rent-by-the-week units. All the action was happening in the second-to-last unit.

The prisoner being held in place was directed into the back seat of the newly arrived cruiser. Then two of the units pulled out, each carrying a cuffed man. There were two officers in the last cruiser. One remained in the vehicle. The other went inside the unit where Marlie and at least one other officer remained. Suddenly, Marlie stepped out into the open, waving at Katie.

"I need you!" she called, continuing to wave her friend over.

"Is it safe?" Katie asked.

"It is now." Marlie grabbed Katie's arm as soon as she was close enough and guided her inside. A dark-haired man wearing a gold hairdresser's smock and cuffs stood in the first room. The officer motioned him towards the door, but the man argued against it.

"No reporters," the officer who held onto the man barked at Marlie.

"Hold on," said Marlie. "This woman has medical training."

Katie could only gawk as Marlie pushed her through the doorway into the second room. Immediately, the sour smell outside became an overwhelming stink of sick. An officer Katie hadn't seen earlier stood, left hand pressed against his mouth. Katie pressed the back of her wrist over her nose and mouth. Amid sweaty sheets lay a woman, dark hair plastered to her head, eyes closed. She was horribly thin. There was a dribble of vomit across the stained pillowcase. Katie stepped closer.

"She's really sick," Katie said nervously. When no one answered, she looked at the officer and added, "She's not going to walk out of here. She needs an ambulance."

"I told you she wasn't faking it," Marlie said.

The officer didn't move. Katie threw her arm out, pointing to the door to make it clear she expected a response.

"Get this bucket of puke out of here. Open that window." Katie laid her hand on the woman's forehead. The sick woman was on fire. "Oh, you poor girl," Katie muttered.

The woman's eyes fluttered. Katie had first thought she was unconscious, but now she considered that the young woman might be too sick to respond. Katie rushed into the tiny bathroom, grabbed a stack of washcloths, and wet them with cold water. With the window open, a dusty-smelling breeze blew in. It was better than the hot, heavy stink from before. Katie pressed one washcloth against the woman's forehead and spoke softly.

"Take a deep breath. I'm right here with you. Help is on the way."

Katie wiped the woman's face, tucking the clean edge of the washcloth into her mouth.

"I'll bet you're really thirsty, aren't you? Take a little suck on that, it'll help wet your mouth. There you go. Cool, isn't it? Take it slow."

She spoke in the same low, confident tone she used with the feral cats. Kneeling beside the bed, Katie could feel whatever had missed the bucket soak through her jeans. She didn't move, but took another face cloth and wiped the woman's arms and hands in another attempt to cool her down.

"Get me a glass of clean, warm water," she said to Marlie over her shoulder.

Outside, she could hear the motel owner as he spoke to one of the officers. The gist seemed to be that the couple was registered, but he had no idea who the big guys were. Katie dunked the edge of the face cloth in the glass and pressed it back into the woman's mouth. Her eyes didn't open. There was no movement, just the slight rise and fall of her chest.

There was so much clatter drifting through the window. Police radios with their static-filled calls, the officer and the thin man continuing to argue, the angry voice of the motel owner. Katie strained to hear the approaching siren of the ambulance.

Please, she prayed silently to the ambulance driver. *Get here soon.*

A man behind her said, "Ma'am, can you back away and let us in?"

Katie got to her feet. Her eyes swept the room as she moved out of the paramedic's way. Along the wall were cardboard boxes filled with items that should have been in somebody's home. She saw the silver flash of pots, magic marker labels that identified the contents as kitchen, bathroom, bedroom. It was all pathetic and sad.

She stepped into the bathroom and closed the door. After she rinsed her mouth and face with cold water, she stepped back out into the main room. The third guy was gone. Marlie and the officer who remained watched the paramedics, who were busy setting up an IV. The woman had been transferred onto the stretcher. Quietly, Katie stepped out the front door, walking past the motel owner and his retainer.

The men's eyes followed her back into the front seat of Marlie's car. Head against the backrest, she waited. She and Marlie might be there a while.

When Marlie returned, Katie had opened the door so she could hold her stained knees outside. As the sun heated up the car, the smell of the woman's sick had grown enough to make Katie gag.

"We have to go down to the Essex Junction police station and fill out a report," Marlie said. "Are you okay?"

"What made you tell that cop I had medical training?" Katie asked.

"Because the twit wouldn't believe the woman might be dying. All he wanted to do was snap the cuffs on her and march her out of there like he was so tough. Some guys are real macho assholes. When they pin the badge on, they lose all their common sense." Marlie started the car. "I'm sorry. I should have thought up a better plan."

"No. It's okay. She needed help. I hope she makes it."

It took longer for Marlie to file her report than it did for Katie to give her statement. While she waited, she went into the restroom and rinsed the knees of her jeans before she returned to the desk.

Only a few feet away, an office door was open. She watched the officer who had argued with the skinny man enter. The officer spoke to someone in the office, Katie couldn't see. He sounded irate. Silently, she scooched her seat closer and leaned as far as she could to eavesdrop.

"The woman, Danielle Tait-Noah, has been admitted to the hospital," said the officer. "Her husband, Ron Noah, says she works with a caterer and lifted a tray of bacon-wrapped scallops. You know, the five-finger discount. The tray had been put aside at a function last weekend. She thought they had just been overlooked, but it seems the scallops weren't forgotten. According to Mr. Noah, they had actually gone bad. He said the woman was pregnant and was already really sick. The seafood put her over the edge."

"But not the husband?" asked the unseen person, who sounded like an older man.

"He said he's allergic and doesn't eat shellfish. He's still acting pretty nervous. What do you want to do with him? He has no priors, and the Morris brothers both said they were just squatting there."

"Cut him loose, get him a ride to the hospital," said the second man. "Have Officer Dowery take him. She's good at making apologies."

"On it, Sarge."

Katie hustled to get away from the door. Her head was bent to reread her report when the angry cop stomped past. On the way home, she told Marlie that she had heard the officer mention Danielle Tait's name.

"I can't believe it." Marlie sounded pleased. "We couldn't find her. I'll drop you off and get down to the office to talk to Sheriff Lewis. He'll want to contact her."

"If you have the chance to speak with Meredith's boys again, ask them if Danielle was sick while she was there. You know, before they left with their father. It sounded like she had been ill for a while," Katie said.

"Yeah, and if Meredith was all nasty to her, maybe her husband might have taken offense and went back to find Meredith."

"Well, that was quite the lunch trip, wasn't it?" Ruth asked after Marlie left, and Katie had told her about the arrest.

Katie gave a weak smile. "Yeah. But next time, I'll drive. Maybe I won't feel so carsick."

* * *

It wasn't until the next day that Marlie showed up at the feed store with more information. It was delivery day in the hardware business, with the tractor-trailer backed up to the loading dock and boxes of inventory stacked in every aisle. Katie worked in one, and Cindy worked in another. When Marlie sidled up to Katie in a sneaky way, Cindy left her area and followed.

"Remember a couple of years ago last spring, when those three guys broke out of Windsor State Penitentiary?" Marlie asked. "There was a statewide alert."

"Weren't they sent to work on a beautification project or something?" Cindy cut open a second shipping box.

"Yeah, they were supposed to paint the garage buildings, I think," Marlie said. "Anyway, they stole a car, drove to Burlington, and hid out. Two of them were B&E nighttime, but the third, Ron Norse, had been in an armed robbery that went bad. He said all he did was drive the car. But they were in an accident, and somebody died. He claimed he saw guns drawn and called it self-defense. The jury didn't see it the same way, but the judge sentenced him to only eighteen months, plus time served."

Marlie stopped talking when Stan's voice could be heard not far away. The women split up, but when his voice faded, regrouped and she continued.

"Anyway, the two Morris brothers, both small-time crooks, got out of prison a few months ago. With no place to go, they decided to look up their buddy. He said they pressured him into letting them stay with him for a few nights. Because his wife was there and felt poorly, he didn't want to argue. The nights turned into weeks. Yesterday, he went to work like any other day. He's a student at the Pierre School of Cosmetology in Burlington. They've only been married a few weeks. The wife works at Lincoln Inn, two blocks away from the motel."

There were footsteps from nearby. Marlie paused, Katie stretched up, peeked over the shelf, then squatted back down.

"Go ahead," she whispered.

"Anyway, his buddies got bored. They wanted money, which the couple didn't have, so they went next door to the Fairground Strip Mall and robbed the Ben Franklin. Then, casual as could be, they walked back to the Cloverleaf."

"Is there a punchline here that I'm not getting?" Cindy asked.

"The business at the end of the strip mall is a bank branch. It has outside cameras. They were caught on film." Marlie grinned.

"No way!" Katie said.

"Talk about stupid," said Cindy.

"What about the woman?" Katie asked. "Is she going to be alright? She was pretty sick."

"She's still in the hospital," said Marlie. "Sheriff Lewis was told that she is pregnant and suffering from acute morning sickness. I made the inquiry call this morning. The hospital person I talked to said she should have been in there getting fluids a week ago. That all those guys who left her alone in there should be charged with endangerment. Once she started to throw up, she just got to the point where she couldn't stop or eat or drink anything."

"Oh, my gosh!" Cindy's hand flew to her mouth. "I had morning sickness, but not like that."

Katie looked up from where she knelt on the floor. Suddenly, she felt a little sick herself and took a big gulp of air. "So, she really could have died?"

"But you saved her," Cindy said.

"No. If they had arrested her, somebody would have realized she was seriously ill." Katie got to her feet.

"The issue was, the only people on-site at that time couldn't see that the poor woman wasn't even able to stand up." Marlie laid her hand on Katie's arm. "You did a good thing. But there's more."

Both Katie and Cindy settled back on their knees among the stacks of product and waited for the rest of Marlie's story.

"When the cops took Danielle's husband to the hospital to be with her, they didn't know he was really Ron Norse. That's the name he used when he got arrested for the car accident. The report came in with a photo a few hours later. Officers went to pick him up, and found out after they dropped him at the main entrance, he never made it upstairs to her room. He's in the wind."

Marlie's radio suddenly crackled. She took a quick look. "Sorry, gotta go," she said, and hurried away.

Cindy went to help Davidson at the cash registers, and Katie reached for the box her friend had cut open. Her fingers trembled, and she knelt on the floor and tried to separate herself from the memory of what had happened at the Cloverleaf. A waft of air blew upward as the flap swept back. Katie caught a whiff of rancid, sick stink. She tried to concentrate on lining up cans of dog food, but her mind wondered where Ron Noah was right now—and where he would have been if the police report from Windsor had arrived at the police station earlier.

Chapter Forty

Sunday, while Katie and Marlie were helping Dorothea at the thrift shop, Ruth's ride home from the knitting group dropped her off at the Dean farm. There she found Grace on the porch, surrounded by bushel baskets of fresh vegetables.

"Whew." Grace wiped her brow. "One day of rain and three days later, we've got more than I know what to do with."

"Davey!" Ruth called out. "Bring your four-wheeler over here."

The Dean family had a pair of farm wheelers made from the frames of Volkswagen Beetles. The chassis had been removed, which left only the seats and rear-mounted engine. A short-sided plank body had replaced the trunk on the front end. The boys used them to haul feed bags and the like.

"I'll take some of this home. I've got time this afternoon to get it ready to pickle," Ruth said. "I stopped down at the Sugarhouse. You'll be able to put a couple of baskets of fresh veggies down there. A lot sold already today."

She pointed out the baskets she wanted and clambered into the passenger seat while Davey loaded the haul for the ride up the hill. Eventually, Katie and Marlie would be home. Ruth didn't have any qualms about badgering them to help.

* * *

Marlie sliced beets to pickle. As she worked, she watched Katie blanch the raw vegetables, then use a thin knife to skin the outer layers off.

"How is it you can do all this stuff so fast?" Marlie asked.

"Monique showed me," Katie answered. "She also left precise directions about the prep and canning of the bread and butter pickles and the first of the mustard-pickled cauliflower."

"Yeah, she showed you once. And it was quick." Marlie put a colander of sliced beets in the sink to rinse.

"I guess I'm just a quick study." Katie shrugged.

For a few minutes, they worked silently. Marlie tried for well-spaced cuts.

"I think," Katie said slowly, "actually, I *know*, when I was little and growing up out here with no one to play with, Gram spent a lot of time trying to teach me. She talked to me all the time like I was grown and understood what she meant. Stuff like how to cook chicken and sew and the proper way to make a bed. We did alright together until she'd try to make me look all girly like my mom."

Marlie knew this was a touchy subject for Katie. She wisely decided to withhold comment.

"Things didn't start to go south until after Poppa passed away. He taught me the same way Gram did, to keep my eyes open and remember." Katie lowered the wire rack into the hot water bath. "He was our safety cushion, kept me and Gram from really having it out." She wiped her hands and moved to stand next to Marlie. Her tone was intimate, like a confession, but she didn't make eye contact. "I've thought about this a lot since I came back, more so in the last couple of months. All the things Gram showed me, tried to tell me. It crushes my heart now, because I can't tell her how much I appreciate what she did. I can't say thank you, or let her know what she did makes me proud." She laughed self-consciously. "I think that's why I want out of here sometimes, for the shame."

With her hands still dripping bright red beet juice, Marlie leaned over and put her head on Katie's shoulder.

"Oh, darlin', she knows every minute. And I know she's proud. We're all proud."

Just as Katie thought tears would flow down her cheeks, a voice in the doorway cut in.

"I don't know who all is proud for what, but this is the last bit of green and yellow beans. I hope we have enough vinegar to get them pickled."

Katie stepped over to the door to take the heavy basket from Ruth. The old woman looked drawn and tired.

"I'll tell you what I'll do for you," Katie said. "Here's a list of stuff we need to finish up. You and Marlie take it down to the feed store. I'll mix us up chili dogs and French fries for supper. Rick will be home soon. If we all work together, we can get this done tonight."

"Are you sure you want me to go now?" Marlie asked. "If you call, Rick can just bring the stuff home."

"Look how tired she is," Katie whispered. "Go ahead. She'll be asleep before you get to the corner."

By the time Marlie and Ruth had returned, Katie had supper ready. Besides the chili dogs and fries, Katie had stir-fried the last bits of all the vegetables in the refrigerator.

"Oh, look," Marlie said. "Five vegetables! We're going to be so healthy."

Charlie grimaced.

Chapter Forty-One

Wayne's new plan was to spend the night in the Schoolhouse Thrift building, but the Sugarhouse Farm stand had been very busy that day. He hadn't felt safe. While everyone was gone, he'd tried the bulkhead door, found it barred, and circled to the front of the house. All the other doors had also been locked, and the easy windows closed, except for the ones in the cattery. Shielded by the hollyhocks and lilacs, he'd hauled a hay bale over. The bale added just enough height for him to slip inside.

There were cookies in the cookie jar and a small piece of meatloaf in the fridge. The cool cellar beckoned, and Wayne had gone down the stairs. Once there, he took a moment to unbar the door in the event an escape was needed. Then he settled down with his snack and a cup of cold tea from Ruth's sun ice tea jug. Solomon was no problem; he knew from past experience. Wayne would share a cookie.

Now, tucked away and feeling safe, Wayne listened to the sounds from upstairs. Hopefully, when supper was over, everyone would move outside to enjoy the evening. If they did, he'd risk a raid of the refrigerator or maybe help himself to anything left to cool on the sideboard. He'd caught a little chill during the rainstorm, and even though he sat quietly, a sneeze jumped out. He was barely able to cover his mouth and nose with his arm in time. Just the same, there had been an eruption of noise.

Above him, the sound of one of the dogs' nails suddenly skittered across the linoleum. Solomon had heard. Now he was at the cellar door, snuffling and carrying on.

"Solomon. Sit," Rick ordered.

The hound quieted down for only a few moments, then began to demand the door be opened. His friend, the cookie man, was down there.

"Maybe you should check downstairs in case a rat came in," the old woman said.

Wayne was already on his feet and moving up the bulkhead steps. Ever so softly, he lowered the hatch door down in place as Rick and Solomon descended. Though Rick didn't find any evidence that a rodent had invaded their walls, Solomon did show him that someone had forgotten to bar the bulkhead door.

From where he hid in the hollyhocks, Wayne heard the heavy bolt slide into place. It was too light to take a chance and run down the short slope and across the dirt drive between the house and the barn. Wayne stayed where he was, confident that the dogs wouldn't find him if he stayed quiet. The big pig that roamed free was another issue, but Bonnie had had supper. For her, it was bedtime. He watched her lumber across the drive, two hundred yards away, headed toward her outdoor pen. She paused, nose stretched to the sky to take a long, woofing sniff. Finally, sure there was nothing for her to check on, she continued. Wayne held his breath until she was safely inside the sty and nestled in her bedding.

That left only the geese, which didn't concern Wayne. As the shadows grew, he darted to the milk house door and inside the barn. Once up in the hayloft, he felt safe.

If he'd still been among the hollyhocks, though, he might not have felt so secure. The spot where he'd hidden was exactly where Splish and Splash bedded down for the night. When they arrived, the human smell had Splish honking furiously, while his mate settled down in her bed.

Rick heard the geese, the barnyard watch dogs, but with the bulkhead closed and all the barn doors shut, he believed everything was tight. Only a fool would try to crawl through the collapsing end of the barn.

Chapter Forty-Two

Every morning when Katie followed Marlie and Rick out to work, she slowed down in front of the Schoolhouse Thrift Shop. They hadn't done much work there since the doors had opened in the spring, and The Sugar Shack Farm Stand had been moved in kitty-corner to the old one-room school. Yet every day there seemed to be subtle changes. The Sugar Shack was open and sold Grace Dean's vegetables, homemade pies, butter, and cheese. Though it sat on a slab of concrete, other than the post and board where the electric meter was set up, it seemed finished to Katie. But she knew her neighbors had a different vision, with a sign and outdoor lighting. Like Ruth, she wanted to see that for the Schoolhouse Thrift as well. *Someday*, she thought. As she drove away, she could see Poppa right there, hammer in hand.

"Maybe," Katie said out the window to the soaring robins, "we could slice a little off the barn loan."

The thought caused her eyes to widen. She hadn't considered any of the little things she could use a few dollars from the loan for.

It was Monique's day at the thrift and farm stand. Katie met the woman and her infant at the turn onto Main Street. Monique flagged her down. In the back seat, the baby blew bubbles and gurgled.

"I left early to catch you," the tall woman smiled. "I made meringues, and I know how much you love them. Peach flavored."

"Oh, I'm going to have to share those with Cindy." Katie moaned.

"There are half a dozen. Share fair," Monique said before she pulled away, The Schoolhouse Thrift, her final destination.

Once clocked in at the feed store, Katie carefully put the container with three meringues in Stan's office with Cindy's name on them.

He's going to eat them all. I just know it.

Her three were hidden on the shelf below her register, safe from both Stan and Davidson. As she got her work area set up, she considered how good she was at seeing what happened on the sides of the road, but never identified people in the cars. Yet, some drivers, like Monique, were able to pick her out. Katie's hands stilled. How many people had seen Meredith drive past in that expensive car? Where would she have been seen? And who would remember?

It seemed every person Katie had talked to knew who Meredith was, and had a high school memory to share, but adult Meredith most often came back as a question. Isn't that the blonde who drives the powder blue convertible? Either the remark didn't say a lot about Meredith's personality, or a lot of people dreamed of owning a powder blue Pontiac convertible. Black top, white interior, whitewall tires. The longer Katie listened, the more she'd heard specific vehicle options added to the list.

When she got home, she popped a pan of lasagna into the oven. None of the high school boys had taken the bait to help Ruth out with the loading and unloading of Irma's junk collection. Both pans had ended up wrapped in heavy aluminum foil in the freezer.

Ruth continued to harp at Rick. "If we can't interest the high school boys, then we need to hire somebody for the outside clean up and the wagon loading to empty the barn, as well. And, I mean, pretty quick."

"I'll ask Isaac," Rick said. "He can load and unload. He knows how to run the tractor, so he can just keep at it until he gets it all done."

Katie ignored the squabble that continued in the living room. There was plenty to do in the kitchen, which restricted her nervous pacing to the worn linoleum. All the footwork didn't get her anywhere. Kittens followed her footsteps back and forth, tripped over themselves and each other, or tried to catch the laces from her sneakers. LG sat on the woodstove, unused during the summer months, and basically ignored Katie unless she got close enough for a grab. But Katie had learned to avoid the sharp hooks the cat kept hidden in her furry paws.

Finally, she snatched the telephone receiver from its chrome cradle and dialed.

"Hi, Corinne?"

"How did I know, Katie, that I'd hear from you?"

Katie was taken aback. She and Corrine Cox had first met when Corinne drove onto the farm as part of Edward Richardson's Vermont Forensics team. Later, they periodically met at town and county events.

Katie tried to laugh, but it sounded forced. "Is that what you think? That I'd only call you if I needed information?"

"No," Corinne answered. "But I know a body showed up in your town. One of your friends said you received last year's Nosy Neighbor of the Year Award."

Katie realized Corinne was enjoying a laugh at her expense. "Oh, ha ha," she said. "You almost had me there."

"So, does this mean you've called me so we can coffee klatch over recent national events?" Corinne asked, with a touch of sarcasm.

"No, you were right. I have questions about Meredith Block."

"Phfft. The investigation is ongoing, Katie. There isn't much I can tell you."

Katie sighed, frustrated. "This time, it's me who knew what you would say. But how about if I ask some general questions?" She twisted the coils of telephone cord around her fingers. "If you can answer yes or no, that's great. If you have to take a pass, that's all right as well."

"Sounds fair," Corinne said. "Go ahead."

"Word has it Meredith was beaten to an unrecognizable pulp," Katie said.

"Ah, that would be a no," Corinne said slowly.

Katie took her friend's reserved answer to indicate that a beating had happened, but it wasn't the worst.

"She was able to crawl some twenty or so feet under her own power."

"That's in question, but the team is leaning toward no."

"She'd been out there for longer than ten days."

"No."

CHAPTER FORTY-TWO

"Okay, let's see…animal damage?"

"Jurie's out."

Katie paused. She'd thought that was an easy one.

"As in, wild or domestic?"

"No comment."

"Did you know Meredith was allergic to bees?" she asked.

"There were a lot of them at the scene. Questions came up in the autopsy that we are still working on."

Corinne's words stopped Katie cold.

"What were they?" she asked.

"We're done here, Katie," Corinne said. "Good night."

Even though it was late enough in the evening for most people to be inside, Ruth and Rick were still seated in the rockers on the porch, swatting mosquitoes.

"You look like you're in a kerfuffle," Rick said. "Did something else disappear?"

"No, not that. Brittany told me that Meredith was allergic to paper wasps. There was Benadryl everywhere in the house, which made me wonder why Meredith would just go charging outdoors. And who else would know she was allergic?" Katie sat down on the top step near her elderly friends. "A few minutes ago, I was blathering to Corinne, and somehow that came out. She said the people in her department recognized Meredith's allergy on arrival. How is that? Did she have it written in Magic Marker across her chest?"

Rick stopped the motion of his chair. "I don't think so. But maybe if she got stung, she would have swelled up. I usually do. It hurts. It's possible that if she was really allergic, it would be more than a little swelling."

"Yeah, but Rick, she was dead. Are wasps like flies, attracted to bodies? Would they sting, and the flesh would react after she was dead?"

"I have no idea," he said.

Ruth was still rocking and knitting. "Funny you should mention bees. We found a mess of dead ones in Meredith's house when we went over to pack it up."

"What? No, Ruth. If there were bees in the house, Meredith would have swatted them dead or something. Brittany said she was absolutely terrified of them."

"That might be," Ruth said. Her chair stopped, and she peered at Katie over the top of her glasses. "But right along the top of the front door, between the wood one and the storm door, was an enormous gray paper wasp hive. It was so big that Marilyn Pierce called Robin. He collects them. He came out and sprayed to kill the wasps that were between the doors. He wanted to take the hive."

Both Katie and Rick stared at Ruth. Katie couldn't believe what she had heard.

"Ask him," Ruth said. "Anyway, some of them must have gotten into the house, and with it so hot and the house closed up, they died."

"Did you find bees all over inside the house?" Katie asked.

"No, mostly in the front hall. Some in the living room. Maybe a few in the kitchen on the windowsills."

"So, more than a half-a-dozen?" asked Rick.

Ruth gathered up her knitting and opened the front door. "More like thirty or forty, I bet. Like these darn mosquitoes, I thought they were everywhere. I'm headed in. I'm tired of the fight to keep them off."

Katie followed Rick. Wasps in the house would have been a very bad thing for Meredith.

The next morning, she told Marlie what she'd learned.

"I hadn't heard Meredith was allergic. Lewis might have and not shared the information," Marlie said. "But maybe that explains some of what I saw."

"Which was?" Katie asked, but Marlie shook her head, unwilling to share. Another bit of silence that told Katie she'd stumbled on something of importance.

Katie left for work shortly after Marlie went upstairs. This would be Marlie's last night shift until the next rotation, which was a good thing. After more than a few nights in a row, her friend looked exhausted all the time.

At the stop sign in town, Katie took a left and drove over to the creamery. Robin Pierce was the manager, and he'd already be there.

"How's that kitten you adopted for your granddaughter, Marah?" Katie asked as she leaned into his office.

"About all grown up, and into everything," Robin said with a smile. "I still see the mama outside, but she won't have another litter of kittens, thanks to Doctor Nguyen."

"I hear you went out to Meredith's house to collect a paper wasp nest," Katie said.

"And it was a big one!" Robin beamed. "Ten inches across, six deep, and attached to both doors. Wasn't easy. Paper wasps are territorial and mean. They wanted to keep it. I can't show it to you because I've got it sealed up until I'm sure there aren't any more critters alive in there."

"That's okay," Katie said. "I was just surprised when Ruth said there were thirty or so wasps in the house."

Robin leaned on his elbows on the desk. "Thirty easy, just in the hall. They can get in through a narrow place. The hive was big enough, so they'd started to ooze in over the top of the door."

"If you were right there, in that house every day, how could you not see something like that?" Katie asked.

"As far as the nest, it looked to me like the front lawn hadn't been mowed for a while, so the wasps hadn't been interrupted there. And the door was stiff to open. Hinges needed to be greased. Mrs. Block probably didn't use that door much. But if she'd still been in the house, as soon as she saw them wasps, she woulda been checking. They're nasty. She had small children. A bee stings you; it loses its stinger and dies. That doesn't happen with wasps. They just keep on and on. As far as them getting in, once one breaches, it's like water flowing. Could have just started, even just that morning."

Katie sucked her teeth as she pictured exactly what he had said. She'd been right up to that door and never seen the nest overhead.

"Why are you asking?" Robin's voice broke into her thoughts.

"When I go out to collect animals, I have to crawl around in some odd places. If I see something like that, I want to be ready," Katie said.

"Good idea."

"And I guess I was surprised when Ruth told me that several of the wasps had gotten inside."

"That's mostly because there wasn't any amount of activity in the house. You know, people moving around, vacuum cleaner running, stuff that would have driven the wasps away," Robin said. "That's one of the reasons the hive between the doors was so big. The wasps were safe, and they knew it."

"Thanks, Robin," Katie said. "Let me know when you're ready for a little brother for Marah's cat."

"As if," he replied to her exiting form.

Chapter Forty-Three

It was a surprise for Katie to walk into the house after work and find the table set and supper waiting to be put down.

"Come on, move along," Ruth ordered. "Get washed up. Go on."

"What's the hurry?"

Rick had come in behind Katie and surveyed this phenomenon as she had. It wasn't as though Ruth never cooked. She could make decent coffee, date bars, and simple meals, but normally she left supper to Katie. Now she laid down several plates, each containing the remnants of a past meal.

"How come we're having Friday night Mulligan stew on Wednesday?" Rick asked.

"Monique will be here for me in an hour. Church business. I've got to be ready to go." Ruth took her place at the table. "Amos will watch the baby, but he's only good for an hour and a half, tops."

Katie washed at the kitchen sink, with Rick in the bathroom scrubbing as well. She could hear him cooing baby talk to Solomon, who was tail-whipping, happy to have him home.

Midway through their meal, Charlie showed up. In anticipation of his appetite, Katie had the wherewithal to set up a plate for Marlie, swathed in Saran Wrap and stashed in the back of the refrigerator.

"Jeez." Charlie washed so fast that his hands still dripped when he sat down. "I didn't mean to be late. We were set up for the cement truck down at the town works garage. I told you we've got to expand the mechanics shed, right? The new trucks are too tall. Any hoot, I had to help rinse out the mixer and pickup." He poured the last four sausages onto his plate. "I got a mess of empty soda bottles for the kitty."

At two cents each, bottle redemption had become a tiny piece of the household revenue. All extra funds were dedicated to a replacement for the thirteen-inch television, which made this Charlie's pet project.

Before Charlie could go any further, a horn blew outside. Ruth dropped her plate in the sink, then grabbed her handbag and a stack of files.

"Bye, honey," Rick said to the empty air as the screen door slammed shut.

Katie muddled around the kitchen while Rick and Charlie spent what was left of their energy on the woodpile. By the time Marlie got home, both men were sweaty and ready for a shower and a nap in front of the television before they went to bed.

"Since when has Ruth had church meetings in the evening?" Marlie asked.

Katie shrugged. "It usually involves some event committee. Tonight is knitting club, so the whole kit and caboodle of them are probably in somebody's living room with a plate of brownies instead of meeting at the library."

Later, as they all settled down for the evening, a car pulled in. Seconds later, Ruth walked inside.

"Whew," she said. "Got sticky out there, didn't it? I'm for a cup of tea."

"If you want a shower," Marlie said, "there's a line. Fortunately, I got to be first, because by now the water is probably a little chilly."

Everyone giggled as Charlie, still damp and fighting his way into a T-shirt over his PJ bottoms, burst out of the bathroom.

"Brr." He shuddered. "I think I'll sit outside for a few minutes and warm up."

Katie sighed. The need for a new hot water heater had just moved up a notch on the to-be-replaced list.

Mug in hand, Ruth sat at the table with Katie while Marlie finished her meal.

"How did the meeting go?" Marlie asked.

"Good." Ruth was all smiles and obviously had something to share. The other two waited expectantly. "We got to meet in one of those new houses across the brook. And you'll never believe who we saw there."

Ruth waited until Katie said, "Okay, nosy-rosy, who did you see?"

"Well, Dorothea said she doesn't have enough time to chair the fall fete committee, so we had to rope in somebody else. But you know how Dorothea is. As soon as we get a volunteer, she'll go on about how it should all happen." Ruth stirred her tea. "That's why we didn't meet over at the church. You know, so Dorothea wouldn't be there while we talked to the newbie."

"For crying out loud, Ruth! Who is the newbie?" Katie demanded. Marlie disguised her grin as she shoved the last forkful of refried beans into her mouth.

Katie's reaction was exactly what Ruth had waited for. She sat back, a full grin on her face, and announced, "The newbie is Amanda Fernald. Gage Fernald's wife. And he was right there in the living room. I could see him from where I sat at the dining room table."

"You went to Gage Fernald's house?" Katie's emotions ran from surprise to a sense of indignation that Ruth would rub elbows with the man who had caused her so much grief.

Ruth totally missed Katie's angst. "That's not the surprise." The old woman leaned forward and spoke softly. "While we were there, the Fernalds had a guest. And it was Sheriff Lewis."

"What?" Marlie almost choked on her last bite. "Are you sure?"

"First of all, who could miss that big mouth?" Indignant, Ruth said, "I told you I could see straight through to the front door. Lewis was right there with that new deputy."

Katie looked at Marlie, whose face was slightly flushed. "Why would the new guy be with Lewis?"

"I was at a car accident over towards Richmond," Marlie said. "Sheriff Lewis doesn't believe Tony can be left alone because he'll get lost. He really is a new guy. Like, fresh out of the academy."

"Yeah, well, I don't think you need to worry about him," Ruth said. "All the time Lewis questioned Fernald, he was busy giving Tony instructions. 'Keep your mouth closed. I'll ask the questions. Take notes. Did you get all of that?' He's so bossy."

"Ruth." Katie tried to sound casual, but ended up coughing loudly to clear her throat. "You didn't happen to hear what Lewis asked Gage Fernald about, did you?"

"To be honest, it wasn't easy to listen. I didn't want him to think I was eavesdropping, so I might have missed a bit. Gwen Johnson went on and on to Amanda about the vendor booths. It was as if Gwen thought the girl was simple. And you know, Gwen is loud."

"Ruth," Marlie said softly. "Back to the story."

"It seems that the sheriff found some things that belonged to Mr. Fernald, and he was there to return them." Ruth shrugged. "However, if you ask me, Lewis seemed really tense about it."

"Huh," Katie said. "I wonder what he was returning?"

This time, Ruth shook her head. "Something smaller than the palm of his hand. Not only that, but I think it was in a plastic bag. I heard Fernald laugh and say he was glad the stuff was finally being returned. Then the young guy said something, and Lewis got all intense. You know, like ugly-looking. After that, I didn't hear much because Gwen said something foolish about the Cat Society table. I had to straighten her out."

"At least Gage ended up with whatever he forgot at the town office, right?" Katie asked. She had a good idea it was the items that had been in Meredith's Lane Chest.

Ruth rinsed her cup. "I guess so. I didn't see him with anything in his hand after Lewis left. But when he went upstairs, he made a heck of a racket and didn't seem too happy." With a yawn, she said goodnight.

Katie and Marlie sat at the table, staring at each other.

"Lewis already questioned Fernald," Marlie said. "He told us that he'd misplaced his wallet at work and never found it. This had to be the stuff from Meredith's chest. But why would Lewis make a special trip out to see Gage? And why take Tony?"

* * *

It wasn't easy to get information from Ruth sometimes. The old woman had a suspicious mind. Katie knew it was all in the presentation. Maybe if she approached the conversation from the perspective of the church ladies' visit to the Fernald house, she could learn what she needed to.

Regular visitors to the farm stand returned their used canning jars and left them in a milk crate by the door. Ruth was elbow deep in hot sudsy water with the milk crate on the floor beside her when Katie sidled up the next afternoon.

"You know," Katie began, "you probably lucked out when you and Monique visited Amanda Fernald."

"How's that?" Ruth asked, not looking up.

"What if he had recognized you as part of my family? You know, equated you with me." Katie grinned. "The last time I saw him, he went away angry at me. He could have gotten all nasty with you, or thrown you out on your butt."

Ruth paused for a moment, then laughed. "I never considered that."

Now came the tricky part, where Katie needed to ask Ruth if it was possible Amanda's involvement with the town ladies was connected to Gage's interest in local politics. If she was, Ruth needed to be warned. But Ruth, head still down over the dishpan, spoke first.

"I thought when Amanda came to us and offered to help, even volunteering to work with Dorothea, it was all some come on, you know? Because of what her husband is up to. But I've met with her a couple of times, and she seems genuine. She talked about how much fun it was to live where she knew people by name, that they interacted with her more than holding an elevator door open like back in the city. She loves her house and confided that a lot of the cool bits and pieces were thrift shop finds."

Ruth tipped the dishpan to let the soapy water whirl down the drain.

"Gwen had this big rah-rah going on about how we needed to be sure that Amanda wouldn't get bored and leave us in a lurch. Poor girl. I think Gwen's attitude blindsided her."

"What did she say?" Katie asked.

"This is her home now. She isn't interested in the idea of a job in the city at some boring office. She wants to be part of the community, so when they have children, this will be the kids' home too."

Katie still wasn't sure. A pretty speech, and Ruth seemed convinced Amanda was the real McCoy. But was her husband? Katie didn't think so.

Chapter Forty-Four

Katie took a call for a raccoon in a garbage can. Marlie, who had just returned from work, ran upstairs to change so she could do a ride-along. On the way back, they drove right past Meredith Block's house. Parked at the crest of the driveway, they saw a flashy Lincoln Mach IV.

"Who the heck is that?" Katie asked.

"I don't know," said Marlie. "But if it's a buyer, they shouldn't be there. Turn around and go back."

Katie pulled in beside the Lincoln. A couple stood in the backyard, both staring at the space behind the garage. As she and Marlie got closer, with Katie trailing behind, she recognized Allison Block. That meant the man was probably Avery. She hung back while Marlie introduced herself and asked why they were on the property.

"I'm Avery Block," the man said. "This property belongs to me."

"I know who you are, Mr. Block," Marlie said smoothly. "I recognize you from when Sheriff Lewis and State Police Corporal Derrick interviewed you after Meredith's body was found. I'm sure you were told this property is still being held as an active crime scene. Access is limited to the house only, and then strictly only by Meredith's representative."

Avery looked down his nose at Marlie, and Katie took offense.

Taking a step ahead, she said, "As long as you're here, Mr. Block, I have a question."

"Who are you?" he asked.

Allison did a quick double-take. Katie tried to ignore her, but felt bad.

She'd liked Allison when they had first met.

"There's a door on the back side of the garage blocked by a big metal cabinet. Do you know anything about that?" Katie asked. "It looks like the cabinet has been moved recently."

"I moved it," Avery said. When his wife turned to look at him, he blushed. "Five or six weeks before her death, Meredith asked me if I'd help her with it. She said the door creeped her out because somebody could break in there and hide, and she wouldn't know it until she was inside the garage. Meredith went so far as to say she thought a shadow had crossed in front of the side window once. But she was probably drunk."

"You never told me you came over here," Allison said. She looked more miffed than surprised.

Avery turned red again. "I didn't think it was a big deal."

"Really?" Acid dripped from Allison's response. "A drive of forty-five minutes out into the sticks—the opposite way from where you live—to move a cabinet for a woman you won't even talk to on the telephone. That isn't a big deal?"

Katie and Marlie listened to the exchange with interest.

The couple stopped talking, but their eyes remained locked. It wasn't a friendly or sexy look, either.

Katie spoke up. "Did anyone know you were here? Anyone who can verify exactly what day you were in Parentville to move a useless piece of furniture around?"

Marlie turned with a gasp. She knew she should stop Katie, but she wanted to know as well.

Avery was struck dumb for only a second. His laugh, hard and cynical, was an enormous expulsion of wind.

"You're not serious, right?"

Katie continued to glower at him. Marlie moved closer.

"You're not, are you?" Avery's grin morphed into a scowl. "Boy, are you wrong, lady. I may have been the bad guy when I left Meredith and married Allison, but Meredith was actually really good for my reputation toward the end."

Katie pulled back. Her eyebrows rose.

"You don't know, do you?" He grinned again. "I'll let you in on a little secret. Back in high school, Meredith was a tease. I don't know if she screwed around with any of the nerds, but with the jocks, she was all come-hither and don't-touch-me. She wanted a husband who would get her out of this hick town. We dated, but I dumped her twice, because she wouldn't put out."

Allison turned away, lips pressed together and cheeks glowing. Katie wondered if Avery's words had embarrassed his wife, or that she wasn't used to such crude language.

Marlie bit the inside of her lower lip. Avery wasn't grinning now. He looked disgusted. Maybe a little sad as well. Katie stood still, practically holding her breath.

Let him talk, she cautioned herself. *Maybe he'll slip up.*

"There were plenty of other girls. I didn't need to do anything stupid. My dad warned me she was a bait trap. When I started college, I was there to have a good time, and who showed up at a keg party? Meredith. But she'd changed somehow. She wasn't some horny girl who couldn't climb up on the horse."

Once again, Allison blushed.

Avery continued, "I don't know how she did it, but she'd gotten classier. Sophisticated, even. She made co-eds her own age look dowdy. A lot of guys were interested in her."

Avery looked around the yard at everything except Allison.

He knows Allison doesn't like what he's saying. I bet she's called him out on it before, Katie thought.

"We dated. One night I passed out in my car and woke up alone, parked behind Woolworths. I called her maybe four or five days later. She didn't take the call. I ran into her on campus. She was enrolled at Champlain College while I was at UVM, but the campuses overlapped. She took one look at me and ran." This time, when Avery laughed, there was only regret. "What a dunce I was."

At the questioning look both Katie and Marlie shot him, Avery shook his head, then looked off down the road.

"I went after her. When I caught up, she was hysterical. It seems I was less of a gentleman than I thought I was. A couple more weeks passed. She called in the middle of the night. She was in trouble and needed some money to handle it."

Marlie sucked in a hard breath.

"She couldn't tell her folks. And there was no way I would tell mine. We got married. Bingo! She lost the baby before she even started to belly up. It was a lesson I didn't see coming."

"Why is that?" Katie asked.

"Because the next time she got pregnant, by the time she was four months along, you could tell."

"Are you saying you think she lied?" Marlie asked.

"Yeah, that's exactly what I said. Two kids later, she's a shrew, and I'm out there with somebody new. We got divorced. Allison's a good wife."

He reached out to touch her arm, but Allison took a step away.

Why? Katie wondered. *She probably already knew all this about Meredith. Maybe...she didn't find out until after they were married that he was a jerk.*

"Now I have to work to keep my reputation, in and out of the office, out of the trash can because of something I did as a stupid kid a long time ago. And here's Meredith again, whoring around every law office in the city. Plus, those were only the guys I knew about. It turned the tables completely around. Anyway, she was good for me because she made herself look so bad. No one remembers that I ran around on her while we were still married." Avery had grown angrier as he spoke.

Katie could understand exactly what Avery meant. And now maybe she knew why Brittany thought so badly of her sister. She opened her mouth, but Avery waved her off.

"I'm done talking with you," he said. "My boys aren't good kids, but they didn't deserve to suffer the death of their mother. Especially not through murder. Allison is strong. She's gotten them to go to counseling, and now we're all working to get better. If the cops want to talk to me, send them. But you? Keep away from me and my family."

He grabbed Allison by the elbow and muscled her toward his car. They were down the driveway, vehicle belly squealing as it bounced on rocks, and gone before Katie and Marlie were back to the truck.

There was nothing to do but leave. Half a mile down the road, Katie pulled the truck to the breakdown lane. This time, she stared off into the distance as she chewed her lip.

"I think I screwed up," she said.

Marlie had been stewing. Her anger overflowed before she could stop it.

"You think? Katie, the only reason we stopped at Meredith's house was to find out who was in the yard and tell them they had to leave. I thought it was a couple of curiosity seekers. Not Avery and his wife! If Avery tells the cops we were there, and it gets back to Sheriff Lewis, he's going to fry your bacon for breakfast! And mine. I'll probably be fired. What were you thinking?"

"I don't know. I guess I wasn't." Katie shook her head. "I'm sorry, Marlie. I know I was wrong, and I take full responsibility."

"As you should," Marlie said. "It wasn't right what happened." Then her tone changed. "But that was a side of Meredith's story, we didn't hear anywhere else, so that's a good thing. I don't think even Sheriff Lewis got wind of any of that."

"True. She didn't want to tell her folks she was pregnant because if she faked a miscarriage a week after she got married, her folks would have questions she didn't want to answer."

"Do you think there's a way we can prove or not prove that? If she didn't go to the hospital, I don't think there'd be any record," Marlie said.

Flipping the directional to pull back into traffic, Katie didn't know the answer.

Chapter Forty-Five

On the way out to check the live traps at the Franklin Road farm, Katie took the approach that would take her by Meredith's parents' home. The only car in the drive was one she identified as belonging to Brittany. Once on the porch, she found Brittany sorting through a box of documents. There appeared to be a pile of pages with school records, photographs, and crumbled pieces of kindergarten refrigerator art, a tiny pile of something other, and a trashcan of shredded bits.

"Looks like good exercise for your wrists," Katie said.

"More junk from Meredith's house," Brittany grunted. "I was for burning it all, but my dad said we should go through it. What's up?"

Katie perched on the edge of the metal sofa swing. "First, I wanted to thank you for letting me talk to your folks. They were so gracious. And also, I was privy to a conversation that occurred with Avery the other day." She wasn't sure why she didn't want to say between herself and Avery, but followed her own instincts. "I have some questions."

"Go ahead."

Brittany wiped her ink-stained fingers across her face, leaving a bruise-colored smudge. She didn't look up from what she was doing, for which Katie was grateful.

"Is it possible that Meredith was pregnant when she got married?" Katie asked.

"Nope."

When Katie didn't respond, Brittany looked up and said flatly. "I know for a fact she wasn't pregnant because of a conversation we; Meredith, myself, and our mother had. The weekend Meredith picked to get married was a holiday weekend. Mom wanted her to wait a week. Meredith said no. She said she'd be on her period that week and it would spoil her whole day. Mom said then wait two weeks. Again, Meredith said no. I guess she figured it was better to spoil her honeymoon than her wedding."

Or, Katie thought, *she needed her period to happen right after she got married so she could tell Avery it was something else.*

"Do you remember ever hearing anything about Meredith having a miscarriage before her first son was born?" Katie asked.

This time, when Brittany sat up, she had a disgusted look on her face. "Katie, my sister, was a brat. I mean the solid gold kind. If she fell down, it was a calamity. If there was blood, she needed a doctor. There is no way in hell if she suffered a miscarriage, the entire village wouldn't have heard about it. She was a self-centered narcissist. I didn't see much of her after she got married, but I still have a lot of friends around here, so I heard stuff. Most of it wasn't good."

Katie was studying her hand, wondering what else she should ask when she felt Brittany's hand against her upper arm. She looked up and found Brittany watching her own hand softly rubbing across Katie's shoulder, a tiny smile on her face. Brittany's touch was light, more a caress than a casual pat. Katie swallowed hard, ready to move away.

"I have a friend," Katie said through dry lips. "A very good friend. Someone I love deeply. I would never do anything to hurt them. I can't allow myself to."

Brittany's hand fell to her side. "I understand. I had a friend like that once."

A late-model sedan pulled into the driveway. The moment was shattered. Katie felt a wash of relief.

"Listen, that's my folks." Brittany looked nervous. "It doesn't matter what I thought about Meredith, or anyone else does as far as that goes. They loved her. What they know is rather limited. Please be careful what you say." She got to her feet. "If all the bad has to come out one day. Let it be then, not now, while they're still grieving."

Katie walked down the steps. "Hi. I'm on my way to check the live traps and saw Brittany's car. I thought I'd say hello. It's nice seeing you as well, and I hate to be rude, but if there are cats, we need to get to the vet's office before they close, so I gotta go."

Mr. and Mrs. Coombs smiled and waved her on.

In the truck, Katie thought, Avery's father was right. Meredith was a bait trap.

Chapter Forty-Six

"Rick?" Katie's fingers refolded the dish towel a third time. "I've got a bank question."

The elderly man swiveled in his seat.

Katie looked at the lists of needed items taped to the side of the refrigerator.

"If I borrowed money from the bank, and there was a little left over that we didn't use for the barn, would I be able to sort of redirect it?"

"I believe as long as the bulk goes to the project you borrowed for, you could. Why?" he asked.

To avoid more questions, she said, "Well, maybe I want to get into the bat removal business. You know, full-length waders, gas masks, a tanker truck."

"I think you need to keep away from that. Maybe Stan knows somebody who can help those New Yorkers with their bat problem," Rick said.

Ruth agreed, but was too busy to add to the conversation as she stirred up a batch of date bars.

"What's the occasion, Ruth?" Katie asked her directly.

"Isaac O'Brien and the new guy Rick hired will be at work down at the barn tomorrow," Ruth explained. "I figured I'd feed them lunch. There's leftover meatloaf for hot sandwiches and boiled potatoes that I can pan-fry. I didn't want to ask you about sweets, so I figured I'd make date bars for dessert and afternoon break."

"So, we'll provide four-star dining *and* pay them for the work?" Katie asked with a smile. "I want that job."

"Not four." Ruth smiled over the hot baking pan. "More like two and a half."

* * *

Katie, Marlie, and Charlie had already gone to work when Rick came back up the road with Isaac in the truck. As it was a Wednesday, Rick's day off, he was available to work with the wood splitter on the firewood pile. The other two, a man and a nearly-grown, would clean up the fallen planks. When that job was completed, they'd shovel out room for the excavator.

Wayne was sitting on the doorstep when Rick walked outside.

"Where's your vehicle, Willy?" Rick asked him.

For once, Wayne had been smart enough to use a different name.

"Still trying to get it to run. My girl dropped me off. She'll pick me up when I call later." The lie slid easily off his tongue. Before Rick could ask another question, Wayne headed around the side of the house. "Time to get to it, I guess."

Isaac had worked with Rick before. He knew to step up. Wayne found it difficult to keep up with the sixteen-year-old boy while under Rick's eye. Even though he was pushed to keep at it, Ruth made up for the toil with food. There was coffee at ten, a hearty lunch at twelve, and more snacks at two-thirty.

"I could get used to eating like this," he confessed to Isaac, who grinned in agreement.

By five, all three were ready to call it a day. Only a steady breeze from the southwest had made the afternoon bearable. Each worker was sweaty and had started to feel the strain in their muscles. Wayne, unused to more exercise than the run from one hiding place to another, felt a wobble in his knees which he fought to hide. Isaac didn't notice, but Rick did. Always willing to believe the best, Rick considered that Wayne had been out of work for a while and gone a little soft.

Katie's car pulled in at the top of the drive.

"C'mon, guys." Rick waved Isaac and Wayne ahead. "Let's get cleaned up and see what Katie will set down for supper tonight."

Wayne was just considering his good fortune when he realized he'd seen Katie before. She had walked out of Meredith Block's driveway and past the

Hunt's house. When she'd looked up the driveway, she'd missed him behind the rhododendron, but he had gotten a good look at her. It was on the tip of his tongue to tell Rick he'd take his day's pay and leave when another vehicle pulled in. The heavy Ford truck belched and farted as the ignition was shut off. Then the door opened, and Charlie shot out like a popgun cork.

"Hey, Wayne, buddy," he said.

Before Wayne had a moment to shut Charlie down, the short, round guy turned to Katie and Rick and said, "Remember I told you about the time I picked up this guy broke down near the farm stand? I drove him into town and dropped him at the church. This is him, Wayne. The Duke."

Wayne could tell from the look in Katie's eyes that the mention of the farm stand had brought up Ruth's complaints about missing produce. Then too, he'd realized when he'd returned to the barn that somebody had picked up the American chop suey bowl and the empty pint jars. Katie was the only farmhouse resident who seemed to prowl around there. She had to have been the one.

"I can't stay," he said quickly to Rick. "You just pay me off, and I'll be gone."

Rick reached for his wallet. "Wait. You've got to call your girl."

"It's late. I bet she's already here down at the end of the road. She won't come up. Shy, you know."

He kept on the move, keeping Rick between himself and Katie. Which meant when the old Pontiac pulled in and Marlie, home from a visit with her grandmother, got out, he was right in front of her.

"You!" she said. "Where have you been? The sheriff looked all over hell and creation for you." Then her eyes narrowed. "Those weren't your dogs that barked up a storm over the ridge. You lied to the sheriff, didn't you?"

That was it. Wayne took off. He ran around the passenger side of the car and across the side lawn while Marlie came around the Pontiac from the other side.

"Solomon, fetch!" Rick ordered.

The big hound knew about this game. Rick threw something, told him to get it, and Solomon brought it back for a snack. With a baying call, he took off after Wayne.

Supper time was when every belly got filled. All the family came together, and Bonnie was part of that family. She had been snuffling around near the hollyhocks when Rick ordered Solomon on. Like the dog, she knew there would be treats if she did the tricks correctly. She wanted in on that.

Wayne looked over his shoulder. Not only was the long-legged hound closing in, but the enormous pig matched him stride for stride. With a strangled scream, Wayne leapt onto the porch. It didn't stop Solomon, who jumped and easily pinned the man against the building, but it did slow down Bonnie. It always took her a few minutes to figure out the technique required for negotiating the three steps.

Ruth opened the screen door, blocking that side, and all four closed in fast. Wayne knew he was all done.

"I'm sorry," he wept. "I tried not to take your food, but I was so hungry."

Marlie, Katie, and Ruth talked at the same time as Wayne blubbered out his confession.

"Be quiet, all of you," Rick ordered. "You too, Solomon. Sit."

Solomon's back quarters went down. Bonnie gave up on the steps, and her butt hit the ground as well. Old Tom decided this was a good time to crawl under the porch.

"What's going on?" Ruth asked.

"That's what I'm trying to figure out," Rick said through clenched teeth. "Charlie, are you sure this is the same guy?"

"Rick," Marlie said. "We need to get hold of Sheriff Lewis."

He held up his hand. "Hold that thought. Charlie?"

"Yeah, I know it is," Charlie answered.

Marlie rubbed her hand over her face.

"So, you stole food from the farm stand?" Rick asked Wayne.

"You can keep my pay," Wayne said. "I'm sorry. I truly am, but I didn't have anything to eat."

"But you took food out of my refrigerator." Katie stepped closer. "You were in our *house*. And you slept in my barn."

"Katie," Marlie said. "You need to stop right there. This is a police matter. Be quiet."

"Yes. Yes, I did. But only the one time." Wayne was sharp enough to know they hadn't figured out about the basement, or that he'd been here for a couple of months. He shouldn't mention it or say another word about how he had lived.

Rick opened his mouth again, but Marlie cut him off.

"All of you, listen to me," she said, stepping forward. "This is the man who found Meredith Block's body. He called the sheriff. Then he gave us this big song and dance about who he was before he took off. Sheriff Lewis has been on the lookout for him. I need to call the sheriff right now."

Rick nodded. Marlie went inside to use the telephone. There wasn't any way Wayne would get past the people and animals that had him with his backbone pressed against the white clapboards.

When she came back outside, Marlie said, "Not another word until Lewis gets here."

It wasn't a long wait. Fifteen minutes later, sirens blaring, Sheriff Lewis pulled into the yard and braked hard. At that moment, everyone started to talk again.

Lewis cuffed Wayne and forced him into the backseat of his car. "How did you find him?" he asked Marlie, still dressed in her civilian clothing.

"I pulled into the yard, and he was just here. I recognized him immediately."

"Yes, that's right," Katie said. "She identified him and said he needed to go into the village and have a talk with you."

"Right." Ruth nodded. "He's been here all day working to ready the barn for the workmen. I tell you what, I had no idea who he was. Marlie came up to settle her account, and bingo, just like that, she was all over him."

Rolling his eyes, Rick shoved Ruth and Charlie in the house, snapping his fingers to send the dog in as well. Katie stepped down from the porch and knocked Bonnie away from the sheriff with her knees.

"You follow me into town," Lewis ordered Marlie. Then he turned to Katie. "I'll be back later for a statement from you people."

Lewis pulled out. Marlie was buckling up when Rick walked over and placed his hands on the door. "What you just heard here? That's your story. It's not wrong. You don't have to say anything beyond that."

"I will if he asks," she said, as she looked up sadly.

Katie had no idea what Sheriff Lewis would ask Marlie once they were in his office. She was terrified that if Marlie had to make a choice between the deputy sheriff job and Katie, that she would lose.

"Then," said Katie. "Think about each question and answer that only."

When they were alone inside the house, Ruth turned to Katie and Rick. "Exactly who is Willy, anyway?"

Rick blew out a breath. "I have no idea."

Katie nodded her agreement. Neither did she, but if he had been sneaking around for a while, she was worried about what he might have seen or heard.

Rick, Ruth, and Charlie were still talking about Willy, with Charlie giving a minute-by-minute on his original pick-up. The mail had been brought in and left on the edge of the table. Even though it appeared to be mostly weekend sale flyers, Katie carefully checked. Letters had been known to get tossed into the woodstove before. Near the bottom of the stack was a long, white envelope addressed to her. The return address was The Howard Bank, South Winooski Avenue, Burlington, VT 05401.

Katie sucked air. Then looked up quickly. No one had heard or noticed what she was doing. The nearest exit from the kitchen was into the cattery. She went there. Out of sight, she tore the end off the envelope and pulled the single sheet out. It was a notice that she had been approved for a $50,000 loan. The only stipulation was that she needed to provide a $10,000 down payment.

Her chest tightened. She'd actually been excited to see that she had been approved. But the down payment ripped the feeling out of her. There was no way she could come up with that much money. LG had followed her and pandiculated up her leg, asking for attention.

Shoving the letter and envelope in her pocket, Katie spoke to the cat. Her voice hoarse with remorse. "It might as well be the moon, Poppa. It's that far away."

* * *

Thirty minutes later, Tony Paquette, the new deputy in town, arrived at the farm. He took statements from everyone, which he wrote out in longhand word for word, then had them sign. He didn't seem to realize that, while he talked to Charlie, Rick hovered close enough to make sure the town driver didn't deviate from the three-sentence speech he'd been rehearsing since Marlie left.

It wasn't until long after dark that Marlie returned. Katie lay in bed, unaware that Rick and Ruth also listened. Only Charlie slept. Walker was sprawled across the little man's feet, and when Solomon's tail thumbed a welcome on the kitchen floor, the old hound figured due diligence was covered. He fell back asleep.

Instead of parking in the drive where the house faced Fire Lane 61, Marlie pulled around between the house and the barn and walked back up to the kitchen door.

"Shh," she said to Solomon, as she used her foot to assure not a single cat snuck out into the night.

The kitchen light had been left on. Marlie was barely inside when members of the household in all manner of nightclothes began to assemble.

"Aren't you guys ready to sleep?" she asked with a groan.

Three heads nodded. Ruth moved toward the refrigerator, but Marlie waved her back.

"Thanks, I'm not hungry," she said.

It was inevitable that Marlie would have to relate the events that had transpired in the sheriff's office, so she filled a glass from the tap and sat down. Katie and Rick took seats, never taking their eyes off the exhausted deputy sheriff. Ruth, once no one was watching, took on the duty of building a sandwich, which she plated, quartered, and slid in front of Marlie.

"It seems that the man you had working for you this afternoon is Wayne Merchant," Marlie began. "He's what my grandmother would refer to as two cards short of a full deck, but basically, I think he's just a victim of circumstances. He ended up here because he was on a jailhouse work crew in Essex. He just walked away. But he had no idea how to take care of himself. He's been able to hide in barns and pilfer food for most of the summer. Anyway, that's the basic stuff. Sheriff Lewis is transporting him back to Essex as we speak because we don't have a holding cell here. Lewis and Corporal Derrick from the state police will be questioning him about Meredith's murder."

She took a small bite of the sandwich and a sip of water.

"Wayne said he didn't kill her, only that he'd tripped over the body and was so scared he couldn't stop himself from calling the sheriff's office. According to his statement, he was down on Route 116 and stumbled onto the Hunts' house. They're away for the summer, but they left a window open. He found food and a dry place to sleep. When Lewis got hold of them, Jacob said they had been there several times and had never found any evidence of an uninvited guest. So, the guy didn't wreck anything, at least.

"From the Hunts, Wayne could see the Block house. He saw the boyfriends going in and out, the kids, all that stuff. He said he didn't see what happened to Meredith, but that one of her boyfriends was rough. Wayne was on the prowl in the neighborhood, looking for an open shed or another place he could hide, when he stumbled on the remains."

Marlie shook her head. "You should have heard the guy trying to explain everything to Lewis. He was terrified. Lewis said something about charging him with murder. I thought he was going to cry. His biggest crime before was drunk and disorderly, leading to destruction of property. He couldn't talk fast enough. Two of us were taking notes. I'll get to consolidate them tomorrow. But he swears he didn't kill Meredith."

"What do you think?" Rick asked.

"He went inside the house after he found Meredith and called," Marlie said. "Angus answered. He said the guy was screaming and terrified. The ability to talk people down on the telephone is Angus's strong point. So, I believe Wayne. He was wrong to lie about who he was to Sheriff Lewis, but by the time we got there after he'd called about finding Meredith, he'd realized we were bound to find out he had escaped incarceration. I'm not sure where that leaves us, except it tightens up the timeline."

"Marlie." Katie's throat was dry, but she needed to know. "Did he say anything about you being here when you found Willy?"

"Not a word, and I'm not bringing the subject up." She sighed. "But I have to be back in the office at six, so I need to turn in." She stood to go, then stopped. "Oh, and Lewis and Tony spoke with Danielle Tate-Noah this afternoon. She's out of the hospital and at her folks' home. Both she and the baby will be alright, but she may be looking for a quick divorce."

They were all saddened by the young girl's plight. But relieved she would recover as well.

"Danielle knew about the boyfriends, but not who they were. Meredith was discreet enough not to bring men around when Danielle was home."

Marlie headed off to bed, leaving the others still seated around the table. Ruth put the empty plate in the sink.

"What a mess," she said. "A young girl who should be all happy about a baby, suffering because the man she chose is a wastrel. Then that guy, Willy! Can you imagine? He was right here, in this house, and we didn't know. Heaven only knows what he learned messing around with our things."

Katie watched Ruth cross the living room towards her bedroom. Turning, she found Rick watching her.

"What indeed?" he asked.

Chapter Forty-Seven

Katie was awake until the Dean's rooster announced the dawn. While she sat in the rocker in front of her window, LG curled up in her lap. When she paced the wide floorboards, the cat found a soft place on the bed and waited. Finally, the rest of the household roused.

"I can't wait any longer," she said to the cat. "I know. Meredith knows. No one else is listening." Feigning fatigue, she told the humans, "I'm just tired, all the stress I guess with the barn and the dog poop calls. I'm a little late this morning. You all go ahead. I'll be ready in a few minutes."

She watched them go and felt sad. She'd lied again. It seemed these days to be a way of life, like when she'd been using drugs. Lies. Lies. Lies. Her eyes felt sunken into her head, her skin taut across her cheekbones. Did it show that she was on the verge of putting everything, even Marlie, on the line?

"This is the last one," she promised herself. "And only because no one else is reacting."

She called the feed store and told Stan she needed to have the day off.

"If you can't get somebody, call me right back," she said. "But there's a bunch of stuff around here I need to take care of right away."

She knew Stan would believe it had something to do with the loan, but that was the way it was. As soon as he was off the telephone, she started to make other calls, a total of seven. Gage Fernald was her last call. She introduced herself as Joy Ash from the Vermont sheriff's department call center. He agreed to meet with her.

This lie hurt her chest. She had one more call to make. If she was even a little wrong, Sheriff Lewis would blow a gasket big-time, because this might cost him the case.

The phone rang. She still had time to hang up. She could cancel it all. Go to work. Let the cops handle it.

"Hello?"

"Good morning, Allison Avery? This is Joy Ash…"

Katie arrived at the town hall just before eleven. Marlie had said Sheriff Lewis declared that every Monday, he would hold a staff meeting from ten-thirty until eleven. She hoped he actually kept that rule. After she selected the most advantageous spot in the parking lot for a quick getaway, she checked the door to the sheriff's office. Locked. A note attached to the glass stated that the office would open at eleven a.m. Katie circled the building, then entered through the town office door. She darted across the reception area. Janice was busy threatening the copy machine with a trip to the junkyard.

"Janice," Katie hissed.

The other woman yelped and jumped away from the copier.

"For the love of Pete, Katie, you scared me to death!" Janice admonished.

Katie held her forefinger against her lips. "Sh. Quiet. I need you to help me."

Janice, like a hunting cat, tiptoed across the floor. Her shoulders were rounded and her neck pulled in. "What?" she whispered.

"A woman named Allison Avery is going to show up in a little while. She'll ask for Joy Ash. Can you tuck her away in the conference room until I'm ready for her?" Katie asked.

"Covert?" Janice asked, mouth and eyes wide.

Katie nodded and turned to the connecting door. The door between reception and the sheriff's office was a tight fit, requiring a firm hand. She knew it wouldn't be as silent as the main entrance, but bumped it fast and hard with her hip, willing to accept the small thud as opposed to a long squeal. Quickly, she slid through and pulled the wooden panel closed behind her. The need to ask for Janice's assistance had brought sweat to her brow.

Here's hoping, she thought. *Janice gets this right.*

Katie hurried across the room, yanked the note off the glass, and unlocked the dead bolt. She moved the chairs along the wall away from each other so her invited guests wouldn't be close enough to chat.

Already the pickup truck with the rack of emergency lights on top had pulled in. Seated behind Angus's desk with a blank form shielding her pages of notes, Katie waited. Her fingertips, sticky with sweat, clung to the paper.

Over the next five minutes, all three of the men she had contacted arrived. With the presence of the fire lieutenant from Charlotte, the owner of the contracting company putting in the subdivisions, and Gage Fernald, they were, for the most part, silent as to their mission. Katie indicated that they should take their seats. The men sat. Only Gage Fernald stood before her for a few long moments. She was sure he recognized her. Katie refused to take her eyes off the paper in her hand. She only needed them to sit there for a few more minutes. The urge to look up had her digging her nails into the palms of her hands, but she knew they were watching her. She couldn't afford a question quite yet.

At 11:32 a.m., the door to the chief's office opened, and Marlie stepped out. The deputy stopped so quickly that Angus, right behind her, bumped her ahead. Marlie stared in shock, but with another jostle from Angus, she moved to the side. Seeing Katie seated at what he considered his desk, Angus edged forward, huffing at her the same way Bonnie did when she was displeased.

Katie waited without saying a word. The only person missing now was Sheriff Lewis. Suddenly, from behind Deputy Tony Paquette, his voice boomed across the office.

"What the hell is this?"

Katie rose to her feet. She didn't look at Lewis. Instead, she faced the three surprised-looking men arranged around the room.

"Gentlemen," she began, with a waver in her voice she hoped they did not hear. "We're all here today for the same reason, and that is to solve the murder of Meredith Block."

"TOOK!" Lewis's face was bright red. He surged forward. One more step and he'd be standing on the other side of her.

Katelyn held up her pages of evidence, some in plastic bags. She started to talk fast.

"Of all the people you've talked to, Martin…"

The use of his first name stopped the sheriff cold. His mouth flopped like a fish, but it gave Katie a chance to continue.

"…these three men are the closest to being actual suspects in Meredith's murder."

The lieutenant and Gage Fernald surged to their feet.

"I can't believe you called me here for this!" Gage's voice had gone deep, not loud, but authoritative. "I'm leaving. You'll be hearing from my firm."

Katie moved to block his path, but spoke to Lewis. "If you don't want me to speak in front of them, can we go into your office? But make them stay here? Can you listen without losing your temper?"

Lewis stood upright and rigid, head tilted slightly in her direction. He pointed toward the seat Gage had abandoned, but Gage stayed where he was. Lewis motioned the deputies toward the outside door, but remained silent.

"I've been talking with Mr. and Mrs. Coombs and their daughter, Brittany—Meredith's older sister. I admit I might have been snooping around a little. When the Lane cedar chest came back to me, I got curious. Three of the guys that Meredith had affairs with…"

A chorus of complaints rose. Now, all three men were on their feet, clustered near the door.

"Wait," Lewis said. "I'm going to need you for witnesses when Ms. Took falls on her face and finally gets her dues."

For a moment, his threat had darting lights blinking in front of her. She swallowed hard.

"As I was saying, three of her boyfriends had nothing to lose if Meredith told the world about the two of them. These three did. When I started to check the facts, I learned more. Mr. Anderson is the man who gave Meredith the cocker spaniel. That seems like the type of gift you would only give to somebody you're in a firm relationship with. Meredith didn't want the guy, and she didn't want the dog. During the two weeks surrounding Meredith's death, the Anderson family, all seven of them, were in Virginia. He had a firm alibi."

"You called my family?" Anderson choked out.

"No, actually, I called the hotel where you were staying. Sheriff Lewis probably did that as well. I knew which one because you had bragged about it to some of the guys you work with. And I know some contractors." She laid her page of notes regarding Anderson on Angus's desk.

Katie turned her attention to the fire lieutenant. "Meredith collected things. She had your Saint Florian medallion. I know it was yours because her habit was to store these things with a business card from the person she'd taken them from. I got a good look at your truck the other day."

She didn't mention how she had actually been driving past the fire station and merely slowed down, that she hadn't even pulled into the lot.

"It's quite tall, isn't it? Those big off-road tires. That tall rack right behind the cab? I believe you had Philip Carwell weld it onto the frame, so it doesn't just come out, right? Then on top you've got four flashing lights. With their individual frames, each one is six inches tall."

"Where are you going with this?" Lewis demanded.

"Meredith's garage measures just under six feet from the ground to the overhead door. The lieutenant's truck is too tall to fit in there. A witness said the man Meredith was seeing at the time of her death parked in the garage. That she would leave her car outside so that the boyfriend's would be hidden. You know, so that if someone like his wife, or one of her friends, drove by, it wouldn't be seen."

She looked back at the fire officer. "I bet I know exactly where you parked."

The burly officer looked decidedly uncomfortable. "There's a cornfield across the road. I'd park in there and cross to the woods. From there, I followed a game trail."

"Same one the witness followed," Katie said, laying that page of notes with her first one. She didn't bother to mention that Marlie had given her the information. "I've walked that path. It's easy, plenty clear during the day and night, and not ten minutes away from the house."

"Then I made some telephone calls," Katie said. "The housekeeper told me she could tell a lot about the guy who was sleeping with Meredith. She said he had black hair and used the same aftershave as her husband. Mennen's Skin Bracer."

At the mention of Mrs. Berstable, Marlie's fingers trembled. She clasped her hands, hoping the sheriff didn't notice.

Katie stopped to study the three men. Two with light brown hair, and Gage, whose short, greasy hair, was very black. She leaned in toward him and sniffed. Even though she stood too far away to detect a single odor in a room full of guys wearing different aftershaves, Lewis caught her drift. He turned to Gage.

"You said you'd lost your wallet in Burlington, that you even had a witness. And that it was possible someone else in the firm, maybe even one of the paralegals, had found it but not turned it in." Her eyes bored into Gage's. "You said there was a lot of money in it. If I called your wife right now, would she agree? Will she even know you lost your wallet?"

Gage swallowed hard. Another note fluttered downward from Katie's hand.

"Now the guys who mowed the lawn, they were a trip," Katie said. "I gathered they saw some very interesting sights and witnessed some notable events just at Meredith's house. But the big piece of information from them is that they wrote up a warning for Meredith the day they mowed out in front of the house and ran into bees. They didn't know where in the yard the bees were coming from, but they weren't about to stick around and look. Meredith wasn't home, so they gave the customer's copy of this same notice to the guy who answered the door." She waved the photocopy provided by Clearcut Landscaping. "The notice stapled to it has the date, time, and description of the man who accepted the notice. He said he'd give it to Meredith."

Even though Lewis reached for the notice, Katie laid it on the desk.

"Brittany told me she picked up every scrap of paper in Meredith's house and took it over to her parents'. I took a chance it hadn't been shredded yet and called Mr. Coombs. I asked if he'd look for it and wear gloves while he did."

Katie held up a baggie with the pink copy of a triplicate form.

"Here it is. There are probably a lot of fingerprints on it, but the person who accepted it knew from then on there was a bee issue right there at the house. And if you've been in Meredith's house, you had to know about her allergy to wasps. She could have cornered the market on Benadryl."

Gage stared at Katie for a long minute. Then he spun around to look at Sheriff Lewis.

"Is that what you think?" he demanded. "That I killed Meredith?" He laughed, loud and hard. "No way, mister. When I pulled out of there that last day, I didn't want to have anything to do with her again. That psychotic bitch was all about how she would call my sister and her husband."

Sweat dripped off Gage's face. He wiped his hand over his brow, then on his clean khakis, leaving a smear down the side.

"I tried to tell Meredith that Avery wouldn't give a fat flying fart who she was messing around with."

Lewis's face screwed up as he tried to figure out what Gage was not saying in the midst of all his blather. But it was Katie that spoke.

"What has Avery got to do with any of this, Gage?" she asked.

This time, when Gage spun, his feet didn't move as fast as his body, which caused him to stumble.

"Everything," Gage said. "Avery Block is married to my sister, Allison. And on top of that, he is technically my boss." Spit flew out of his mouth, landing inches from the toe of Katie's shoe.

She looked down at the glistening bit of wet, focused on the reflective sparkle from the overhead lights. With a deep sigh, she raised her head.

"Your sister?" Katie looked up toward the ceiling, brow furrowed. "So, *your* sister is Allison Block. *Her* husband is Avery Block. *He* was Meredith's ex-husband and *is* your boss. That's all correct, right?"

Gage nodded. His skin had taken on a yellow tinge. The other two men took a step away from him, and Marlie moved with them.

"I just knew one of you had every reason to hate Meredith enough to kill her. You were angry, she threatened you, whatever. But maybe what she actually said wasn't as dangerous as her implied threat," Katie mused.

While she was silent, contemplating her last words, the group in the room nervously looked from one to the other. The question of whether she was through pointing her finger was on each face.

"Kaitlyn Took," Sheriff Lewis said. "I want you to shut up right now. Go into my office and wait."

"Sheriff," Marlie began.

"No. This time it's for real. Not only has that woman stuck her nose into an official investigation and compromised everything we're doing, but she took it on herself to falsely accuse three private citizens." Lewis pulled his handcuffs from the leather pouch on his belt.

"Kaitlyn Took, I'm arresting you for hindering an investigation."

"When you get done," Katie said evenly, "You might want to step into the conference room and have a conversation with Avery's wife. I bet she knows exactly what happened to Meredith, her husband's ex-wife. The woman who was out to tarnish his reputation, corrupt his children, and create scandal anywhere she could. I'll bet the best part for Meredith was that she kept Allison's home in a constant uproar. Oh, and you might want to ask Allison where she got all the scratches on her arms and legs."

Everyone else in the room seemed to fade away. Except Martin Lewis, eyeball to eyeball with Katie. On the other side of the wall was the town clerk's office. A loud thump sounded through the wall, as though something large—like an adult woman, maybe even the town clerk—had fallen off a desk. Marlie sucked in a deep breath.

"Crap," Sheriff Lewis said.

Chapter Forty-Eight

The next day, just before lunch, Stan came out and told Katie the two of them would step out and take a ride.

"Where?" she asked warily.

"Sheriff Lewis called requesting your presence," Stan said, closing the door of his office behind himself. "I don't think you should go alone, and I can't get hold of Rick on his delivery route, so I think I'll tag along."

During the short ride over to the sheriff's office, Katie explained to Stan what had happened the day before.

"It's best that you know," she said. "You might not be happy about what I did, but if you get caught unawares by Lewis, you'll be angrier."

They were approaching the turnoff and Stan slowed down. "Did Lewis talk to Allison? What happened?" he asked.

"I don't know. He made me leave. Marlie got home late, and she wasn't talking." Katie chewed her lip. She specifically didn't mention that on Marlie's return, it was Katie who had stayed away.

There wasn't room for Lewis, Katie, Stan, and all three of the deputies, including Marlie, who refused to make eye contact, in the sheriff's office, so they stood in a loose circle in the main room. Marlie looked wrinkled and spent, as did Tony. Both Lewis and Angus had on fresh uniform shirts.

"As you're sure to hear soon, with Corporal Derrick from the State Police involved, we questioned Allison Block." He stared down at his toes and sucked his teeth. "After several hours with us, then with her own attorney, she confessed to being with Meredith when she died."

"Was with, or murdered?" Katie exhaled the question.

"Voluntary manslaughter. As in a crime of passion, that ends up with one person dead," Lewis said.

Katie waited.

"According to her statement, Allison went over to see Meredith. She was angry. Avery had decided not to return the boys. The older one, Shawn, wanted to be with his mother, where he had free range. He threatened Allison with what Meredith would do to her and to her marriage. Allison and Avery had been experiencing some issues for a while, because Meredith would call, demand something of Avery, and create chaos. Meredith was also out in the community, both here and in Burlington, taking every occasion to identify herself as Mrs. Avery Block. The list of complaints that circled back to Allison, which she had kept a written record of, proved Meredith wasn't exactly spreading goodwill."

He pulled a photocopied page out of a military-green folder.

"Allison Block told her husband shortly after they were married that Meredith Block had made numerous calls to their residence when Mr. Block was at work. Initially, Allison believed she should report the calls to her husband. But every time she did, he would contact his ex-wife. That wasn't what Allison wanted, but probably exactly what Meredith did. Eventually, Allison stopped telling him."

"They're rich. They probably have a telephone answering machine. Why didn't she let the machine pick up the calls?" Katie asked.

"No idea. Some people are just gluttons for punishment. Anyway, during that period of time, Meredith was still working. Allison said that Avery was at the court building one day, and Meredith, who didn't work anywhere near his office, walked in. Supposedly to deliver paperwork. She cornered him in the main corridor. There was a short but heated conversation. According to Meredith's office, she was never sent to the courthouse. Avery complained to Meredith's boss, and she got fired." Lewis paused. "I talked to the man. He told her why he was letting her go. It couldn't have been a long jump for Meredith to realize that Avery was probably looking for a reason to fire her that wouldn't get him in trouble with his superiors or end up in a lawsuit. From there, it's possible that Meredith believed this had happened because

Allison harped long enough to get her way. We'll never know, and you have to remember that Meredith had a drinking problem."

Katie took a half step ahead before she spoke. "So, Meredith's pissed off because she got thrown to the curb for a more upscale wife. She lost her job, and I bet there was a gossip line burning up between lawyers' offices as it spread all the bad about her." Katie ticked things off the fingers of her right hand. "By this time, Avery has told her that her children will not be back, but she's already riled them up enough to make life miserable for Allison. What's left? Oh, yeah, we just heard from at least three guys that she messed around with that, and as soon as they realized she was a powder keg, they dumped her."

"The au pair was gone," Marlie said. "The housekeeper. And any extra money Avery provided. We haven't seen financial records yet, but Meredith was probably deep in the red."

"We've found evidence that she had a drinking problem," Lewis added. "In Allison's statement, she said Meredith called her up, all apologetic. Said she understood why Avery wanted to keep the boys. Allison admitted she wanted Shawn to go back to his mother, but would be willing to keep Alex. Because of this, she wanted to keep the lines of communication open with Meredith."

He replaced the pages in the folder.

"Meredith called Allison on a day Avery was in court and would be out of reach. She said she had made plans to get help and had packed the boys' favorite things. Could Allison drive out and pick them up before three? Allison said when she got there, the house was an absolute mess, and Meredith was totally sloshed. Once inside, it was evident nothing was ready for her, and she called Meredith out. Allison admitted she told Meredith that she and Avery were all done playing games. Meredith wouldn't get another cent, and Allison planned to file charges.

"Meredith picked up a baseball bat and charged at Allison, who ran back out the kitchen door. She said Meredith was fast, even though she was loaded, and cut her off from her car. So, Allison ran around the garage to get away. Before she got to the back, Meredith grabbed her arm and stumbled.

There were a few slaps and some punches thrown. Meredith still had the bat, but when Allison pulled away, Meredith fumbled and dropped it. Near the front of the small shed, Meredith caught up with Allison and tackled her. They fell onto the ground, still duking it out. Allison said Meredith was beneath her, and all of a sudden, she began to scream and really thrash around. Allison got a couple of stings on her lower leg where she lay on the ground. She jumped up and ran away."

"Ground wasps!" Katie said.

Sheriff Lewis nodded.

"Allison said from where she stood, trying to swat the wasps off her, she could hear Meredith's continual screams. She said she yelled at Meredith to get up and run away. Allison stated to us that she did not know Meredith was allergic to bees. When she finally got up the nerve, Allison ran to where Meredith lay, grabbed her by the arm, and kept going. She dragged the other woman around the side of the garage."

"Was Meredith conscious?" Katie asked.

Lewis shook his head. "Even while she swatted away bees that were stuck onto Meredith, Meredith swelled up like a balloon. Allison said she'd never seen anything like that and didn't understand what was happening. It had only been a few minutes since she had received the first sting. Then Meredith convulsed—Allison's words—and stopped breathing."

"So, Allison just ran off and left her?" asked Katie.

"That's what she says."

"Do you think Allison knew that Meredith was already dead?" Stan asked.

"I'm not an expert," Lewis said. "That would have to come from forensics or the coroner's office. But in my own opinion, yes. Allison said Meredith swelled up like a balloon in practically seconds. The timeline we put together from Allison's statement between the stings and her getting Meredith to the side of the garage provides enough lag so that Meredith could have expired."

Sheriff Lewis stared at Katie. He knew something he wasn't telling her; she was sure of it. Katie rubbed at her chin.

"When Edward Richardson and his forensic team were inside the house, they took fingerprints, right?" Katie asked. "Have you seen that report? Is there a set of prints that might match Allison Block's?"

"Yes, I have. And, no, there isn't," said Lewis.

"How is it that she was in the house with Meredith and never left any prints? Not even on the doorknob."

"My question," Lewis said, "is how come, in a house where numerous people went in and out, the only set of prints on the doorknob and the pipe rail onto the deck belong to Wayne Merchant?"

There was another pause. Katie's eyes narrowed. Sheriff Lewis didn't flinch from her scrutiny, but when she chanced a peek at Marlie, she could see where Lewis and Derrick had unearthed that fact the day before. Finally, Tony spoke up.

"That can't possibly be right."

"It could be," Katie said. "If the chase scene was actually Allison running after Meredith, and Allison went back and cleaned up."

"Then why would Allison bother to drag Meredith away from the bees?" Tony asked.

"Because she hadn't meant for Meredith to die," said Lewis. "Just scare her enough to make her back off."

"I can't imagine seeing a swarm of bees, because it would be a swarm, attack somebody else, and not react," Katie said.

Beside her, Marlie let out a slow breath. "If Meredith had enough stings, she could have swollen up enough to die of asphyxiation."

Katie recalled her conversation with Corinne. She had to have known. Why hadn't Corinne said anything. *Because,* Katie thought, *she knew there was more to the telling.*

"According to her sister, one sting would have been enough." Katie looked out the window. Across the intersection, Delia Fortin's flowers were in full bloom. *And probably,* Katie thought, *full of bees.* "Did you ask Allison if she went back into the house?"

"Too bad you're such a pain in the ass, Katie," Lewis said. "You would have made a good deputy."

Both Katie and Marlie blinked in surprise. It wasn't often that Lewis said something nice about somebody. And never Katie.

"That's exactly where Allison's lawyer told her to stop talking." Lewis turned back toward his own office. The interview was over.

"I'll meet you outside," Katie said to Stan. She went through the connecting door and found Janice seated at the desk below the heating vent. "Did you get a bruise when you fell off that chair?" Katie asked.

The town clerk blushed to a dark red.

"I wanted to speak with you before you left," Janice said. "If you haven't been paid for collecting the cats yet, you might want to get on that."

"Why?" Katie asked.

"The real estate company had planned to keep the property and break it up into house lots. That's why they wanted to get rid of the cats," Janice said. "But the perk test for drainage came back. It seems the underlying ledge is too close to the surface to put in multiple systems. Which means the property can't be subdivided. They need to find another buyer or lose their investment."

"Good thing Ms. Frith demanded a contract, isn't it?" Katie said. "I'll get it done this evening. Thanks Janice. Oh, and I've got some poop chits as well."

Chapter Forty-Nine

When Marlie showed up at the sheriff's office the next morning, Tony was manning the desk.

"Hey," she said. "What happened to Angus?"

"Sheriff Lewis changed the schedule again. Angus gets to have a turn on the night shift. He'll just call one of us to notify," Tony said. The smile on his face made his dimples even deeper than normal. "Angus isn't happy that he'll have to take a turn on nights."

"O-kay," Marlie said slowly. "That is funny, but why are you so cheerful?"

"Sheriff Lewis has a guest, and it's Commissioner Ryan," Tony stage-whispered.

Marlie swung back around. Her visual search through the window finally settled on a dark blue Crown Victoria across the parking lot. There were no emblems on the car, no government plate, nothing that indicated the top man for the Vermont Sheriff's Department was in their hole-in-the-wall town. Before she could ask what had brought Commissioner Ryan's visit, both he and Sheriff Lewis stepped out of Lewis's office. Marlie tried to read her boss's face, but it was blank. Ryan, on the other hand, had a hearty smile.

"Well, I'm pleased to see you both here," he addressed the deputies.

Both Marlie and Tony stood at attention. Their eyes traveled from Lewis to Ryan. Ryan harrumphed and tugged the front of his jacket down.

"This is not the way we normally handle things," he said. "There's an application and vetting process, you know? However, we've had a particularly high loss of deputies and have a need to get things squared away before the next group is ready for their on-the-job training."

Marlie nodded. She didn't know what Ryan had to say next, but he looked at Tony, and her heart sank.

"With the amount of people moving into the county, the commission has elected to establish another deputy slot in this office."

Marlie had to will herself not to cry.

"Deputy Paquette, I am authorized to offer you that position. Temporarily, at least, until the next meeting and vote," said Ryan.

Tony blushed so fast and so red, Marlie could have sworn she felt the heat on her arm.

"Thank you," he said. "Thank you."

Then Ryan turned to Marlie. His smile wavered. She couldn't swallow.

"Deputy Foster, it has been brought to our attention that your assistance in the case involving Meredith Block was invaluable. And that you alone were able to curtail, or possibly control, the vigilante group that insinuated themselves into the investigation."

"Group?" she croaked. Her eyes flicked to Lewis.

He remained impassive.

"Because of that," Ryan said, "the commission wishes to offer you the full-time deputy position. Would you be willing to transfer out of Irasberg and the Northwest Territory to work in Chittenden County?"

"YES! Absolutely!"

The words burst from her lips and, though he looked a little startled, Ryan smiled back.

"It's the same deal as Deputy Paquette," Lewis said. "There will be a vote and paperwork, so nothing is finalized until then."

"I understand completely," Marlie said. Nothing could dim her joy.

Chapter Fifty

A week later, Katie and Charlie stopped at the Fernald Road farm. They collected only one crate with a cat and found two traps that had been sprung but were empty.

"How is that?" Charlie asked.

"Most likely something bigger than a cat, maybe a raccoon, was drawn to the mackerel, came at the trap from the side, and rocked it. That would set off the trigger." Katie dumped the bait out of all the traps to prevent a coyote or some larger animal from ripping them apart. She used a stick to spread the ripe fish around. "This way, they all get a sniff, maybe a little bite, and they come back another time for more. But I don't think we'll catch many more cats, anyway."

She had noticed that the for-sale sign was gone, so a buyer must have signed the Realtor's contract, which meant her job was finished. Janice had taken to processing Katie's chits daily to make sure she got paid. She and Ruth had looked for more nests the other day, but had seen only a couple of cats and no pregnant females.

"I'll come back and reset these three traps in the morning, probably for the last time," she said.

They left the farm, and at Valley Wide Veterinary, Katie told Lois about this would be her last drop. Then she and Charlie drove into Charlotte for the AA meeting, after which there would be cannoli, a new favorite at the farm.

"I have to stop eating these," Marlie confessed when Katie and Charlie opened the box that evening. "My uniform pants are already starting to groan."

"Ah, come on." Ruth bumped shoulders. "Look how much exercise you get on the job."

But Marlie shook her head ruefully.

"Lately, I spend a lot of time in the driver's seat. When I worked on the desk all the time, I figured it would be constant action out in the field. Not true."

"What's the news on Allison being charged for murder?" Katie asked.

She knew from Corinne that the autopsy had shown evidence that Meredith had taken a beating from a heavy, cylinder-shaped object. Most likely, the bat that had never been found. There had also been faint evidence in Meredith's remains of tryptase serum and IgE, an indication that her death might be attributed to an anaphylactic reaction. It would be a debate between Allison's lawyer and the state in which Meredith had died from the beating or the stings.

It was still a sore spot for Katie, who didn't understand all the finer nuances of the law. As far as she was concerned, if Allison hadn't put Meredith in a position of danger when she chased her with a bat, Meredith wouldn't have died. That made Allison guilty of murder.

"Allison didn't go there with a plan to kill Meredith," Marlie said slowly. It was a comment she had made multiple times and knew Katie would argue.

"No." Katie didn't raise her head, intent on collecting the crumbs from her cannoli. "But she didn't call for help when she saw something was wrong. And she had enough clarity of mind to go back to the house and wipe all her prints away."

The two women were silent.

"Oh," Marlie said. "I wanted you to know that dog poop complaints are down now that fines are being issued and those being fined are listed in the monthly newsletter. Also, Wayne had his day in court, and he's been remanded back to jail with an extension of three months for escaping. I think they went easy on him because Sheriff Lewis issued a letter stating Meredith's body might not have been found for weeks if it weren't for Wayne. And there was a sentence in there about trauma."

"How do you know that?" Katie asked.

"Angus is just learning to type. I'm good at it," Marlie said.

Ruth, who also sat at the table with the other members of the household, recognized this stalemate. Though she wished the courts would make a quick decision, there were still a lot of facts to be debated and discerned.

"So," the woman began cheerfully, "besides the heartwarming news that Gage Fernald no longer lives in town, though Amanda has plans to stay, Delia Fortin gave me a call today. That was quite a surprise. She's not big on using the telephone, old as she is."

Rick asked, "What's going on there? Is she looking to steal your chutney recipe?"

"Idiot!" Ruth retorted. "Actually, she said that she and Arthur would like to come for a visit on Sunday. For dinner, specifically."

Katie's head jerked up. "To eat? Here?"

"Yes, to eat." Ruth rose from the table. "I told her that would be lovely. Don't get in a dither. You have a couple of days to get ready."

"I guess my question is, why do they want to come out here?" Katie asked.

She watched Ruth collect and rinse the small plates, looking for something on the older woman's face that would hint of an ulterior motive. Ruth, however, turned back to her in all innocence.

"You may find this hard to believe," she said with a smile. "But I think Delia is fond of you. Every time she gets in an uproar because her cat is up on a roof, or stuck in a tree, you rush over to help her. It's hard for her to get around. Arthritis is crippling. But you never put her off. On top of that, Arthur respects you. Ask Rick. The old guy has come to your support a number of times."

"It's true." Rick swirled the last dregs of coffee around in his mug. "I've been right there a couple of times when somebody like Gage Fernald would open his mouth about what you do, or whatever, and Mr. Fortin would step right up and shut him down. He doesn't say much, but he can be very articulate."

Katie felt a blush run along the ridges of her cheeks, and thought. *I have to admit, I'm fond of them as well.*

* * *

On Sunday, just as Katie checked the roast and browning potatoes and pronounced them soon to be done, a well-maintained Buick LaSabre pulled into the driveway. Ruth stepped outside to welcome their guests, and Marlie set a vase of wildflowers on the table.

"Stop fidgeting," she said as Katie gave another tug to the cotton dress Ruth had demanded she wear. "You look fine. These people like you, Katie. Relax."

She entered the living room as the guests came in the front door. Both diminutive people, Mrs. Fortin, wore a long-sleeved cotton dress with a tiny swirling flower pattern and a hat of navy blue that matched her handbag. Her husband wore a dark suit with a vest, and a shirt with a high collar that kept his chin firmly in place. They looked adorable and very Old World. Katie couldn't help but smile.

She had been in the Fortins' big house on Main Street. She knew they had a kitchen and a large dining room filled with a maple table and chair set, buffet, and three China cabinets filled with Mrs. Fortin's extensive collection of figurines. Inviting them to have a seat at the farmer's table with its mismatched chairs and dishware had her teeth on edge. But they sat, ate, drank, and chatted through the entire meal, which included an upside-down pineapple cake, which Muriel Fortin said was her father-in-law's favorite.

When they finished, Mr. Fortin said, "Now, there is business."

Katie started to rise with Ruth and Marlie to clear, but Mr. Fortin waved her back into her seat. Rick sat quietly in his chair, unsure what to do. Charlie followed his lead.

"Did you know that I recently purchased a derelict farm?" Arthur Fortin looked directly at Katie. She shook her head. "Yes, he continued. "It is on Franklin Road. Good land for beef stock, but not dairy cattle. The house needs work, but my boys will soon be at it."

Katie felt her eyes widen. He meant the property where she had been trapping cats.

"I tell you, this is a busy time of year, with the last hay and crops to be harvested." He shook his head. "So much to do that I have hired a company to dismantle the barn on the farm. It's no good, except maybe for the superstructure. Then I have a small barn in a different place that they will move to Franklin Road. Can you believe that? To move a barn?"

"I can't imagine," Katie confessed, confused why Mr. Fortin, who rarely talked at all, was telling them of his business dealings.

"This is why I am sitting with you." He leaned forward. With the plates and silver removed, there was room for his forearm to rest on the table, hand wrapped around his coffee cup. "Now you and I can talk business. These men who come to work for me will need a place to stay for six or eight weeks. And they will need to be fed. I heard you plan to house a group here while they work on your barn."

Katie was about to say the renovations weren't yet a done deal, but she didn't. The bank had come back with the offer of a loan, but needed a down payment she didn't have. Mr. Fortin held up his hand.

"I have already purchased a herd of beef cattle that will be housed at the farm. Not many to begin with, because the land has been fallow for a long time. It will take a lot of work. In the spring, I plan to bring in young stock. Heifers. You already have a heifer pasture you aren't using."

"How do you know all this?" Katie asked. She shot Rick a questioning look.

"This whole community is made up of farmers," Mr. Fortin said. "If it pertains to our livelihood, we know many things. Besides, I have lived here more years than your life. Regardless, I have a proposal for you."

"Really?" Katie's tongue rubbed against the back of her teeth.

"If you wish to borrow money from the bank to fix your barn, they will want to see earnest funds," Mr. Fortin said. "Maybe ten thousand dollars. Which is what I propose to advance on contract."

Katie's breath had caught at Mr. Fortin's last words. She didn't need another contract. But his offer was exactly the amount Mr. Tanner from the Howard Bank had quoted. Which Katie didn't have. Once again, her gaze flipped to Rick, who looked as stunned as she felt. If Rick hadn't told Mr. Fortin, was it possible someone from the bank had?

"Now, you have something I want. I wish to bring in these same men to work on my barn. Mine is work that can wait for the winter season. But I don't want to pay an exorbitant amount for them to have a place to sleep and supper in their bellies." Mr. Fortin's gaze held Katie's. "I propose they stay in your new boarding house for a price you and I will agree on. It can be deducted from what I advance you. Also, in the spring, you would set up the heifer pasture, and I would receive a ten-year agreement to use it from May until October. By my calculations, that would leave about five thousand dollars left. The bank interest rate is eight percent. With the start of the new year, you will pay me monthly what you can. Plus, six and a half percent accrued monthly against the remainder."

Rick cut in, "You need to understand, Katie, that it will be on us to prepare the heifer field for next spring."

She nodded her understanding before addressing Mr. Fortin. "In regards to the monthly payment, if I have more or less available, I can give you what I have?" Katie asked.

"Yes. I hear that like myself, Katie, you have your fingers in many pies." Mr. Fortin smiled.

Katie sat for a few moments, eyes glued on her grandmother's Dutch boy and girl salt and pepper set. It was a huge chance. She could fail miserably if she couldn't make both bank payments and pay Mr. Fortin as well. Behind her, Marlie and Ruth stood in front of the sink. Across the table, Rick was intent on his own fingers. This time, the decision had to be hers.

"Mr. Fortin," Katie said slowly. He looked back, impassive and waiting. "What you're proposing is an enormous step for me." She sensed everyone around her holding their breath, worried she might decline.

"However, I'll accept your offer. With the stipulation that, if we're pasturing your heifers, I will be able to run a few beef head in with them."

"Done," said the old man.

Katie held out her hand across the table, an agreement seal she had witnessed her grandfather use many times.

Arthur stood, walked over to where she sat, and solemnly shook her hand. Then he said with a twinkle in his eye, "I told you I would be your banker."

Around the room, a collective breath was released, and every face held a smile. As did Katie, remembering once again what a true gentleman her elderly friend was.

Acknowledgments

I never could have gotten this far without the people, some of whom I've lost, but all who supported me for years. My parents, Ray T. and Therese J. (Fortin) Menard. My ten younger siblings, who provided fodder. My grandparents, who gave me the backbone and, therefore, the courage to venture forth.

Glenn R. Sennett, life partner. The man who lets me spend all my time concocting the next tale. He feeds the cats and dogs, does the dishes, and will grocery shop. What more could I ask for?

My daughters, Mylinda T. Piadade and Tiffany R. Kendall. The grandkids, Cody Billodeau, Izzabella Verrill, and Gracin Verrill. And of course, Reagan Billodeau.

Verena Rose from Level Best Books, who let me fledge and then caught me when I was out of breath. Deb Well, who is right there to tell me yes or no, and teach as she goes. Shawn Reilly Simmons, whose covers are the absolute best, and is never too busy to answer a question.

Lisa Matthews, How to Kill Your Darlings Editing. She knows my punctuation skills are non-existent.

Anne Garland, Donna Fontana-Smith, Trish Esden, Paula Munier, and Donna Howard from The Eloquent Page Bookstore. All listening, reading, critiquing nicely, and encouraging.

The people who follow me, read my books, the librarians and book sellers who are willing to offer advice and provide me space to introduce the world to what I do.

Hello! My name is DonnaRae Menard, and I'd like to introduce you to my books.

About the Author

DonnaRae Menard is a born in the hayfield Vermonter, with a penchant for recycling found junk into something useable, stray animals, and often, sob stories. She has always worked some unusual jobs. Her large family and well-worn work history provide fodder for much of what she writes. Her first writing recognition came in high school when she was caught penning malicious abstracts of fellow students. DonnaRae writes in four genres: cozy/caper, thriller, historical fiction, and fantasy. She was an International Competitor with Toastmaster International, and is a member of Sisters in Crime, New England Chapter, Guppies, League of Vermont Writers, Mystery Writers of America, and the Registrar for New England Crime Bake. A hybrid author who self-publishes as well as being contracted with Level Best Books for two series; An It's Never Too Late and The Pig & I, as well as with Of Metal and Magic; The Waif and The Warlord, she's always willing to talk about her on-the-page friends and the high jinks of barnyard critters.

AUTHOR WEBSITE: Donnaraemenardbooks.com

SOCIAL MEDIA HANDLES:
Facebook: DonnaRae Menard Author,
Bluesky: drmenardbooks_blsky_social

Also by Donnarae Menard

AN IT'S NEVER TOO LATE MYSTERY SERIES
Murder in the Meadow
Murder on Eagle Drop Ridge
Murder in the Village Proper
Murder on the Small Farm

THE PIG & I MYSTERY SERIES
Snuffling Up Bones

DETECTIVE CARMINE MANUER SERIES
Patterns
Hunters

The Waif and the Warlord

COURIER TO THE DEAD SERIES
The Morality Issue

LYNN STEEVES SERIES
Beneath the Fountain

GWEN HANSON MYSTERY SERIES
Dropped from the Sky

WOMEN WARRIORS SERIES
In the Shadow of Pharoah
Strength of the Myan Leopard
Wu-Lee

Dreams Of A Mad Woman

It Takes Guts

Willa

9 781685 129910